Cold Case

Second Edition

Cold Case

Second Edition

Mike Faricy

This is a work of fiction. All of the characters, organizations, and events portrayed in this novel are either products of the author's imagination or are used fictitiously.

Library of Congress Control Number: 2023915752
paperback ISBN: 978-1-962080-37-8
e-book ISBN: 978-1-962080-38-5

MJF Publishing books may be purchased for education, Business, or promotional use. For information on bulk purchases, please contact the author directly at mikefaricyauthor@gmail.com

Published by

MJF Publishing
https://www.mikefaricybooks.com

To Teresa

"Isn't he just the cute hoor"

Acknowledgments

I would like to thank the following people for their help and support:

Special thanks to my editors, Kitty, Donna and Rhonda for their hard work, cheerful patience and positive feedback.

I would like to thank Ann and Julie for their creative talent and not slitting their wrists or jumping off the high bridge when dealing with my Neanderthal computer capabilities.

Special thanks to Ann for her patience.

Last, I would like to thank family and friends for their encouragement and unqualified support. Special thanks to Maggie, Jed, Schatz, Pat, Av, Emily and Pat for not rolling their eyes, at least when I was there, and most of all, to my wife Teresa whose belief, support and inspiration has from day one, never waned.

Prologue

He took the bottle from the ice bucket, deftly tore off the foil covering the cork, and pointed the bottle toward the entrance to the kitchen. He edged the cork up until it exploded and shot into the kitchen. "No, Maddie, now not another word. I'm cooking dinner for you. It's the least I can do. You've been so kind. I've got a special family recipe in the oven. It will be ready in an hour. Until then, your job is to get comfy on the couch, tell me about your day, and try this champagne. I hope you like it,"

"Oh, wow, that was so cool, and you didn't spill a drop."

"Practice makes perfect, now not to worry, there's plenty more. I've got two more bottles in the refrigerator. I got these last month in Chateau Thierry," he lied. "A little town about sixty miles north of Paris. A lovely place. I took the train up there, spent the night in a seventeenth-century B&B. Then back to Paris the next day. I thought this would be the perfect night to open a bottle or two."

"It sounds wonderful. I want to hear all about your trip. I was so worried when I didn't hear from you. I thought maybe I said something, and you decided you weren't interested anymore."

"Last minute flight. I meant to call, but my phone wasn't working in Paris. Let me just fill our glasses. They're in the kitchen. I'll be right back." He hurried into the kitchen, glancing over his shoulder to make sure she hadn't followed. He tore the nine dollar price tag from Liquor City off the bottle, moved her champagne flute off to the right-hand side, and slowly filled it with champagne. He filled his flute, then took her's in his right hand, swirled the champagne for a moment, picked up his flute with his left, and hurried back into the living room.

"Here you go, darling. In the few weeks we've known one another, you've come to mean so much to me. Now, a toast to you. I, I love you," he said, holding his champagne flute out to toast her. He leaned down and kissed her on the forehead.

"Oh, wow," she said, as his beard lightly tickled her forehead. She clinked her crystal flute with his and took a sip. "This is just what… I mean, you've no idea. I've wanted to hear you say that from the moment we first laid eyes on one another. I adore you, and these last weeks have been so special. You've made me feel like a princess. You've been so kind, so gracious, so loving."

"Believe me, you're the one who's been so wonderful. Now," he said, extending his flute as they clinked crystal once more, "to both of us and for a wonderful future. Drink up now. As I said, I've got two more bottles and a delicious meal coming. Let's both relax and enjoy the evening."

"Oh, I will, and dinner smells delicious."

"An old family recipe. I know you're going to love it, and I'm quite sure you've never had anything like it."

"What is it?" she asked and took a large sip.

"Oh, no. You just wait. Finish that glass while I get the bottle," he said and hurried into the kitchen. He came back with the champagne bottle, topped up her glass, and placed the bottle in the ice bucket. "Another toast, this one to my princess," he said, extending his flute once again. She raised her flute a bit too fast, and champagne spilled over the side.

"Oh, shit, sorry about that." Her speech was beginning to slur, and she moved her head from side to side for a moment in an attempt to regain her balance.

"Not a problem. Finish that up, and I'll refill it for you."

Maddie attempted to gulp down the champagne, oblivious to it running down her chin. He took the champagne flute from her hand, refilled it, and set it on the coffee table. She seemed to be fighting to keep her head up as he walked into the kitchen. He pulled the garlic bread out of the oven, took the frozen pizza out of the freezer, placed it on a cookie sheet in the oven, then set the timer.

He'd been watching porn on the computer for twenty minutes before he checked on Maddie, now comatose on the couch. As he pulled her up onto her feet, she mumbled something incoherent. He draped her over his shoulder and carried her into the guest room. He laid her on the plastic-covered bed and attached her wrists and ankles to the leather restraints. He placed a length of duct tape over her mouth then headed back into the kitchen to turn off the timer and take the pizza out of the oven.

One

This was going to be complicated. I'd dated Allison Dankwell three times, right before I met Taffy. On top of being an absolute control freak, Allison is just plain nuts. About a week after I met Taffy, she suddenly became Taffy's Facebook friend. Maybe two weeks after that, they met for coffee. Whacko Allison has been in the picture ever since. Tonight was going to be the first time I'd actually seen Allison since I nicely told her it wasn't working out and then ran as fast as I could to my car and locked the doors.

"What's wrong with you, Dev? This is going to be fun. Besides, Allison has turned out to be a great new friend, and I want to give her support."

I put the blinker on, turned into the parking ramp, and waited for the line to inch forward. "You know how I am about concerts, Taffy. The tickets cost a big chunk of change. We have to pay for parking, and once we get inside, two things are going to happen. First, whoever is in front of me will stand for the entire concert. Second, there'll be some drunk next to me who'll sing along off-key to every song."

"God, Mr. Crabby, sorry if I ruined the night you had planned with all those classy guys at The Spot bar.

Maybe just let me out here, and I'll find a ride home afterwards. Look at all the people here for the concert, Dev. The place is jammed. Hello, get with the program. You're always listening to music from thirty years ago. The stuff you like is almost older than me."

I looked around as we inched our way into the parking ramp. There was a line of cars on either side and a long line of cars behind us. I was boxed in and couldn't leave even if I wanted to. I saw no point in telling her, ninety-nine percent of the traffic was people coming to watch the first preseason hockey game. "I didn't mean it like that, Taffy. I'm here with you. I'll be nice. It's just not my thing to do is all."

"Mmm, well, maybe I'll just remember that next time I don't want to do *something*," she said, emphasizing that last word and sending a very clear message.

"Okay, okay. I'm looking forward to it," I lied, hoping there weren't any sharp objects in the place that Allison could use to stab me. "I'll be Mr. Positive."

"Oh, really," Taffy said then folded her arms over her chest and stared ahead.

We parked up on the fourth level. At least half the people getting out of their cars were wearing Minnesota Wild jerseys or hats.

"Oh my God, this is so wonderful. All these people coming to hear Allison."

There was no point in telling her most of these people would run the other way once they heard Allison sing. I wasn't sure how she got the gig with a pickup band in the River-View room, but I had my suspicions. We took the elevator down to the second floor and then walked through the concourse over Kellogg Boulevard one-story below. The line of traffic going into the parking ramp was three times longer than just fifteen minutes ago.

"Oh, I'm so excited for Allison," Taffy squealed. "This is going to be the start of a great career. Finally, the break she's worked so hard to get."

That didn't quite match up with the history I knew. Allison had started a restaurant, actually her version of a food truck. She put on a bikini and sold hotdogs from a Styrofoam cooler she had in her car for two or three days before the city confiscated the cooler and fined her. She had a lap dance business for maybe a week. Somehow, she had found her way into a vacant apartment and advertised on the internet until the neighbors got together and physically threw her out. The painting business lasted, I think, just a day before her first customer, her sister, fired her. After school daycare was a disaster, teaching kindergarteners how to mix martinis. The dog care business tanked when her dog impregnated the two dogs she was supposed to be watching. Now, she somehow talked four guys into forming a pickup band so she could sing. God only knew what it would be like.

We came to a side door along the concourse with a handwritten sign on a piece of paper torn from a spiral notebook. The sign was taped to the door with two pieces of blue masking tape.

ALLISON DANKWELL
RIVER-VIEW ROOM

"I guess we go in here," Taffy said and gave a questioning look at all the people walking past, headed for the hockey game.

"Maybe we just have special upfront seating," I said and opened the door. We walked down two flights of stairs to a basement room. A woman was seated at a card table in front of the door. A gray metal cash box sat on the table with a sign that read, '**$10.**'

"Is this where Allison Dankwell is singing?" Taffy asked.

The woman sipped from a glass of dark liquid I doubted was tea and said, "It is. Just ten dollars each, please."

Yeah, I'd need a drink too, just to build up enough courage to tell people they had to pay to hear Allison. I pulled out my wallet and handed her a twenty.

"Just through that door," she indicated with her head. "They'll start in about thirty minutes."

"Thanks," I said and held the door open for Taffy.

We walked into the River-View Room, and the first thing I noticed was there weren't any windows, as in no actual view of the river. All sorts of tables and chairs were scattered around, looking like a hodgepodge of furniture donated for people in need. At the far end of the room sat a small portable bar on wheels with maybe a dozen people standing around it.

Taffy looked stunned as we headed toward the bar. I heard her mumble under her breath, "Oh, my God. This is not good."

"Oh, Taffy, so nice you came. Allison will be so pleased," an older woman said. I recognized her as Allison's battle-ax mother, although I'd only met her once.

"Oh, hi, Mrs. Dankwell. How nice to see you. How are you?" Taffy said.

"Just fine, dear, just fine. And this is?" she said, giving me a quick once over and frowning. From the unimpressed look she gave me, it was suddenly obvious where Allison got her personality.

"This is a friend of mine, Dev Haskell. Dev, this is Allison's mom."

I smiled, hoping she didn't pick up on my name. "It's very nice to meet you, Mrs. Dankwell."

"Yeah, that's what everybody says," she said, not joking. I was introduced to Allison's two sisters, an aunt, Mrs. Dankwell's neighbor, who had a walker and couldn't escape, and some guy named Jasper. The six other people turned out to be three high school friends and their not too happy looking husbands. I got an overpriced glass of wine for Taffy, a beer for me, and drifted toward the three husbands complaining to one another over in a corner.

It was closer to forty-five minutes and two beers before Allison and her band appeared. There wasn't a stage. A set of drums and a piano were arranged in a corner, and four guys took up positions. Two guitar players, a five-string and bass, plugged into two small amplifiers. One of the amps gave off a high-pitched squeaking sound that got everyone cringing. Once that was turned down, Allison stepped up to the microphone.

"I'd just like to thank everyone for coming tonight," Allison said and flashed a half-second glare in my direction. "Thank you all and just screw everyone else." She turned toward the band and slowly counted, "One, two, three, four," before she burst into a dreadful, off-key rendition of 'Do you Believe in Magic.' It was a good thing there weren't any sharp objects around, or I might have slit my wrists. I noticed the woman with the walker rubbing her ears until it dawned on me, she was really turning off her hearing aids. Even the pickup band shot one another looks that said, "What the hell?"

Things went downhill from there. I don't think I've ever heard so many wonderful songs absolutely abused and destroyed, but Allison just kept on singing. There were always at least two people at the bar getting refills just to ease the pain. I stopped at three beers, only because I was driving.

It felt like a long week had passed before Allison finished up abusing Linda Ronstadt's 'Long Long Time.' The musicians fled the scene out a side door as Allison took a bow. Everyone clapped, but I think only because they were thankful she was finally finished. The three girlfriends smiled, waved, and caught up with their husbands already storming out the door.

Taffy took a deep breath, smiled, and said, "Oh, Allison. I just don't know what to say."

"So, what did you think?" Allison said, looking at me again with the glare.

"You've certainly got your own unique sound."

She eyed me, but clearly wasn't sure how to respond.

"Wonderful, darling, just wonderful," her mother said and turned to the woman with the walker. "What did you think, Marilyn?"

"I think you should take me home," Marilyn said.

God bless her, that brought things to a close.

"Dev, would you mind? I'm going to grab a ride with Allison."

Oh great, probably a 'tell-all' moment with Allison after which Taffy would dump me. "You sure? I mean I thought we might—"

"Dev, I'm going to grab a ride with Allison." She leaned toward me and whispered, "She needs some support right now."

She needed a dozen kicks in the ass, but I said, "Not a problem, I've got an early morning tomorrow. Mrs. Dankwell, nice to meet you. Allison, congratulations on your first show." They both gave me the evil eye. I leaned in to give Taffy a kiss. She turned her cheek at the last moment, which pretty much served as the icing on the cake for the night. I walked as fast as I could to my car, drove home, and then Morton and I watched a movie of no redeeming social value.

TWO

It was just a little after five the following afternoon. I was sitting on a stool at The Spot bar, chatting with my office mate Louie Laufen. Morton was stretched out at my feet, waiting for the next deep-fat-fried pork rind from Louie. He'd already eaten the better part of the bag. I was in the process of listening to Louie tell me about his latest DUI court case.

"So, they pull him over, and he gets out of the car, naked."

"The guy is naked?" I asked.

"Well, he had on tennis shoes and black socks."

"Where were his clothes?"

"In the back seat. In fact, that was exactly what he told the cops when they asked him the same thing. Then he went on to explain that it was his birthday, and he just assumed it would be okay to drive around in his birthday suit."

"You're making this up. You gotta be. Was there a girlfriend in the back seat?"

"If only, it probably would have helped my defense. He's going down on the DUI, unfortunately his second. I'm just hoping to get the Indecent Exposure charge dropped or maybe pled down to obscenity. I mean, he had no intention of getting out of the car except that the police pulled him over and then requested that he step outside his vehicle."

"And that's when they realized he was driving around naked?"

"Yeah," Louie said, nodding, maybe bouncing the theory off me to get my reaction before he presented it to a judge.

"Any chance of PTSD or some form of mental instability?"

"So you're thinking my effort to plead down to obscenity isn't going to fly."

"I'm thinking it might just do more harm than good," depending on who the judge is.

"Unfortunately, I can't disagree," Louie said and took a sip from his glass.

"I think you're both full of shit," the guy on the stool next to me said.

I turned to face him, and he started to laugh. "Hi, Dev. Long time no see," he said and held out his hand. Ben Jackson, a retired homicide detective. I recognized the twinkling blue eyes and the scar through his bottom lip. Last time I saw him, he was a big muscular guy. Now he looked lean and almost frail.

"Ben Jackson. How have you been? I thought someone told me you moved down to Florida."

We shook hands, and Ben said, "You heard right. We moved down to a little town called Venice. Finally had enough of the tax rates and the winters up here. We've been Florida residents for the last six years. We're just back in town for a niece's wedding tomorrow. Thought I might look you up."

"Amazing you found me here at The Spot."

"Not really," Ben said and didn't laugh.

"How have things been going? Oh, hey, this is a friend and my office mate, Louie Laufen. He practices law."

"Nice to meet you," Ben said and nodded. "Yeah, I recognize the name. You represent a lot of folks on DUI charges, don't you?"

Louie nodded.

"Listen, Dev. I was thinking of you the other day. I got into this mystery series and thought you might enjoy it. Wanted to give you this book." He opened a grocery bag and pulled out a paperback. The cover was solid black with the title, One After Midnight, in bold red letters.

My first thought was *'Why would I want to read this,'* but I smiled and said, "Oh, gee, Ben, you didn't have to do this. I have to tell you, I don't really read too many books, and I've got a lot on my plate right now."

"Yeah, Dev, sure you do. Come on. Don't kid a kidder," he said and waved Mike the bartender over with a nod of his head. "Let me buy a round for these two ne'er'-do-wells and better give them another bag of whatever they're feeding that poor dog on the floor."

"Pork rinds," Louie said.

"Obviously, a health food," Ben said, meaning anything but. He opened the book and placed a business card inside. "Listen, give me a call when you're finished with the book. I'd love to hear what you thought about it."

"Did you write this thing?" I asked as I took the book from him.

"Me? Hell no. I've neither the time nor the inclination. This one is actually the first in a series. I think you might find it interesting."

"Well, thanks for thinking of me, Ben. Much appreciated," I said and smiled.

Ben shook his head, tossed a ten on the bar, and looked at Louie. "You must be one hell of a patient guy to put up with all of Haskell's bullshit."

"Some days are easier than others," Louie said, and the two of them laughed.

Ben slid off his stool just as Mike delivered our drinks, then reached behind, pulled a bag of pork rinds from the rack, and dropped it in front of Louie. "Good seeing you, Dev. I'll be waiting for that phone call. Keep the change," he said to Mike and headed out the door.

Louie opened the bag of pork rinds and stuffed three or four into his mouth.

I looked at the book and shook my head. "What the hell am I going to do with this?"

"Maybe read it," Mike said. He picked up the ten-dollar bill and said, "I need another two bucks for the bag of pork rinds."

Louie quickly set down the open bag.

I dug into my wallet and pulled out a five-dollar bill, the only bill I had in my wallet. Mike took the five and slapped the edge of both bills on the bar, indicating 'thanks for the tip' then walked over to the cash register.

We chatted for another five minutes, and then I slid off my stool.

"You heading out?" Louie said and took a sip.

I drained my beer mug. "Yeah, Taffy's fixing dinner tonight for Morton and me. We have to be over there in an hour, and I'm thinking it just might be a good idea to take Morton on a little walk before we head over."

"See you in the morning?" Louie asked.

"Yeah, we should be in around nine. You have a good evening."

"I intend to," Louie said and raised his glass.

Three

We pulled up to Taffy's building right on time and headed inside. She buzzed us in, and we took the elevator up to the third floor. She and her dog, Muffin, opened the door to her condo as we were walking down the hall.

"Amazing," she said, shaking her head. "For all the goofy stuff you do, you're almost always on time."

"It's from all that military training I had."

"Hmm, too bad they didn't spend time in some other areas."

As we stepped inside, I handed her the bottle of wine I'd picked up. Morton and Muffin were already engaged in chasing one another with a chew toy. Muffin currently had the thing in his mouth and had just shot around the back of the couch. Morton was too large to fit behind, and he met Muffin coming out the other side.

"Come on out to the kitchen," Taffy said.

"The place smells wonderful. What are you making?" I asked. I noticed there were three places set on the kitchen counter.

"Chicken curry. I actually made it yesterday. I don't know what it is, but it just seems to taste better on day two. Open that wine, pour us each a glass, and we can sit out on the balcony. How was your day?"

"Wonderfully uneventful. How about you?" I noticed there were three wine glasses on the kitchen counter.

I was just about to ask who else would be joining us when Taffy said, "I got called into my boss's office this morning."

"Oh? Everything all right?"

"Even better than that. We have a team coming in to interview three candidates for a management position, and he wants me to be one of them."

"What? Oh, congratulations. That's fantastic news." I twisted the cap off the wine bottle and filled two glasses. I handed a glass to Taffy then raised mine in a toast. "Here's to your success. When does this happen?"

"Interviews are two days from now."

"Do you know who you're up against?"

"No. It's all hush-hush. As part of the interview process, you're sworn to secrecy. I called my folks, and I've told you, but that's all."

"Oh, Taffy, that's really great news. I know, if they have any brains at all, you're going to be the person they choose. Congratulations! Well done, you."

The intercom suddenly signaled someone down at the security entrance. "I'll get that. Why don't you head out to the balcony? I'll join you in a minute."

"Who's coming?"

"Dev, the balcony," she said and pointed to the double doors leading outside.

"Okay, okay, I'm going."

I was thinking it was Taffy's mother who would be joining us. A nice enough woman who had told Taffy more than once she could do better than me. Unfortunately, I was wrong. About three minutes after Taffy buzzed in whoever was in the lobby. I heard the squeals and shrieks at the door. Taffy and Allison. I was going to need something stronger than wine.

"Oh… you," Allison said a few minutes later as she stepped out onto the balcony. She sounded more than a little disappointed and made a face like someone had just farted in church. As the three of us sat out on the balcony in the setting sun, Taffy told Allison what she was going to wear to her interview. She told her about the hair appointment and pedicure she was going to get tomorrow evening, the night before the interview. She went on and on, and I smiled, nodded, and watched the occasional person walking past on the street below. It was more of the same over dinner. Taffy limited herself to one glass of wine for the entire evening. Allison had pulled the wine bottle closer to her and had talked nonstop for the past half-hour. I cleared the table, loaded the dishwasher, and washed the curry pan. Once I finished cleaning the kitchen, I thought I might encourage Allison to hit the road.

"Congratulations on your performance last night, Allison, very umm, unique. Hope you enjoy the rest of the evening. It was nice to see you again."

"Yeah, that's what everybody tells me," shades of her mother I thought.

"Allison, pour yourself another glass of wine and join me in the living room," Taffy said. Then she pasted a smile on and said, "Thanks for joining us, Dev." With that she shooed Morton and me out the door.

So much for a romantic evening, but then I couldn't blame her. The interview was a really big deal, and she'd worked hard to get this far. It was obvious a kiss wasn't in the cards, so I wished her luck, and we drove home. We settled in front of the tv, and after twenty minutes of going through all the series and movies I had no desire to watch, I turned off the tv and, against my better judgment, opened One After Midnight.

I put some coffee on a little after ten and kept reading. It was an interesting story, not the least of which because it was set in my town, Saint Paul. I recognized the streets, the church where the wedding was, the descriptions of buildings, even the seasonal weather. It was just like being there, although since it had been published in 2006, a few things were different. Someone used a payphone. There was no mention of the internet. At one point, the victim was trying to make a decision in a Blockbuster Video store. Yeah, it was dated, but it was still interesting. Eventually, I was nodding off, with less than sixty pages left to read. I plowed through and then was left hanging when the perpetrator, the man who stalked and then murdered the young woman, got away with the crime. To say I was disappointed was an understatement. I went up to bed, and I think I was asleep before my head hit the pillow.

I was in the midst of a dream. The victim in the book was in Blockbuster Video, and I spotted her as I stepped in the door. I tried to warn her, but she kept moving to a different aisle, and I couldn't get close enough to talk to her. I was about to climb over a rack of videos when my alarm went off.

Morton slipped his head beneath the pillow as I crawled out of bed and headed for the shower. He came downstairs an hour later. I gave him his perfunctory scratch behind the ears then let him out the kitchen door. I fooled around on the internet for a bit, sent Taffy an email thanking her for dinner, and let Morton back in. I grabbed the book I read last night, and we headed down to the office. I was putting the coffee on just as I heard Louie making his way up the stairs.

He opened the door a moment later, red-faced and gasping for air. He made his way around his picnic table desk and more or less collapsed in his office chair. I took his coffee mug, dumped the remnants in the sink, refilled it with fresh coffee, and set it in front of him. He nodded thanks and took a couple of sips before he was able to talk.

"You going to give me the details of last night's adventure?"

"You mean with Taffy?"

"You've got more than one?"

"Nothing to tell, Louie. She's got an interview tomorrow morning for a promotion, and it was pretty much the only thing on her mind. Not that I can blame her. But she was completely focused on that. She already had the outfit picked out she was going to wear. She's getting her hair done and a pedicure tonight. She'll probably sleep about fifteen minutes the entire night, not all at once, and then breeze through the interview. I've seen her like this before. It would drive me crazy, but it's just the way she operates, and she's nothing if not successful."

"What are you going to do with the book that retired detective gave you?"

"Maybe give it back to him. I finished it last night around two this morning."

"You actually read the thing?" Louie asked.

"Yeah, to tell you the truth, I was more or less hooked. The story takes place in town here, and there were all sorts of places I recognized. The thing was a little dated. I mean, it was written about fifteen years ago, but I still enjoyed it."

"Dev, up late and finishing a book. Who knew?"

"Well, between Allison's horrible singing and Taffy focused on her job interview, I've got the time. Matter of fact, let me give Ben a call right now. I want to tell him I finished the book. I know he gave it to me thinking I'd never open the thing." I opened the book on my desk, took out Ben Jackson's card, and dialed the number.

Ben answered on the third ring. "Jackson."

"Hi, Ben. Dev here. Just wanted to say it was nice to see you last night, and I wanted to thank you again for the book."

"Dev, You have to read it. I'm telling you, it—"

"I finished it last night, Ben."

"Finished it?"

"Yeah. I enjoyed the hell out it. A great read. It might just get me back into the reading mode."

"Seriously?"

"Yeah, I'm not kidding you. I put the coffee on and finished it a little after two this morning. It was a really good read."

"Tell you what, Dev. I want you to do me a favor when you get home tonight."

"What's that?"

"Check your mailbox."

"What?"

"Something wrong with your hearing? I said check your mailbox. I'm leaving a little something for you."

"Oh, you don't have to do—"

"At my age, Dev, I don't have to do anything I don't want to do. You just check your mailbox. Anything else?"

"No, sir, I guess not."

"You got time for coffee tomorrow?"

"Always for you, Ben."

"Good. Call me in the morning, and we'll get together. Talk to you then."

I worked through the day checking job applications and verifying employment records. Louie suggested we head over to The Spot around half-past-four, but I was anxious to get home and check the mailbox, so I begged off.

I parked in the driveway, let Morton in the front door, then checked my mailbox. There were two credit card offers, the power bill, and another book, this one entitled, Two After Midnight. The cover on the book was essentially the same, the title in bold red letters with a solid black background. I closed the door behind me and headed into the kitchen. I let Morton out into the back and tossed the mail on the kitchen counter. I debated opening a beer, decided it might make me sleepy, and grabbed a water instead. I sat down on a kitchen stool and started to read the first page.

Four

I heard Morton scratching at the back door and glanced at the clock on the stove. It was after eight. I glanced out the window, and it was almost dark. Morton had been in the backyard for the better part of three hours, and I'd been engrossed in Two After Midnight.

Morton gave me a look then stepped inside and stood in front of the kitchen counter looking at the cookie jar where I kept the dog biscuits. I couldn't blame him. I'd completely lost track of time. I tossed him a biscuit, placed the Lean Cuisine Taffy got me in the microwave and got lost again in the book.

It was similar to the first story. The chief protagonist was the same guy, seemingly a nice, social kind of guy, who met young women and courted them, apparently with the idea that he would eventually murder them. Once again, the tale was set in Saint Paul, and the descriptions of street corners, bars, and restaurants matched my experience.

The microwave started beeping, and I pulled out the Lean Cuisine. Morton waited around for a taste. Eventually, I heard him give a loud sigh, and he made his way into the living room, climbed onto the couch, and stared out the window. I continued to read.

In the book, the couple were attending a Saturday wedding. The protagonist begged off alcohol because he was driving while, at the same time, making sure his date's glass was never empty. Prosecco seemed to be her drink of choice, and there was plenty of it. She was dancing on a table toward the end of the reception, and he carried her out over his shoulder to all sorts of cheers from her friends and headed out the door. They drove back to her home, where he placed her in bed, basically unconscious from Prosecco. He proceeded to spend the next few hours going through her computer, her files, desk drawers, bank statements. You name it. He photographed a number of documents and copied her computer password. He took her house keys to a twenty-four-hour shop and had copies made. He left a nice note next to a glass of water and a bottle of aspirin on her bedside table and went home around four in the morning.

He phoned her at eleven that morning, offering to take her out to breakfast. He guessed she was still in bed, maybe with a cold compress over her eyes. She answered her phone with a groaning voice. She begged off from his offer for breakfast, apologized for her behavior the previous night, and disconnected. He called his mother and offered to bring dinner over, ever the perfect son.

I realized my dinner had been sitting on the counter for at least a couple of hours. It wasn't even warm, it was cold. I nibbled away at it while reading. After a couple of yawns, I put the coffee on, had a candy bar, and continued reading. The book ended basically the same way as the one the night before. The guy murdered the woman and was never caught. I finished a little earlier than last night and headed up to bed at half-past-one. Morton was stretched out on the bed and didn't so much as move when I climbed in.

My alarm went off at seven. I stumbled into the shower, where I remained for a good twenty minutes. I dressed and headed downstairs, leaving Morton in bed with his head shoved under the pillow. I made a fresh pot of coffee, ate two pieces of cold pizza for breakfast and sent Taffy a text message, *'Wishing you all the best in your interview this morning.'*

I heard Morton jump off the bed a half-hour later. He made his way into the kitchen, stretched, then strolled over to me for his perfunctory morning head scratch before I let him out the back door.

I received a short text back from Taffy, *'Thx'*. I Googled the author of the Midnight series, a guy named Virgil Tueur. Based on his picture, I placed him at maybe forty. Dark, curly hair combed back with a full beard. Google had a list of his books, there were six, and a very short biography. It turns out he was from Saint Paul, which explained the excellent job on his descriptions of places. The biography described him as 'extremely private.'

I let Morton in, fed him and after thirty minutes, we headed down to the office. We arrived before Louie, who had once again neglected to turn off the coffee maker. I dumped the scorched remnants into the sink and made a fresh pot. I was on my second cup when I heard Louie coming up the stairs.

He entered red-faced, set his briefcase on his picnic table desk, and collapsed into his desk chair, gasping for air. I got up and poured some fresh coffee into his mug. He pulled the mug toward him, took a sip, grimaced, and said, "Not bad."

"How late were you at The Spot last night?" I asked.

He took another sip of coffee and said, "I was there until close, whenever that was. You meet up with Taffy?"

"No, she's focused on that job interview today. She was getting her hair done and a pedicure or something last night. Probably tried on a dozen or so outfits this morning and I bet she left her place dressed in the one she originally chose. I stayed home last night reading."

"Sounds like Ben Jackson all of a sudden turned you into an egghead," Louie said and slurped more coffee.

"Mmm, thanks for reminding me. I'm supposed to call him this morning for coffee." I checked the time on my phone, it was nine-fifteen, and I called Ben.

Five

Ben said he'd meet me at Nina's for coffee around half-past-ten. I arrived fifteen minutes early, and he was already waiting. Based on his almost empty coffee mug and the crumbs on the plate in front of him, I figured he'd been sitting there for at least a half-hour.

"Hi, Ben, you been waiting long?"

"Not a problem, it's interesting people-watching in this joint."

I could relate to what he said. Maybe two-thirds of the tables were occupied by people on a laptop. I knew for a fact a number of them had been here for at least an hour and, in some cases, more than two hours. Great work if you can get it, I guess. "I'm grabbing a coffee. Can I get you another?"

"Decaf americano," he said then focused on two guys just sitting down a couple of tables away. They each had a coffee and a laptop. I went and got two coffees, and by the time I got back to the table, I had completely forgotten which one was the decaf. I didn't see any point in mentioning that to Ben.

"I want to thank you again for the books, Ben. I hesitate to say I enjoyed them. I mean the guy murders a woman in each book, but I really got into the story, very realistic. I felt like I was right there. You know anything about the author?"

"You mean this fellow, Tueur?"

"Yeah, Virgil Tueur," I said.

"I know a little bit. He is, or at least was, a local Saint Paul guy. Did a lot of in-depth crime reporting for newspapers. He was an independent, meaning he wasn't on anyone's payroll. He'd submit stories to a variety of papers around the country. They were in multiple parts, a series if you will. A paper would run a new part for four or five days in a row. Trips he'd taken to New York City, New Orleans, San Francisco, Mexico, and even Europe. He did a lot of writing about local mobs, that sort of thing. I've read a number of his articles, always entertaining and interesting. Of course, this was before the newspaper industry took a dive. That first book—"

"One After Midnight," I said and smiled like I'd just given the correct answer in a spelling bee.

"Good answer, you get a gold star," Ben said. "His first book was written back in 2006. The next one, Two after midnight, was written about 2008. After that second one was published, his writing career on the book side began to take off. It was right around that time that he stopped writing the newspaper stories and became a full-time book guy. As near as I can tell, he hasn't looked back. He's been on all sorts of tv shows. He was even interviewed by what's her name, real popular woman with a tv show. She's got some damn book list and—"

"Are you talking about Oprah Winfrey?"

"Yeah, that's the one. Anyway, she interviews him, and apparently his books really take off. This is right around the time Kindles are introduced and all that internet stuff. I guess he's been living the life ever since."

"Sounds like the ultimate success story. So, why are you giving me these books, Ben? And don't get me wrong. I loved them. I haven't read a book in years, and I finished these two in record time. I stayed up late and put the coffee on just so I could finish the damn things. But why me?"

"You like 'em?"

"Yeah, obviously. I picked up on a lot of the places he describes. I've been in a lot of the bars and restaurants. The guy spends probably the first third of the book looking around for just the right woman. His main character, it's interesting you never learn the guy's name, but he stalks his victim, dates her for about three weeks, and then he kills her. He's an absolute nutcase."

"And don't forget he gets away with it," Ben said. He reached down on the chair next to him and picked up a book, Three After Midnight.

I held my hands up. "Ben, you don't have to go buying me books. I like the stories, the series, I guess. It's cool they're set here in town, but at the end of the day, this guy is basically a serial killer, and he's getting away with it."

"First of all, Dev, I didn't buy this one for you. God, you think I'm nuts? I got them for me. I've read them all. So do me a favor, just read this one and give me a call. We're in town for two more days, and then we're fleeing Minnesota. The mid-western winters have lost all appeal for me."

"It's a week past Labor Day. We won't have snow for seven or eight more weeks."

"Yeah, maybe, but why take the chance? Give me a call when you finish this book. I gotta take the wife over to her sister Suzi's place today," he said and rolled his eyes. "I'll be waiting for your call, and thanks for meeting me this morning." With that, he stood, extended his hand, we shook, and he headed out the door.

I watched him through the window as he crossed the street and disappeared from sight. Another book, he must think I've got all sorts of time to burn. I checked the thing to see if it might be autographed. It wasn't. It was published in 2012. I figured it couldn't hurt to just read the two-page prologue, so I turned to it and started reading.

"You mind if we join you? Is anyone sitting here?" a guy asked.

I looked up. He had brown hair, a sparse beard, and was holding a laptop computer with a sandwich and a coffee balanced on top.

"Sorry to bother you, but you're next to one of the outlets, and I have to charge my laptop, and these are the only two seats available." The young girl behind him nodded. They might have been twenty and looked like college kids.

"Yeah, not a problem, grab a seat," I said and looked around. The place was jammed. A line six people long stood at the counter waiting to order food and coffee. Every table looked to be taken. Three groups of people were standing, drinking coffee, and chatting away. I looked out the window, and all the tables along the sidewalk were occupied. I glanced at the book in front of me. I was already on page sixty-three. "Besides, I was just leaving," I said and stood.

"Are you sure? We're not chasing you off, are we?"

"No, no. Just a quick break, but it's time to get back to the office. Enjoy your lunch," I said and hurried out the door. When I got back to the office, Louie was gone. The coffee pot was empty, and the burner was still on. Morton ran past me, down the stairs, and barked by the front door. I grabbed his leash and hurried after him. We made it about two feet around the corner before he assumed the position and did his business.

"Thanks in advance for picking that up," a guy said as he walked past. Thankfully, I had a bundle of poop bags attached to Morton's leash. I tossed the bag in the trash bin on the corner and hurried back upstairs.

Six

Morton assumed his position on his bed and resumed his love affair with the rawhide chew. I put on a fresh pot of coffee and picked up where I'd left off in Three After Midnight.

I heard Louie groaning a couple of hours later as he made his way up the stairs. He was red-faced as always when he opened the door and proceeded to collapse in his chair. I kept reading.

Eventually, I looked up and said, "So, how did it go?"

"You mean with my birthday suit client?"

"No, your appointment with your tax accountant. Yes, the birthday suit client, what happened?"

"He'll have six months to be thinking about the wisdom of his actions. Once he's released, he'll be dealing with four years of probation to remind himself, not to mention his increased car insurance rates that will run somewhere around ten grand over the course of the next seven years. On a more positive note, I was able to avoid having him charged as a sex offender, so he won't have to go through that process."

"They were going to charge him as a sex offender?"

"Well, that was their plan, and they were asking for a two-year sentence."

"Remind me to stay dressed whenever I'm behind the wheel."

"I see you're still reading that book," Louie said.

"Actually, no, this is the third book in the series." I went on to tell Louie about my meeting with Ben Jackson over coffee. "I get the feeling there's something out there he wants to tell me, but every time I try to broach the subject, he hands me another book and tells me to read it. The good news is I like reading the books. The author really writes a great story about how this creep thinks, the things he does, drugging these women and then murdering them."

"And it's a local guy that writes the books? What'd you say his name is?"

"Virgil Tueur, I don't even know if that's the right way to say it. Ben was telling me the guy wrote stories for newspapers back in the day. The kind of thing they'd run for five or six days."

"Did he write for the Minneapolis or the Saint Paul paper?"

"Neither one, I guess he was more of a freelance type of guy. It was a different world back then just ten years ago. Anyway, nice job on getting Mr. Birthday Suit six months instead of the two years."

"Let's just hope this time it registers with him. If he gets nailed again, he's going to be looking at three years just for DUI. God help him if he doesn't have clothes on," Louie said and opened his briefcase, signaling the conversation was over.

I went back to reading. It seemed like just a couple of minutes later when Louie asked, "Hey, you thinking of maybe going over to The Spot for one?"

I think I could count on one hand the times I'd only had 'one' at The Spot. "Tell you what, I was gonna call Taffy and see if she wanted to grab some pizza or something. I gotta take Morton for a walk. Why don't you head over, and I'll stop in either way and let you know what's up. I just want to finish this chapter."

"Okay, one way or the other, I'll see you over there," he said. He tossed a file back in his briefcase and headed out the door. I watched him out the window as he waited for a bus to pass and then made a beeline for The Spot.

I stopped reading at the end of the chapter. I checked, and I only had a hundred and six pages left to read. I phoned Taffy to see if she wanted to go to dinner, just the two of us.

She answered on the fifth ring, just before I was dropped into her voicemail. "Hi, Dev, what's up?"

"I wanted to see how things went on the interview with your boss today and thought maybe you'd like to grab dinner somewhere. There's a great pizza place called Mario's that gives you this Italian bread with olive oil and balsamic while you're waiting for—"

"Mmm, thanks, but I'm just beat after stressing over the interview for the past two days. Would it be all right if I took a pass?"

"Yeah, sure, I guess. Everything all right?"

"Yeah, just really beat. I won't hear anything for another day or two. I just need a night to decompress and watch Beauty and the Beast or something."

"You're watching Beauty and the Beast tonight?"

"I need a break, Dev. I'm still stressed out."

"Okay, okay, no pressure. Enjoy your evening, and I'll talk to you tomorrow."

"Yeah, okay, thanks for understanding."

I figured, if I wanted any more positive feedback, I could always call bitchy Allison. Man, a ninety-second conversation, I wondered what Allison might have told her. I grabbed the book, clicked Morton's leash onto his collar, and we headed out the door. We took a roundabout twenty-minute walk through the neighborhood then made our way into The Spot. Morton's tail started wagging as I opened the front door. Louie was sitting at the far end of the bar. He saw me walk in and signaled Mike to get me a beer. I stopped and chatted for a moment with two guys seated at the bar. By the time I sat down next to Louie, a beer was waiting for me, and Louie proceeded to open a bag of pork rinds. Morton immediately sat and paid rapt attention to Louie.

"God, it's just amazing. He's so much smarter than you are, Dev."

I took a sip of my beer and said, "On most days, that's not very hard to do."

Louie grabbed two pork rinds and lowered his hand toward Morton. Morton lapped them up and then settled onto the floor beneath our stools. "So, you grabbing dinner with Taffy tonight?"

"No, I talked to her on the phone for a minute. She's still stressed out from the interview, won't know how it went for a couple of days, and she just wanted to chill out at home."

"You going over later?"

"You kidding? Absolutely not. She's going to be watching Beauty and the Beast tonight. I had to go through this once before. She sits on the couch, hugging a pillow, crying, repeating lines, and singing all the songs. Believe me, no one in their right mind would want to be there. I think I'll go home and finish my book. I'm gonna call Ben Jackson later to meet for coffee tomorrow."

"I thought you met with him this morning?"

"Yeah, I did, but I told him I'd give him a call for tomorrow and link up. He and his wife are heading back to Florida the day after tomorrow, and I want to thank him for the books. It's nice to see the guy after five or six years. Anyway, we might not be in tomorrow until ten or so. You in court?"

"Not until the afternoon," Louie said and took a sip.

We chatted on about nothing for the next hour and another beer, and then Morton and I headed home. I let

Morton out the back door, settled in on a kitchen stool, and started reading. More of the same, the bars, the restaurants, the streets. At one point, the author mentioned construction on a particular bridge, and I remembered it exactly as he described it. The time it took to resurface, the new attractive wrought iron railings put in place. The railings were ten feet high. But what most people didn't realize was they were put in place to stop folks from jumping off the bridge and committing suicide.

I let Morton back in and then went online. I got onto the Amazon site, clicked on books, then entered the author's name, Virgil Tueur. The entire series of six books came up on the screen. I purchased the last three in the series and sent them to my Kindle. Much as I liked reading the paperback books, the Kindle made it so much easier. The titles and the covers were the same, Four, Five, and Six After Midnight, with the title in red letters on the black background.

I checked the time. It was eight-forty-five. Maybe too late to call Ben, so I sent him a text message. My phone rang about five minutes later.

"Ben?"

"Hi Dev, got your text. How's it going?"

"Good, hey, I just finished that third book, and before you say anything, I've got the next three loaded on my Kindle, so don't give me the fourth one. You got time for coffee tomorrow?"

"If I live that long. We've been at my sister-in-law's all day, and the girls are still going strong trading stories from a half-century ago about who did what to whom. Yeah, how about same time, same place?"

"We could do that," I said. "Or if you wanted to meet an hour earlier, say maybe nine, I could meet you then."

"Terrific, see you at nine tomorrow morning."

"And Ben, I'm buying tomorrow."

"Gee, a coffee, that's big of you, Dev. I'll see you in the morning."

I went upstairs, turned on my Kindle, and settled into bed.

Seven

I woke the following morning just a little after six. I was still dressed with the Kindle resting on my chest. Morton was stretched out next to me taking up two-thirds of the bed. I grabbed a shower, went downstairs, put the coffee on and turned on my computer. I raced through my emails, sent Louie a message reminding him we wouldn't be in before ten. I poured myself a coffee, turned on my Kindle, and got back into Four Before Midnight.

I let Morton out the kitchen door once he had his stretch and I scratched him behind the ears. I put two slices of bread in the toaster and went back to reading. Morton scratching at the kitchen door got my attention. I let him in, filled his food and water dish and checked the time. It was just a little after eight-thirty, and Nina's coffee shop was just a two-minute walk from my place. I wanted to be there before Ben, so I headed out the door.

I ordered coffee and a pastry, sat down, and waited. I didn't have to wait long. Ben walked in before I was halfway through my coffee. He was wearing a heavy black wool coat and a surprised look when he saw me smiling at him.

"You just coming home from last night?" he asked.

"I wish. No, I live up the block and figured I'd get here before you. What can I get you?" I asked as I stood.

"Relax, you don't have to get me anything. I'll just—"

"After you gave me three books, the least I can do is buy you a coffee. What do you want?"

"You sure?"

"Ben, I told you I'm buying. Name your poison."

"Okay, if you insist. I'll have a decaf americano and a slice of that apple strudel."

"Coming right up, sit down and hold this table for us until I get back." I stepped to the back of the line and gradually made my way up to the front. "Two americanos, one of them decaf, and two slices of the apple strudel, please."

I took the strudels over to the table then hurried back to grab the coffee. By the time I got back to the table, Ben had eaten half his strudel and was eyeing mine. "Hey, forget it, Ben. No way, this one's mine. Besides, my girlfriend says I need the sweetening."

"Probably the least of the things that need to be fixed with you," he laughed. "You said you got the fourth book?"

"I'm a big spender, Ben. I bought four, five, and six."

"When will they be delivered?"

"Last night, about fifteen seconds after I ordered them. I got the eBooks on my Kindle."

"Fifteen seconds? God, the technology nowadays, I tell ya."

"Here's what you can tell me. This is not a complaint, but why did you seek me out and give me the books? I hasten to add, I'm loving the series. Really, I love it."

"That's good. They're all set here in the saintly city."

"Yeah, I know that. I told you that's part of what I like about them. Honest to God, I feel like I'm right there."

Ben nodded, took a loud sip of his coffee and then a bite of his strudel. Once he swallowed, he took a deep breath and said, "What if I told you each one of those books is actually an unsolved case?"

"What?" I half-shouted, apparently loud enough that folks around us shot me a quick look.

"Yeah, believe it or not, each one of those books represents an unsolved case here in town. Unfortunately, I happen to know that because I was working some of the damn cases. They were tough. At one point, we must have had a dozen guys on them, and, in the end, we still came up with nothing."

"But this guy is a serial killer. Couldn't you put that together and—"

"Dev, it's not like he was doing this every week. The first two cases are two years apart, 2006 and 2008. The third case is four years after that, in 2012. The next two are three years apart."

"So did you have any suspects, some guys you thought might have—"

"It was a couple of years, four to be exact, before the author's name came up. Just a fluke, one of the guys on the investigation team had a college kid who read one of those books. We started going through them, the books, and they were like reading a file on the cases we were working."

"Did you arrest him?"

He shook his head and said, "No. We brought him in, talked to him. He told us he had inside information. Someone working the investigation who fed him tidbits, but we could never find out who it was, and to this day, I don't believe the bastard. I still think he was lying."

"Does that mean you think he's the murderer?"

"If he's not, he knows who the hell is. We took him to court but lost on the grounds of privacy. We watched him. Hell, we watched him for two years, spent hundreds of thousands of dollars in time and came up empty-handed. We searched his house, searched his lake place, and found absolutely nothing. We interviewed anyone we could find who knew the son-of-a-bitch and got absolutely nowhere. Everyone said he was just a really nice guy."

"Is that why you gave me the books?"

He smirked and said, "I gave them to you on advice."

"Advice? Who in the hell—"

"This bastard still keeps me awake at night, Dev. And let me level with you. I got cancer. We're actually up here because I've been going to Mayo for treatments. I just finished up my second round of Chemo, and I'm crossing my fingers on the follow-up exam. I'm hoping they'll work, but hell, in the end, I don't know. I do know one thing. I don't want this bastard still walking around when I'm gone."

"Ben, I had no idea. I didn't know. I'm so sorry you—"

"Don't go giving me the pity party routine, Dev. I'm still here."

"Yeah, okay. So, who'd you talk to that mentioned my name?"

"Your buddy, Aaron LaZelle."

"Aaron?"

He nodded and smiled. "I told him I was looking for someone who, mmm-mmm, maybe would cut some corners, not be bound by the rules, and nail this guy. Your name came up."

"You got any notes?"

"Funny you should ask," he said and pulled a manila envelope from inside his coat. "Some private notes and two USB flash drives. Aaron said to tell you all the cold case files are available, just check with him. One more thing," Ben said.

"Yeah, what's that?" I said, picking up the manila envelope and peeking inside. It looked like about twenty sheets of paper along with the two flash drives.

"The most recent book in the series is Six After Midnight."

"Yeah, I just downloaded it last night."

"Well, when you read it, check the publication date. It was published six months before the actual murder."

"Six months? Couldn't you guys nail him on that?"

"You'd think so, but no. At that point, it was 2019. I'd been retired for five years. I know they had a number of people on it, and, unfortunately, came up with the same results. Namely hands-off." He glanced at his watch and said, "Oh, sorry. I have to head out. We're down in Rochester this afternoon for what I hope will be a quick check-up and then off to Florida tomorrow. You got any questions, don't hesitate to call. And Dev?"

"Yeah?"

"Thanks in advance for doing this. Gotta run, good luck," he said. He pulled on his heavy wool coat, shook hands with me, and headed out the door into the sunshine and the mid-seventies temperature.

I sat for a good fifteen minutes just thinking, going through the twenty or so pages of notes but not really reading anything. Eventually, I slipped the notes back into the envelope and headed out the door.

I grabbed Morton, and we drove down to the office. Louie was seated at his desk, going over a file. The coffee was on, but there was just barely a swallow or two left in the pot. As soon as we stepped into the office, Morton hurried over to his bed and what was left of the rawhide chew. I tossed Ben's envelope on my desk and said, "Louie, exactly when were you going to turn off the coffee?"

"What? You don't want any?"

"Are you kidding? There isn't enough left in there to pour into my mug."

He shrugged and said, "How does this sound for an idea? You make some more."

"Yeah, I guess I'll have to," I said and set about making a fresh pot. I turned it on, settled in at my desk and pulled out Ben's notes. I read for a couple of minutes then said, "Hey, Louie, sorry I was so bitchy. I just got handed a project that's way out of my league."

"It wouldn't be from Ben Jackson, would it?"

"How'd you know that?"

"Just a wild guess, but I kind of thought he wanted something."

"Yeah, it's a cold case, or actually, a half-dozen of them, apparently all related and driving him nuts. It turns out, he's up here for chemo treatment and wants me to solve the damn things."

"You going to do it?"

"I guess I'm going to have to try."

"Well, let me get you some coffee while you read through that file," Louie said as he waddled over to the coffee pot and filled my mug. "Here, my good deed for the week," he said, setting the mug on my desk.

Eight

Going through Ben Jackson's file was like reading a summary of the After Midnight books. The six victims all had traces of Rohypnol in their system, which suggested they had taken or been given 'roofies,' whether they knew it or not. They had all been sexually assaulted while alive. Each victim had ligature marks about two inches wide on her wrists and ankles. In the books, the victims had their wrists and ankles attached to leather restraints after they'd been served champagne laced with Rohypnol. As I read through Ben's notes, more and more items and descriptions struck me as having been taken directly from the books. Not only the restraints, but the traces of Rohypnol and champagne in the victims' systems. The victims' clothing was left neatly folded next to the bodies as though they'd undressed themselves. Sweaters, blouses, skirts and undergarments were described in the books although the colors had been changed from what was found at the actual scene. Each victim was dressed in a 1960s style white nylon slip, and they were all wearing a white lace wedding veil. It was nothing short of amazing. Another thing that changed was the victim's name and hair color and, in two cases, the race. One of the actual victims was Hispanic and another was Asian. All six women had been described in the books as Caucasian. Three of the six women had tattoos, but no mention of tattoos was made in the books I'd read thus far.

I did find out the author's actual name wasn't Virgil Tueur but rather Virgil Hayes. Not that it was unusual for an author to use a pen name. On a whim, I Googled the French to English translation and input the name Tueur. It translated to 'Killer.' After the better part of an hour, I called Aaron LaZelle, my pal in homicide, and the guy who passed on my name to Ben Jackson. I ended up leaving a message. Aaron phoned me back about an hour later.

"Hi, Aaron," was how I answered my phone.

"Returning your call, Dev."

"Yeah, I had coffee this morning with Ben Jackson. He—"

"Did he give you his notes?"

"Yeah, along with two flash drives I haven't opened yet."

"Dev, the flash drives contain crime scene photos. Not for the faint of heart."

"Are you familiar with the cases, Aaron?"

"Somewhat," he said. "The last one was a year ago. The one prior to that took place the year before, in 2018. Jackson stopped in to see me about a week ago. He'd finished up down at Mayo clinic and ran things past me. You're welcome to look at the cold case files, and I'll help in whatever way I can. The department's spent hundreds, no make that thousands, of hours on these investigations, and we've come up empty-handed each and every time. Frankly, I'm of the opinion that focusing so much time and effort on that author character—"

"Virgil Hayes."

"Yeah, that's the guy's name. I'm thinking he may be completely innocent. Jackson was all worked up about the publication date on the last book, but we checked with the publisher, and they said that was actually a typo in the book. The publication date was officially 2020."

"Okay, but doesn't it take them at least a year to go from the initial manuscript to actually getting the book out there? That would suggest this Hayes character had to submit the written work something like twelve months earlier."

"Correct, but the problem is the book doesn't follow the particular crime as closely as the early books did. In my opinion, he somehow had access to our investigations; that seems to be a given. I'm not sure how and I don't like saying it, but I believe that's the case. I do know this; the intricate details he had to the actual murders worked to make the books that much better and increased his sales. He would mention the fact that we viewed him as a person of interest whenever he was interviewed on radio or tv, and all that seemed to do was give him a bigger bump in sales."

"Was there a search of his home?"

"More than once, along with his lake place up in St. Louis County, and we came up with absolutely nothing each and every time. Not so much as a victim fingerprint. At this stage, I don't see him involved. Well, other than he was apparently somehow privy to the inner workings of our investigations."

"Ben mentioned you gave the okay for me to view the case files."

"Yeah, absolutely, another pair of eyes, even if it's you, can only help." I ignored that last comment. "You thinking of coming down this afternoon?" Aaron asked.

"Yeah, I can be down there in the next half-hour or so."

"I'll get it cleared. Ask for Manning when you get here. I've got a budget meeting I have to be in about ten minutes from now."

"Manning? Come on, Aaron. He'll probably put me in an interview room and let me sit for two hours if he doesn't just try to arrest me for these murders. The guy hates me."

"Calm down. I'll tell him to escort you down to the file room and be on his best behavior. Okay?"

"There isn't someone else who could do it, Andretta, or Williams? Hey, I know, Lin Nguyen. She could take me down there and—"

"I'll tell Manning to be nice. Touch base with me when you're finished," he said and hung up.

Detective Manning has had an in for me ever since the day we met. God only knew why he'd didn't like me.

He's tried to pin every crime in the city on me. I was determined not to let him stop me from going over these cases.

I sent a text message to Taffy, *'Stay positive. You got this. Interested in dinner tonight?'* I waited for the next couple of minutes but didn't receive a response. I took Morton for a quick walk around the block, left Louie a note, and headed down to the police station.

The visitor's parking lot was full, but there was another lot for department personnel and people on official police business. The lot was paved as opposed to the visitor's lot, with its gravel surface and potholes that were large enough to swallow an entire vehicle. I pulled into the back of the official business lot, parked and made my way to the front desk. There were at least twenty people standing around in the front lobby chatting. All dressed in suits or sport coats and carrying briefcases.

I hurried up to the front desk. Fortunately, my friend Gary was working. As per usual, he sat partially hidden behind stacks of about three dozen files and didn't notice me as I walked up.

"Hi, Gary," I said.

He looked up, wearing a scowl that quickly changed to a smile when he recognized me. "Hi, Dev, I got a call you'd be coming in. Everything okay?"

"Yeah, just want to look at some cold cases for my reading pleasure. What's up with everyone hanging out in the lobby?" I said and indicated the crowd of nicely dressed folks chatting back and forth.

"Mmm, Minnesota public defenders meeting or seminar or something like that. Suddenly, they're all happy to be here instead of complaining we've arrested their always innocent clients. Hey, let me just make a call upstairs and get someone to escort you down to the file room."

"Hopefully, Manning will be busy," I half-joked.

Gary shot me a look that suggested I was probably screwed.

"They'll send someone down. Might as well grab a seat. It might be a couple of minutes."

It was more like a half-hour. I glanced over at Gary a couple of times, but he seemed focused on his files and didn't look up. By now, the lobby was more empty than not. An older woman seemed to be napping in a chair. A younger couple were quietly arguing two rows over. All the public defenders had headed off to some room about fifteen minutes ago. I was thinking of grabbing a coffee from the machine just to stay awake when an all too familiar voice shouted, "Haskell."

Oh, hell. Pain in the ass Detective Sergeant Norris Manning. The top of his bald head was the color of pink lemonade and, as I hurried out of my chair, his icy blue eyes focused on me like lasers.

"Hi, Detective Manning. How are you today?" I asked, trying to sound nice.

"Busy," was his one-word reply. He used the card hanging from the lanyard around his neck to unlock the security door. It buzzed, and the lock clicked. Manning opened the door and stepped into the secure area. I had to run the last few steps to catch the door before it closed. He led me down the hall toward the elevators. I noticed the three people we passed stared at the floor rather than look at Manning and have to say something. I sure as hell couldn't blame them.

Fortunately, the elevator doors opened as soon as he pressed the down button. Manning stepped inside and immediately pressed the button for the second basement level. He didn't say anything during the thirty second ride down. He stepped out of the elevator and headed down the hall to the file room. Once again, he used his card to unlock the security door and stepped inside. I was right behind him and stepped into the file room.

"I've got Devlin Haskell here to review files on a half-dozen cases," Manning said to the officer behind the counter. "I believe Lieutenant LaZelle called down and gave you a list of the files."

"Already got 'em pulled," the officer said.

"Okay, I'll leave him with you," Manning said and turned toward me. "Take as long as you want. Nothing leaves this room. You need paper and a pen for notes?"

I was actually taken aback by the question. Who knew Manning could be halfway nice? "No, sir, I'm good to go," I said and patted my pocket with the small notebook and pen.

"Okay, good luck. Oh, you have any trouble parking? We have a number of public defenders meeting for a seminar today."

"No, I grabbed a spot at the back of the official business lot."

"Good move. All right, any problems or questions, maybe check with Leo here," he said and nodded at the officer behind the counter. "Feel free to call Lieutenant LaZelle, but he's in a budget meeting, and they usually go for most of the afternoon. Anything else I can do for you?"

"No, thank you. I'm sure this is more than enough to keep me busy," I said, hoping I hid the surprise in my voice at Manning suddenly being nice.

"All right, then. Good luck," Manning said and headed out the door.

"Why don't you go ahead and grab that seat at cubicle three, and I'll bring the files out to you," Leo said.

I settled into the chair, and about thirty seconds later, Leo came over, pushing a cart filled with files and boxes. He proceeded to arrange them in three stacks on the table where I was seated.

"Whoa, that's a lot of information."

"This is just about half of them. I'll bring the rest over once you've had the chance to go through these. Our policy is we close to non-department folks at five this evening," he said and pulled the empty cart back behind the counter.

Nine

I grabbed my pocket notebook and pulled the top file off the stack. The photo that appeared when I opened the file looked like it could have been a high school yearbook picture. Marlis Goodman was just twenty-two years old at the time of her murder. She was originally from Winona, Minnesota, a town about a hundred miles south on the Mississippi River. She studied for two years at a state university and worked for fourteen months as a bank teller. She lived in a one-bedroom apartment on Sylvester Avenue. Her body was found in a city park on the eighth of August, 2006. She was dressed in a white nylon slip and wedding veil, and her clothes were stacked and neatly folded two feet from her body. She had ligature marks on her wrists and ankles. Traces of Rohypnol and champagne were found in her system.

No one interviewed had any knowledge of problems with acquaintances, cohorts she worked with or neighbors. Her boyfriend at the time was in the Air Force and stationed in Italy. They had not seen one another in eight and a half months. There was no mention of Virgil Hayes or his pen name, Virgil Tueur, anywhere in the file.

Crystal Higgins, age twenty-nine, lived in a duplex in the suburb of North St. Paul, the town where she was born and raised. She worked as a paralegal for a large law firm in downtown Minneapolis. Her body, dressed in a white nylon slip and wedding veil, was found in a city park in June of 2008, not the same park where Marlis Goodman's body had been found. Like the murder two years earlier, her clothing was folded and neatly stacked next to her body. Crystal had ligature marks on her wrists and ankles. Traces of Rohypnol and champagne were found in her system. Once again, family, friends, and co-workers had no knowledge of problems with anyone. Again, no mention was made of Virgil Hayes, and no correlation was suggested between the murder of Crystal Higgins and Marlis Goodman two years earlier. Detective Ben Jackson was listed as one of the investigating officers.

I found pretty much the same thing with the murder of Jia Kahn, a thirty-one-year-old St. Paul native working as a realtor. She had the same ligature marks as the earlier victims, approximately two inches wide, on her wrists and ankles. Rohypnol and champagne traces were found in her system. Just like the two cases before her, she was found in a white nylon slip and wedding veil in a city park in November of 2012. Her clothing was neatly arranged next to her body. Once again, not the same park as the previous murders. No mention of the two earlier murders and no mention of Virgil Hayes or

Virgil Tueur in the file. Detective Ben Jackson was listed as one of the investigating officers.

It was getting close to five, and I was not only tired but depressed after reading three of the six files. I went over to the counter and told Leo I was finished for the day, but I'd be back tomorrow.

"Okay," he said, sounding happy I didn't want to try to stay after five. "Let me call Detective Manning, and he can escort you back upstairs."

"I have to get in touch with Lieutenant LaZelle. He said something about meeting me down here. Let me give him a ring," I said, hoping I could dodge Manning.

Leo gave me a skeptical look but said, "Okay, give him a call."

I dialed Aaron's number and prayed he'd answer. He did, on the fifth ring, thankfully. "Yeah, Aaron, I'm finishing up for the day. I've gone through the first three cases. You wanted to see me."

"You come across anything that caught your attention?"

"Not really, but I've only reviewed the first three, and they covered a span of six years. I'm a little surprised they weren't at least connected, given the nylon slip, the wedding veil and the body left in a city park, the clothing folded nearby, and the Rohypnol and champagne, but then I'm saying that with the knowledge of what we already know. I'll be back tomorrow to go through the next three. You said you wanted to see me."

“I know what you’re saying, but that was a period when the city, in its wisdom, was making all sorts of budget cuts. Remember we had bodies stacked up in the hallway of the city morgue. Don’t worry about stopping up tonight. You pretty much told me what I thought you’d say. Did you let Leo know you’d be back tomorrow?”

“I did, but I’m thinking he should hear that from you, too.”

“He will. Let me send someone down there to escort you out. Can you be back down here around ten tomorrow morning?”

“Yeah, that should work fine.”

“Okay,” he said.

“Hey, before you go—”

But he’d already hung up. I sat and waited for the next twenty minutes until Manning made an appearance. He arrived only because Leo wanted to go home and had finally called him.

Manning opened the security door and motioned me toward him without uttering a word. I followed him out the door and onto the elevator. We had another quiet elevator ride up two floors. He escorted me off the elevator and out to the lobby.

“Have a pleasant evening, Detective,” I said and smiled.

“Yes, and you do the same, Haskell. Enjoy and be careful.”

The way he said it made me look around, expecting someone to knock me on the ground and handcuff me, but nothing happened. I watched him as he disappeared behind the security door, making sure he was gone before I headed out of the building. I crossed the street and walked toward my car in the back of the 'Official Business' parking lot. I climbed in behind the wheel then stared at the windshield and the piece of paper held in place by my windshield wiper. I climbed out and pulled the parking ticket from beneath the wiper.

A sixty dollar parking ticket for parking without an 'Official Business' parking pass. The ticket was handwritten, and I was pretty sure it was Manning's handwriting. I tossed it on the passenger seat and drove back to my office.

Louie was eating a submarine sandwich at his picnic table, and Morton was asleep on his bed. Louie took a large bite and then asked, "Mmm-mmm, everything go okay?" At least that's what I think he said. It was tough trying to understand him through a mouthful of sandwich.

"Yeah, I was going through cold case files. It's going to be a long process. How'd your day go?" My phone suddenly rang, and I said, "Hold that thought for a minute."

"Hi, Taffy, how are you doing?"

"Completely stressed out and in a holding pattern."

"Meaning you haven't heard anything?"

"Exactly. Why in God's name is it taking so long?"

"They probably have to review everyone's interview, compare notes, talk to the powers that be. It all takes time. Hey, you interested in some dinner? We'll get your mind off of this, and maybe you could just, you know, lay back, relax, and enjoy yourself," I said, hoping she picked up on the message suggesting some late-night action.

"Well, actually, I'm having dinner with Allison tonight. You can join us, I guess. I mean, you know, if you want to."

She made it sound like it wasn't the best idea, which was probably right, but I didn't really care. It had been the better part of a week since we'd been together and longer than that since she seemed happy. I was even ready to put up with Allison, at least for a while. "Yeah, that sounds great. I'd love to join you."

"You would?"

"Yeah, just tell me where, and I'll meet you two there."

"Okay, you're sure?"

"Very sure. I'm looking forward to it. Where and when?"

"We have a seven o'clock reservation at the Thai Garden."

"The one on University Avenue?"

"Yes," she said, sounding surprised I knew the place.

"I'll see you there at seven," I said and disconnected.

"Hot date?" Louie asked and stuffed the last bit of the submarine sandwich into his mouth.

"Not exactly. I'm meeting Taffy for dinner, but that permanently unhappy pain in the ass, Allison, is going to be there, too. I don't know what it is, but all of a sudden the two of them seem to be inseparable."

"Maybe it's just a stress thing from the job interview."

"Well, she's certainly stressed out from that, but Allison has been cramping my style for the last couple of weeks, and it's driving me nuts. I think she's actually stalking Taffy."

"Does Taffy know you dated Allison?"

"No, at least not that I know of, and before you say anything, I know I should have told her right away, but by the time I found out Allison had injected herself into Taffy's life, it was too late. Now, telling her we dated would just sound like one big, well-kept secret and probably the worst thing I could do."

"Give it some time. She finds out about this promotion, one way or the other, she'll probably calm down. I don't know. What if you lined up a getaway weekend with Taffy? You know, someplace out of town where you could show her a good time without Allison butting in."

"You know, Louie, that's a really good idea. She likes birds and flowers and stuff. Maybe get a weekend place up north, just the two of us. Take it easy. Relax, maybe stay in bed late and work up an appetite."

"There you go. Just a suggestion, but maybe don't mention it tonight, at least not while that Allison woman is around. Next thing you know, she'll be getting a room right next to you and ruin the whole thing."

"Yeah, Allison's an absolute stalker and certainly capable of doing that. Hey, I better get Morton home, take him for a walk, and get cleaned up. You around tomorrow morning?"

"Yeah, I don't have court until the middle of the afternoon."

"I should be in around nine, but I've got to be back at the police station going over three more cold case files at ten."

"I'll expect a full report on the night's activities tomorrow morning," Louie said.

Morton opened his eyes at the sound of me picking up his leash. He hopped off his bed and hurried over by the door. I snapped his leash on, and we headed home.

Ten

We drove home, and I took Morton for a walk then grabbed a shower. I pulled on clean black jeans and my favorite pearl-button cowboy shirt. The shirt was black with white leaf embroidery on the shoulders. It had slit pockets and white pearly buttons. Each cuff had three buttons. The outfit made Taffy laugh, and I hopped it would help put her in a more positive mood. I added a pair of crocodile cowboy boots, checked myself in the mirror, and knew I was ready to go.

I was the first one at the Thai Garden, and the receptionist escorted me to a table next to a window looking out onto University Avenue. I held off ordering anything since Taffy and pain in the butt Allison would probably show up at any minute. I was almost dead from starvation by the time they arrived forty minutes later. They both took a seat across the table from me. Allison was next to the window. Maybe with any luck, there would be a drive-by shooting, and she'd get hit.

"What?" I said as Taffy stared with her mouth open.

"What in the hell are you wearing?" There wasn't a hint of funny in her question.

"You like it? It's my cowboy shirt, and check these out," I said, lifting my leg along the side of the table so she could see my crocodile boots.

"I don't know, Taffy, I think you've got an awful lot of work to do. God, incredible. You look homeless," Allison said and shook her head.

My mood immediately changed. "So, what took you two so long?"

"Oh, we stopped along the way. Allison has a date tomorrow night with a guy she met online, and she wanted to have just the right look," Taffy said.

Nothing like, 'Sorry we're late,' or 'Allison is a major pain in the ass.' I figured it really didn't matter what Allison wore. Once the guy met her, if he had any brains at all, he'd run for the door. "So, interesting, you met this guy online. Do you know his name or what he does? What made you decide to contact him?"

"It just happens to be the other way around, Dev. He contacted me. They all do once they see my post," Allison said. She smiled and nodded, setting the record straight.

Yeah, right. I had my doubts. I figured she probably posted a naked picture of herself along with the promise to pay anyone a hundred bucks if they'd spend ten minutes with her. "Wow, impressive. You must have really clicked with this guy. What sites were you on?" I asked and thought I'd check out her info and maybe leave a snarky, anonymous review warning any guy foolish enough to be interested.

"I'm just on one site, but it's the best one," she said, not sharing any further information. She turned and faced Taffy. "You think I should have gotten those shoes?" That led to ten minutes of fashion talk. I sat and stared out the window. The restaurant was jammed, and I finally caught the eye of our server.

"Are you ready to order?" she said as she stepped over to our table.

"Yes," I said.

"No, I think just the bottle of wine for right now. The 2016 Merlot," Allison said, glancing at the wine list. My stomach growled. The waitress smiled and hurried off.

"Oh, Taffy, you won't believe this wine. It's to die for. It's from this Napa Valley vineyard, Howell Mountain. Delicious, a hint of cherry and blackberry," Allison said and droned on about some trip she took out to California for a week with a stockbroker. She never did mention whatever happened to the guy, since he obviously wasn't on the scene now. I figured, if he didn't slit his wrists, he probably put Allison on a plane back to the twin cities then immediately changed his name and is still hiding out in California.

The waitress came back with the wine. She displayed the label to Allison, who nodded and said, "Lovely, that's exactly the wine I had on a recent trip to Napa Valley." She made it sound like Napa Valley was a weekly event.

The waitress smiled, uncorked the bottle, poured Allison a taste, and waited.

I thought I was familiar with the routine, but Allison sloshed the wine around in her mouth, swallowed, and then said, "Mmm-mmm, no, I don't think so. This isn't the one I was thinking of." Vintage Allison. So now what? The bottle's open. She didn't say it had gone off, she said, 'It isn't the one I was thinking of.' Oh, and by the way, when in the hell did she become a wine connoisseur? When I dated her, she was drinking martinis and cosmopolitans two-fisted.

The waitress looked like someone had just shot her with a taser.

"Maybe we could drink it anyway," I said.

"Oh, I don't know. The hint of cherry just isn't there," Allison said and glared.

That was all the encouragement I needed. "We'll take the bottle," I said. "I'll have a Tiger beer. You two ready to order dinner?"

"We haven't even looked at the menu, Dev," Taffy said.

"Okay, I'll have the spring roll starter along with that beer. You two want a starter?"

Now Taffy glared at me. Allison looked like she wanted to kill. The waitress fled the scene. I filled their wine glasses, making sure Taffy had just a little more than Allison. The girls went back to discussing fashion and the pros and cons of Allison buying a pair of shoes.

I stared out the window until my beer and spring rolls arrived. There were three spring rolls on the plate.

Against my better judgment, I said, "You two want to try these spring rolls. They're really good here."

"No," they replied in unison and went back to talking fashion.

I watched the passing traffic out the window as I slowly ate my spring rolls and sipped my beer. The ladies were now on their second glass of wine and still talking fashion and shoes. I finished my spring rolls and beer and waited a few more minutes for a break in the conversation that never came.

"Excuse me, ladies, but I've got an early day tomorrow."

"Yeah, sure you do. The homeless shelter probably closes their door at eight-thirty, so you better hurry if you want to get a bed tonight," Allison said. They both laughed at that and took a healthy sip from their glasses.

Instead of responding, I said, "No, really, actually I do. Enjoy your evening. Give me a call, Taffy." I stood and headed toward the front of the restaurant.

Our waitress was standing at the cash register, and I said, "I'm sorry, I just got a call and have to get back to surgery. I'd like to pay for the wine, my beer, and the spring rolls."

She smiled, rang the bill up, and said, "One twenty-five."

A hundred and twenty-five bucks? I handed her my credit card and said, “Could I have a receipt for that, please?”

Fortunately, my credit card went through, I signed, and she handed me the receipt. Not bad, a hundred-dollar bottle of wine, and Allison was going to send it back because the ‘hint of cherry’ wasn’t there. As if she would know what a hint of cherry tasted like. I was tempted to go back to the table and shove the receipt down Allison’s throat. Instead, I smiled at the waitress, told her thanks, and headed out the door.

I had to walk past the windows and the table Taffy and Allison were seated at to get to my car. They were sipping wine, and I saw Allison’s lips move as I approached. Taffy suddenly looked the other way. Allison kept talking, but she moved her hand under the table and gave me the finger, wiggling the middle finger up and down, so I’d be sure to notice it.

I got in my car, drove down the street to McDonald’s, ordered a Quarter Pounder with cheese and bacon, a chocolate shake, two chocolate chip cookies, and headed home.

Morton was stretched out on the couch, and I let him out the kitchen door. I spread the McDonald’s out on the kitchen counter, fired up my Kindle, and started reading Four After Midnight.

Eleven

The story was more of the same. Mister Charming was beyond gracious for maybe three or four weeks before he had the victim over for dinner. He always says he has a family recipe in the oven as he hands a champagne flute drugged with Rohypnol to his unsuspecting victim. Once she's passed out, he tosses a frozen pizza in the oven and proceeds to take his time murdering the victim. At this stage, the guy has a proven system. I made a number of notes as I read through the book and paged back through the first three books to check on similarities and some of the finer points.

I heard Morton scratching at the door and glanced outside. It was already dark, and I let Morton back in the kitchen. He gave me a look that suggested he was less than happy with me. I tossed him a biscuit, which he caught in midair and then hurried into the front room so he wouldn't have to share with me. I went back to my Kindle.

It was well after midnight when I went up to bed. Morton was stretched out on the bed, and I moved him over to make room for myself. I was up well before my alarm went off, showered, put the coffee on, and went online to read more about serial killers. Morton wandered downstairs around half-past-seven and allowed me to give him a scratch behind the ears before I sent him into the backyard. I let him inside a few minutes later, and he immediately began inhaling his breakfast while I was online reading up on the traits of serial killers.

I sent Taffy a text message asking her to call me, and we headed down to the office a little before nine. As we left, I bagged Morton's morning deposit from the backyard and tossed the bag on the floor of the passenger seat.

Amazingly, Louie had remembered to turn off the coffee maker last night. I'd just put on a fresh pot of coffee when I heard the stairs creaking as Louie made his way up to the office. Morton raised his head and stared at the door, waiting for Louie to stumble in.

He didn't disappoint as he stepped into the office red-faced and gasped, "Made it," as if he was congratulating himself for accomplishing a marathon or some major endurance test. Along with his briefcase, he was carrying a white paper bag from the bakery. The bag appeared to hold at least a half-dozen doughnuts. He tossed his briefcase and the doughnut bag onto the picnic table and collapsed in his chair. The coffee was in the middle of brewing. I dumped the remnants from his mug down the sink and refilled the mug with freshly brewed coffee.

Louie nodded thanks as he took hold of his mug, and after a couple of swallows, he said, "You up for some sweetness?" He pulled a chocolate doughnut from the bag and handed it to me. My stomach growled in response as I took the doughnut from him.

"You know," Louie said. "I was thinking last night about this business Ben Jackson has you involved in."

"The murders?"

"No, Dev, the home run numbers in the American League. Yes, the murders. Did he tell you anything about them, or have you looked into the traits of these serial killers?"

"In a word, no. I've checked into the traits a little, but as soon as I'm finished with my initial review of the files, that's the next thing I'll be doing. Since no one has been arrested, the guy, and I'm guessing it's a guy as opposed to a woman, is still out there. The last two murders were only a year apart, which might suggest he's feeling the urge to kill more frequently."

"Yeah, or, you said there were six murders, it might suggest he's on the far side of the learning curve. Maybe he's got it down to a system, and it's just that much easier."

"They still don't know where the murders have been committed, let alone by who. And this leaving the bodies to be discovered in a city park. It reminds me of Jack the Ripper, leaving the bodies on the streets and alleys of London."

"Yeah," Louie said. "Now that you mention it. It also seems to suggest he might just have a fairly high opinion of himself. You know, taunting the cops with yet another body. Basically telling them, 'Good luck in catching me. Here's another one, and there's nothing you can do about it.' Man, there are some really screwed up people in the world," Louie said and reached in the bag for another chocolate doughnut.

I pulled into the visitor's lot at the police station just before ten. I dodged two potholes and found a spot in the back of the lot. I grabbed the bag from the floor of the passenger seat, waited until no one was wandering around the 'Official Business' lot, and then hurried over through an opening in the hedge. I found what I was looking for parked in the middle of the lot, a black Ford Escape with the license 719MEW. Detective Manning's car. I opened the bag with Morton's deposit and carefully smeared it on the backside of the driver's door handle. I quickly smeared the remnants of the bag on the windshield wipers and then hurried back through the hedge into the visitor's lot.

Twelve

Gary was doing whatever it was he did with files, and he looked up at me and smiled when I called his name. He phoned Manning, who made me wait close to a half-hour before he came down to escort me to the file room. This morning, I didn't care. Just like yesterday, he shouted my name and quickly stepped into the secure area, so I had to run to catch the door just before it closed.

Leo was behind the counter, and I could see the files stacked up on the cart when I stepped into the file room. Manning gave me his usual lecture about not taking anything from the room and then left without saying another word. Leo directed me to the first cubicle and rolled the cart with the files over to me. He stacked the files on the table, asked if there was anything else I needed, and then headed back behind the counter.

The fourth murder victim was named Trudie Mandel, a dark-haired woman with striking blue eyes, who worked for the county. She had just turned thirty-two years old when she was murdered in April of 2015. She had been divorced seven months earlier, back in September, and her former husband had moved to Atlanta at the first of the year. Her body was found in a downtown city park across the street from the Landmark Center. A normally very busy area, the small park was surrounded on four sides by the downtown public library, the St. Paul Hotel, the Landmark Center, and the Ordway Theatre. All busy places that, together, added a fair amount of foot traffic traveling through the park for the better part of eighteen hours a day.

The fact that a women's body was left in the park, not to mention seated on a park bench, suggested she was placed there between maybe two and four in the morning. It also seemed to reinforce Louie's suggestion, at least to me, that by leaving the body in a very public place, the perpetrator was taunting the police.

A number of things stood out in the case file. There was the link to the three previous murders based on the trace of Rohypnol and champagne in the victim's blood, the clothing stacked nearby, the white nylon slip, and the wedding veil, matching the previous murders. The ligature marks were the same as the three preceding cases. The body was once again left in a city park, but in the previous cases, the parks were large, and the victims' bodies weren't left in an obvious place. This time, the victim's body was arranged on a park bench in a small, very busy area. As with the previous cases, I made a list of family and individuals interviewed. The Trudie Mandel case was the last one where Detective Ben Jackson was listed as one of the investigating officers.

Lucia Ruiz was twenty-nine years old, a native of St. Paul, who worked as a midwife. Her body was discovered in a city park on the west side of the city in July of 2018, a full three years after the Mandel murder. Once again, the similarities of Rohypnol, traces of champagne, white nylon slip, wedding veil, ligature marks, and the location of the body in a city park linked her to the four previous cases.

Additionally, for the first time, the name of Virgil Hayes, also known as the author Virgil Tueur, was listed as a person of interest. The police interviewed him twice. I read and reread the transcripts of both interviews. He came across as concerned and actually offered to help the police in their search for the killer. He gave the police a list of attributes that he applied to the serial killer in his books: pleasant, smooth-talking, manipulative, insincere, a bit of a loner, and someone who had experienced early behavioral problems. Hayes' home on the River Boulevard, one of the high buck streets in town, as well as his lake place up in St. Louis County, had been searched twice. Both times, the authorities came up empty-handed. He was previously married and had divorced in 2004. His former wife, Louise Thompson, returned to her hometown of Santa Barbara, California in 2005 and remarried in 2007. She had not had any contact with Hayes since she remarried. I made a note of her phone number, should I ever need to call her.

Hayes did not seem stressed nor agitated by either the police interviews or the searches of his home and lake place; and in fact, he mentioned the police involvement in a number of later media interviews. A series of eleven radio interviews, one of which was on National Public Radio, and two television interviews, one of which was with Oprah Winfrey, were included in the files on disks and two videotapes. Fortunately, the internet links were listed, and I copied them down to listen and watch later. Ben Jackson had retired by this time, and he was not listed as one of the investigating officers in the Lucia Ruiz murder.

I sent Taffy another text message, worked through the noon hour, and grabbed a Snickers bar from a machine for lunch while I reviewed the final case, the murder of Madeline Long. Madeline was thirty-five years old and originally from Chicago. She attended the University of Minnesota and stayed here after graduating with a degree in education. She had gone on to earn a master's degree from the University of St. Thomas and was an assistant principal at a Junior High. She lived in Woodbury, a St. Paul suburb. The picture in the file appeared to be an enlarged copy of another image and was slightly blurry. Although blurry, Madeline Long appeared to be very attractive. Similarities to the previous cases began with the ligatures. Rohypnol and champagne were again found in her system. Just like the previous victims, she was attired in a white nylon slip and a wedding veil. Her body was found in Como Park, overlooking the lake in May of 2019. Interviews once again pointed to no difficulties with workmates, neighbors, social friends, or family.

Virgil Hayes was again interviewed as a person of interest, but that was about as far as it went. He offered to take a lie detector test, but there was no record of one having ever been given. Reading through the transcripts of his interviews, there were actually three, he repeated pretty much the same thing he'd said when being interviewed regarding the murder of Lucia Ruiz the previous year. But then again, that seemed to make sense, since he was pretty much asked the same questions.

He claimed to have been home at the time of the Long murder, as well as the two previous days, working on his next book. Verification was determined by tracking his cellphone and the operation of his laptop computer, a MacBook Pro. This would have been the same book Ben Jackson said was published prior to the murder and that Aaron LaZelle said had a printing error in the publication date. I made a note to check the book on Amazon.

I finished up around three in the afternoon, returned the files to Leo and called Aaron LaZelle. Unfortunately, I had to leave a message, so Leo phoned Manning. I sat in the file room for the next forty minutes, twiddling my thumbs, before he bothered to show up.

Actually, that was okay. When he stepped into the file room, pushed the door open, and stepped back into the hall, signaling I should hurry up, it made me smile. We rode the elevator up to the main floor in silence, and

I even said thank you to him and smiled as he opened the door to the lobby. I could tell he was dying for a comment about the parking ticket, but I wasn't about to give him one. The only thing I was upset about was that I wouldn't be around to watch him open the driver's door on his Ford Escape. I thought about going over and letting the air out of two of his tires, so even when he changed one, he still couldn't drive anywhere, but decided against it.

My car hadn't been towed, I didn't have a ticket on my windshield, and all the tires looked good, so I headed back to the office. Morton was apparently in charge, and he met me at the door. I got the message, clicked the leash onto his collar, and we went for a twenty-minute walk.

When we got back, Louie was seated in his office chair with his shoes off and his feet up on the picnic table. One black sock was ankle length, and the other was a knee-high. His big toe was visible through a hole in the knee-high. The white bakery bag was still on his desk, only now it was empty, and crumbs were all over his desk. "So, did you solve the case?" he asked.

"No, about all I came up with was a lot more questions and a laundry list of people to talk to."

"What about the writer?"

"Virgil Hayes? He seems to have an airtight alibi for the last murder. He was working from home on the day of the murder and for two days previous. They corroborated he was there by checking his cell phone and computer. His name didn't come up in any of the interviews of friends, family, and work colleagues. He's mentioned as a person of interest in the last two murders, but he checks out. They searched his home and lake place twice and came up empty-handed both times. After two searches, you'd think they would have found something."

"Anyone ever consider he might have a third property or an accomplice?"

"No mention of either in the notes I read."

"Might be something to check into," Louie said just before he snuggled down in his chair and closed his eyes.

Thirteen

Taffy phoned just as Morton and I were about to head home. I let her call ring four times before I answered, hoping she got the message I wasn't happy about last night's dinner at the Thai Garden, and even less happy that it took her all day to call me back.

"Haskell Investigations," I answered.

"Hi, Dev, I'm returning your call," she said, like her actions last night were no big deal.

"Oh, Taffy, thanks for finally calling me back. Did you two enjoy your dinner last night at the Thai Garden?"

"Yeah, it was okay. You didn't have to leave, you know."

"Well, I got the distinct impression from both of you that I was the odd man out. You barely even said hello to me, and then once you were finished telling me I looked like I was homeless, you went on for the next half-hour about buying outfits and whether Allison should buy a pair of shoes. You made it pretty clear I wasn't adding much to the evening. Besides, I had to make it into that homeless shelter before eight-thirty."

“Hey, I told you we were going shopping, but you wanted to join us anyway. What was I supposed to do?”

This was not sounding like the woman I thought I knew, and I changed the subject. “You interested in dinner tonight, just the two of us?”

“No.”

“You want to think about that for a moment?”

“I don’t want to do dinner tonight. What’s the big deal?”

“Okay, then. Nice talking to you.”

“Don’t be like that, Dev. Besides, I’ve got something lined up with Allison. She’s on her date with this new guy. She really likes him, and I’m just going to help her get ready. She wants to look her best.”

I thought if the guy had any sense, he will have already packed a bag and was heading for the airport. “Well, maybe we could grab something later, just the two of us.”

“Thanks, but no. I’m still stressing over the interview, and I haven’t heard anything from my boss yet.”

“All I can say is, if they don’t give you the promotion, you might want to think about working somewhere else, because they’d really be missing the boat.”

“Oh, thanks. That’s nice of you to say. Hey, I better run. Allison’s getting picked up around eight, so I have to get over to her place. I’ll talk to you later.”

“All right, have a good—” She’d already hung up.

"That sounded like it didn't go too well," Louie said. His feet were still up on the desk, and his eyes were closed.

"Get this. That obnoxious Allison has a date tonight, and Taffy's helping her get dressed. Man, she's getting crazier by the day. This guy must be a real nutcase if he wants to date Allison, either that or a glutton for punishment."

"You know what they say," Louie said. "Never try to figure out people's relationships or their taxes. Any idea what the guy does?"

"I haven't been told his name, let alone anything about him. No doubt, the two of them are worried I'd figure out a way to get in touch with him and warn him off."

"Well, then it sounds like he's going to get what he deserves. Speaking of which, you interested in some in-depth conversation over at The Spot?"

"Yeah, I think I could join you for one. You ready to go now?"

"I will be as soon as I get my shoes on."

Mike was bartending, and he must have seen us coming across the street. When we stepped in the door, my beer and Louie's drink were already waiting for us on the bar, along with a bag of pork rinds for Morton. "How are things going?" Mike asked.

"Different day, same shit," Louie said.

"Yeah, same for me, only shittier," I said.

Mike shook his head. “You two are a couple of real live wires.”

I laid a ten on the bar. Mike grabbed it and hurried down to the far end. I tore open the bag of pork rinds and handed a couple to Morton.

Louie took a sip from his drink and said, “You going over more of those cold case files tomorrow?”

“There’s six of them, and I went through the last one today. Not that I won’t revisit them, but I’ve got enough general information. The cases have some commonalities. I’d like to talk with family members and acquaintances to see if I can pick up on anything. Something that Taffy and Allison said last night rang a bell with me.”

“Really? What was that?”

“They’re all worked up about Allison meeting this perfect guy online. I didn’t see any mention of that in the files, but maybe it was something like that. This guy seeks out his victims on a dating site. All but one of the women were single, and well, that one was actually single too. She’d been divorced six or seven months earlier. The oldest one was thirty-five, a number in their twenties, all prime dating age. I know it’s a little like grasping at a straw, but maybe online dating is the common denominator.”

“But weren’t a couple of the murders actually before the internet really exploded?” Louie asked.

“Yeah, one in 2006 and another in 2008, but there were dating meetups back then, and I think Match.com was going. Remember the deals where you’d spend like five minutes at a table and then move to the next table, meeting ten or twelve people on a Saturday afternoon or a Wednesday night. There used to be all sorts of dating ads in the personal's column in the back of the paper. I don't know. Maybe the guy started there, and the online deal just made it that much easier for him."

Louie drained his glass and signaled Mike still down at the far end of the bar.

"Hey, none for me. We're going to head home. I've got some more online work I can do tonight. Are you in court tomorrow?"

"I don't think so," Louie said, "unless I get a call about a plea I'm waiting for a response on. I'll be in around nine, either way."

"First one in makes the coffee," I said and drained the last two swallows of beer, waved good-bye to Mike, and headed out the side door.

Fourteen

I cooked up a chicken breast with roast peppers for dinner while Morton was out in the backyard. I suddenly remembered that Detective Manning had probably had the interaction with Morton's deposit on his car door handle by now, and that brought a smile to my face. I called Morton in and tossed him two dog biscuits. He caught the first one in midair and the second on the first bounce then hurried over to a distant corner, so he wouldn't have to share with me.

I fired up the computer after dinner and pulled out my notes from the cold case files. The first thing I did was click on the links and listen to the radio interviews of Virgil Hayes. There were eleven of them. Two were a half-hour long. Three more were maybe twenty minutes, and the rest were right around ten minutes long. There was no specific mention of the After Midnight series being based on the murders, but when the interviewer didn't bring it up, Hayes mentioned it and went on to tell about his home and lake place being searched twice. He mentioned being questioned by the police and said they rousted him out of bed in the middle of the night and questioned him for a number of hours.

He more or less portrayed himself as a self-taught authority on serial killers and presented himself as someone who had attempted to assist the police. That really didn't match the portrayal I picked up from the cold case files listing him as a person of interest, but I have to say he sounded very credible. His Oprah interview apparently lifted him to the top of the ladder of writing success, which wasn't really a surprise.

I went onto the Amazon book site and checked out all six of his books. Each one was rated in the top twenty-five in the serial killer genre. Books three through six were listed as best sellers with over a million copies sold. The books were available in print, eBook and audio. I read his author page on Amazon. It listed him as having been nominated for a Pulitzer, along with winning a number of awards I'd never heard of. He was originally from Chicago, attended the University of Iowa, and had lived in St. Paul for the past twenty-some years. I couldn't find a Facebook page or a Twitter account for him.

I made a mental note to drive past his home on the River Boulevard tomorrow morning on the way down to the office. I turned off my laptop and stretched out on the couch in front of the tv. I woke up at close to two in the morning and went up to bed. Morton was stretched out on the bed with his head on my pillow. I moved him over and laid down, still dressed.

I woke a little before six in the morning. I was wide awake, and there was no hope of going back to sleep, so

I got up, hopped in the shower, then dressed and headed downstairs. Morton joined me about two hours later. After scratching him behind the ears and praising him for a minute, I let him out the kitchen door and went back to my computer.

Virgil Hayes was listed as the owner of the property on the River Boulevard. The home was built in 1924, and his property taxes were twenty-two-hundred dollars per month. Not bad for a writer. I fed Morton breakfast, had an ice cream bar for myself, and then headed toward Virgil Hayes's house in the opposite direction from my office.

I slowed down as I drove past his home, a large two-story white stucco place with green trim and a red tile roof. I turned at the corner and headed down his alley. He had a backyard surrounded by an eight-foot high white stucco wall and a double garage. I noticed there were outdoor motion sensors mounted on either corner of the garage and probably more mounted on the house.

I drove down the alley, back onto the street again, and past his home. Three newspapers were rolled in plastic bags and sitting on his front steps, which didn't really seem strange for a former newspaper guy and writer. The house appeared to be very nice, and with annual property taxes of over twenty-six-grand, it should be. We sped along the River Boulevard and down to the office.

We were the first ones in, and I set about making coffee while Morton returned to attacking his rawhide chew. At nine, I began calling people from the list of contacts I'd written down from the cold case files. I purposely did not call the parents of the victims. I planned to get to them later, maybe. But right now, I wanted to talk to friends and acquaintances, the people who might know the things that parents wouldn't necessarily be privy to, dating in particular. I began with Madeline Long's friends, she being the most recent victim, and worked through the three most recent victims on the list. I'd lined up four appointments by the time Louie made it up the stairs. His wrinkled suit looked like he'd slept in it, and when he stumbled into the office in his usual red-faced condition, he simply nodded and then collapsed in his chair. I was on the phone talking to a woman named Susan O'Mara, a friend of Madeline Long.

"Yeah, Susan, an hour from now would work just fine. Dunn Brothers Coffee on Snelling and Grand. I know the place. I'll be wearing a Saint Paul Saints jersey and black jeans."

"Perfect," she said. "I'm wearing a green t-shirt with a rainbow and the word 'Good' below the rainbow. I hope I can help. It's so damn frustrating the police haven't been able to arrest anyone."

"Believe me, they haven't given up. They're still searching and going over what they do know. That's part of what I'm doing."

"See you when I see you," she said and disconnected.

I got up, grabbed Louie's empty coffee mug off the picnic table, filled the thing and set it down in front of him. He nodded thanks. After three or four sips, he said, "So, how's it going?"

"Setting up appointments with people who knew the victims, hoping they might mention something that clicks, and suddenly everything is gonna fall in place."

"You think that'll work?"

"No, but you can always hope."

Fifteen

I parked in the parking lot next to Dunn Brother's Coffee. It was a warm sunny morning, and there were seven people sitting in chairs alongside the building. The three tables in front of the shop were occupied. I stepped into the coffee shop and immediately spotted Susan O'Mara in her green t-shirt with the rainbow. We waved at one another at almost the same time, and I headed over to her table.

"Hi Susan, I'm Dev Haskell. I was going to order a coffee. Can I get you something? Another coffee or a pastry?"

"I'm actually drinking a Twining's Breakfast Tea if you wouldn't mind."

"Got it. You sure you wouldn't like a pastry?"

"No, thanks," she said.

"I'll be back in a moment." Fortunately, there was only one person ahead of me, and he was only ordering a black coffee. I ordered my coffee and Susan's tea and was sitting down with her a few minutes later.

"Mmm-mmm, thanks for the tea," she said after taking a sip.

“Thanks for taking the time to meet with me. I hope you don’t mind me asking you questions. I’ve gone over the investigation into Madeline’s murder, but it’s important I get information from people like you who knew Madeline.”

She nodded and said. “I’ll tell you everything I can think of. God, I really miss her. We met in high school back in Chicago. Our lockers were next to each other. We always called her Maddie. She’s kind of the reason I ended up here in St. Paul. I visited her when she was attending the U of M and ended up getting a job here. The company put me through school, and I’ve been working for them for the last eleven years.”

“What do you do?”

“Anything they want, I’m in the IT department. We manufacture medical products, syringes, thermometers, that sort of thing. Everything’s made in China now, but we sell all over the US, Europe and South America.”

“Did Madeline, err Maddie, ever mention anything about a relationship, dating anyone, or meeting someone? She ever mention anything about someone following her?”

“No, nothing like that. We both were on Match.com, and we’ve had dates. I was off for a while after what happened to her, but I’ve been back on for a couple of months. Like I told the police, I’m not aware of anyone she was really seeing. You have all these people you meet online, and it’s like they just want to be your best friend, only online. I keep thinking, God would you ever just get to the point and ask me out? I don't need a damn pen-pal. Then, if they seem really nice and you set up to meet them, you know, at someplace like here, the second you see them, you automatically know it's simply not going to work."

"Maddie and I used to joke about it all the time. I don't know, online dating is just what it is. I've always thought, since Maddie was an assistant principal, maybe someone who had a kid at her school killed her. Some whacko father or something. She was at a junior high, and I couldn't believe the stories she'd tell about all these pain in the butt kids. Then she'd always remind me that, once you meet the parents, most of your questions are answered."

"Right now, the thought is it might have been a serial killer," I said.

"Yeah, I heard that, but how would a serial killer find someone like Maddie? She didn't really go to bars. There was alcoholism in her family, her father, so she was usually our sober cab driver. When we'd go out, she was quite happy just drinking a coke."

"Did she do any drugs?"

Susan shook her head. "No, that wasn't her thing at all. She'd put up with us drinking, but if anyone suggested drugs, she was out the door. When I heard they found Rohypnol in her system, I couldn't believe it. Maddie was a woman who wouldn't take aspirin for a headache."

"Traces of Rohypnol and champagne have been found in the system of all the victims. We're guessing they were served a drugged drink. All the women match what you're telling me about Maddie. They're employed, working hard, successful, single, and between the ages of twenty-five and thirty-five. You did mention she was doing online dating."

"Yes, but with pretty much the same lousy results as I have. At the end of the day, there just is no one you're interested in."

"Is it possible she may have met someone but wouldn't say anything until she was sure it might be a good match?"

Susan seemed to think about that for a long moment before she said, "Yeah, I suppose that could have been the case. I mean, if I had a flop date, I'd call her that night or the next morning and tell her, just to have someone laugh with me, and it always reminded me that you're not alone in the way it always seems to work out. But as you're saying that, I'm thinking if she had a good date, maybe she wouldn't say anything because she didn't want to hurt my feelings or depress me. I mean, if you're out there doing online dating, let's face it, you're actively looking for someone, and that damn biological clock is ticking. Don't I know."

"If she wouldn't tell you, can you think of anyone she might tell?"

Susan shook her head. "No, sorry, but I really can't. And if you're thinking about her mom, most women from our mom's generation don't get the online thing. They grew up meeting their guys at parties or dances. That's just not how it works today, and God love 'em, but they don't get it. Put my mom at the top of that list."

"Might she have been into something you didn't know about? I mean, if she wasn't wild about drinking and was an absolute no on drugs, I don't know, could she have been interested in rich guys, or dangerous guys, or a doctor, or an author, maybe movie star?"

"Yeah, she might have been interested in someone like that, provided they were nice. But just to go after someone because they were, you know, in a band, or made a movie, or something, no, that's not the Maddie I knew. She was just a really nice person, a dear friend, and I really, really miss her," she said, and her eyes began to tear up.

"Well, let me end with this. First of all, thank you for taking the time to meet with me. I know it hasn't been easy. If there's one thing I can promise you, it's that I will do everything I can to find out who did this. I promise."

She smiled, squeezed my hand, and said, "Thanks. If I can think of anything, I'll call you."

"Please do. Anytime. Day or night."

We walked out together. Susan gave me a hug out on the sidewalk, then headed off around the corner. I went back to my car. My phone rang just as I climbed in behind the wheel.

"Haskell Investigations."

"Dev, Aaron, are you coming down today?"

"I hadn't planned on it. Why, what's up?"

"I got a call from Ben Jackson's wife this morning. They were planning to head back to Florida this morning, but Ben's back in Mayo."

"I thought he was going down for a quick checkup yesterday just to see how the chemo treatment was working."

"Yeah, that was the plan. Unfortunately, the checkup discovered cancer on the kidneys, lungs, liver, and pancreas, not good news."

"Oh, no, did they give any prognosis?"

"Not yet, but my sense would be, they may suggest hospice care."

"Any idea when he's being released from Mayo?"

"At this point, no. I told Gretchen, that's Jackson's wife, to keep me posted."

"How'd she sound?"

"About like you'd expect. You picking up anything on the cold cases?"

"I just finished meeting with a friend of Maddie Long's. She didn't really have anything to add. Everything she said pretty much matched the interview I read in the file. I've got calls out to a number of people. Hopefully, someone in the next couple of days will say something that might open a door. I just don't know. We'll just have to wait and see."

"I hear anything from Gretchen, I'll let you know. Keep me posted on any progress you make."

"Will do. Thanks, Aaron," I said, and we disconnected. I was dying to ask him about Manning and the dog shit but didn't want to tip my hand. Besides, Aaron wouldn't really appreciate what I'd done.

Sixteen

I had just pulled up across the street from my office when my phone rang again. "Haskell Investigations."

"Yeah, Dev Haskell, please. I'm returning a call he left for me."

"You got him."

"Oh, hi. I'm Tom Chambers. You left a message saying you were looking into Maddie Long's murder."

"Yeah, Tom, thanks for calling me back. I wonder if we might get together today or tonight. You're not being investigated or anything like that. I'm just looking into Maddie's case and trying to get a handle on who she was, what she was like."

"I talked to the cops and told them everything I could remember."

"Yes, I know you did. In fact, I read the transcript, and you were very helpful. The problem is, no arrest has ever been made. No one has ever been charged. The police are still more or less in the dark. I'm just wondering if we could get together. I'll buy the coffee or a beer."

He half-laughed at that and said, "Thanks but not necessary. I tell you what, are you free now?"

“Yeah, sure,” I said.

“I’ve got a painting business, and I’m working now. Do you know the Highland Park area?”

“I do.”

“I’m painting a place over on Pinehurst and Davern. The number is seventeen-sixteen, on Pinehurst. It’s a big brick place, third house from the corner. If you want to come over, I could use a break, and we can talk if that works for you.”

“Seventeen-sixteen,” I said, writing the number on the back of the parking ticket I was pretty sure Manning had given me. “I can be there in about fifteen minutes.”

“Good, just ring the doorbell. Oh, and maybe pick up a coffee on the way if you want. I’ve got some here, but I’m not sharing,” he said and laughed.

“I’ll see you shortly,” I said and disconnected. I knew approximately where the house was, and I had to pass a Caribou Coffee to get there. I grabbed a medium decaf americano and headed over to meet Tom Chambers. The house was a three-story red-brick structure with white trim. A white panel van with the words Chambers Painting along the side of the van was parked in front of the house. I parked across the street, grabbed my coffee from the console, and walked up the front sidewalk. When I rang the doorbell, I could hear it chiming inside.

A dark-haired guy I pegged at maybe mid-thirties and dressed in white painters pants and a white t-shirt appeared at the door a moment later. “Mr. Haskell?” he said.

“Yeah, Tom?” I said and held out my hand.

He shook it in a vice-like grip. “Please come in, perfect timing. I just finished washing my brush. Doing the cut-ins before I roll the walls. Any trouble finding the place?”

“No, I had pals living up in this area in high school. I knew a number of girls from around here who didn’t want to have anything to do with me.”

“I know how that goes. Let’s head back into the kitchen, and we can talk.”

“Thanks, Tom. Call me Dev, by the way. How long you been painting?”

“Oh, a number of years, maybe ten plus. After the 2009 crash, the company I was working for went belly up. I started doing odd jobs just to stay afloat, drifted into painting, and suddenly I’ve been doing it for over a decade.”

“Business good?” I asked as I followed him through a dining room and into the kitchen.

“Yeah, I’m always booked out four or five weeks in advance. I work on my own. Someone calls, I put them on the list, and if they have someone else do the work in the meantime, I just go on to the next name. I’m making more money than I was in an office, and I like being my own boss.” He unscrewed the lid from a thermos and filled it with steaming coffee. He pulled a sandwich from a brown paper bag and unwrapped the cellophane.

"Hope you don't mind if I have a bite. You mentioned Maddie Long on the phone."

"Yeah, let me be upfront and tell you I'm not with the police. I'm a private investigator. A retired cop I know worked some cases linked to Maddie's and asked me to look into them. So that's what I'm doing. I've read the case files the police have. They know I'm doing this, and they have tried to help me in any way possible. That said, I'm just trying to talk to folks like you, see if they might remember anything that wasn't covered by the police. I'm trying to get a feel for the type of person Maddie was. Really, anything that might come to mind would only help."

Chambers nodded, took a bite of his sandwich, and followed up with some coffee. "I didn't really know her that well. We had four, no wait, five dates, over almost as many weeks. She was nice, and she was fun. On our first date, I suggested we meet at a bar, Plums, as a matter of fact, not too far from here. I had two beers and was thinking of ordering a third when I noticed she was still sipping the same glass of wine. That's when she told me she wasn't into the drinking thing. Not that she had to be, but you know, idiot me set it up to meet in a bar. Anyway, we went to a movie another night, out to dinner twice, and then to a hockey game. I guess that pretty much covers it. I was maybe thinking, you know, with some time, maybe something might turn up the heat a little, but then, after the hockey game, she more or less distanced herself, and a couple of months after that, I met the woman I've been dating ever since, Rachel. We've been going out for mmm, not quite a year."

"How'd you meet Maddie?"

"Oh, same way I met Rachel, Match.com."

"Were you on that site a lot?"

"No, not a lot. More like from time to time. I haven't been on there now for close to a year, ever since I met Rachel."

"You said she distanced herself. Any particular reason?"

"No, not really except I'm into sports, hockey, football, baseball. From time to time, I enjoy meeting friends at a bar. If I'm at someone's house for a Bar-B-Que or they're over at my place, we're drinking beer. The girls are drinking wine or that prosecco shit. Maddie wasn't into that, and that's okay, but it was obvious she was gritting her teeth and smiling all the while she wasn't enjoying the night. I liked her, but we were just into different things. I think we always would have been friends. She mentioned having me paint her living room, but nothing ever came of it and then, well… If you're looking for something she might have been doing that was, you know, super kinky or way out there, I never picked up on anything like that," he said, shaking his head.

"You think she may have gone back to Match.com to meet someone else?"

"Oh, yeah. As a matter of fact, I know she did. I checked her site a few times, and she was back on. You familiar with it? The website?"

"No, not really. I seem to be able to get into enough trouble just meeting women in person."

"Well, when you log on and go to someone's personal profile, it tells you how long since the person has been on the site. I think it's hourly for the first twenty-four hours, then it lists days for maybe the next week or two, and then it lists the number of weeks. At one point, I was on there just about every day, certainly four or five times a week. But then I met Rachel and well, we're getting along great. It would only screw things up if I went back on there now. Even if I went on to erase my information, it would say I was on there an hour ago or three days ago, and if Rachel ever saw that, she'd probably dump me in a heartbeat."

"Yeah, I know how that works. They never forget, do they?"

"You're telling me," he said shaking his head.

"The cops ever ask you about the online stuff?"

He took another sip of coffee and seemed to think about it for a moment. "It's not that they didn't ask me. It was more a case of me mentioning how I met Maddie, and then that opened up the discussion. In fact, I wanted to make sure they knew that I had met Rachel online after Maddie and I drifted apart. I wanted to be sure they knew that Rachel and I were dating."

"Were you ever at Maddie's place?"

He shook his head. "No, it just, I don't know. I think we were both trying, but each time we went out, it was an okay night but never fantastic. We were both polite and all of that, but for whatever reason, nothing was really clicking. The last two dates, I picked her up at her place, but she was waiting for me to pull up and then ran out the door to get in my car. When I took her home, I just dropped her off. It was the old, 'thanks' and a peck on the cheek when we said good night. Like I said, nothing against her, but it just never went to the next level for either one of us. I can tell you this, whoever killed her, I'd gladly take them out in a second. She didn't deserve what happened to her. None of those girls did."

"Yeah, and unfortunately, we think that guy is still out there. Tom, I want to thank you for your time."

"Sorry I couldn't help, but like I told the cops, I just don't have any real information. We didn't really have a relationship. We were more like casual, short-term friends. You know?"

I did know, and I nodded. "Thanks again. I'll let myself out, and you can finish that coffee in peace." I held out my hand, we shook, and I headed to the front door.

I was almost to my car when he shouted, "Hey, Dev, if I can ever be of any help getting this bastard, give me a call."

"Thank you, Tom. I'll keep that in mind. Good luck to you now."

Seventeen

I drove back to the office and parked across the street. When I stepped into the office, Morton was asleep on his bed next to the file cabinet. He opened one eye and then closed it and went back to sleep once he saw it was me.

I began calling acquaintances of Lucia Ruiz, the woman who had been murdered in 2018, the year before Maddie Long's death. I left messages on the first two calls and got a live voice on the third call.

"Hello?"

"Hi, I'm calling for Camila Vasquez. My name is Dev Haskell."

"This is Camila. How can I help you, Mr. Haskell?" There was noise in the background, either a tv or little kids.

"Camila, I'm a private investigator working with the Saint Paul police department. I'm reviewing the case of Lucia Ruiz, and I—"

"Can you hold on for just a moment, please?" Her voice was suddenly muted, suggesting she maybe put the phone against her thigh or something, although I could still hear her. "Hey, Mommy is on the phone. We need to use our quiet voice." There was a long pause before she came back on. "Sorry about that. There's a lot of energy today. You mentioned Lucia?"

"Yes, I'm a private investigator, and I'm looking into her case, along with some others, and—"

"There's a total of six now, right?" She asked.

"Yes, that's correct. I'm wondering if we could talk. I've read the transcripts of your interview two years ago, but I wanted to talk to you. Maybe there's something you might remember or something that maybe would—"

"Why me?"

"Why you?"

"Yes, are you talking to anyone else?"

"Everyone I can. I've talked to two other people today on a related case and left two messages regarding Lucia's case. You're the first person to answer the phone with the calls I've made this afternoon."

"I spoke to the police two years ago."

"I'm aware of that. In fact, that's how I got your name. Like I said, I read the transcripts of your interview, and I was hoping we might chat. I know it must be difficult, but if I could at least meet you and tell you what we know or don't know, it could help. Maybe something might come to the surface and—"

"You're suggesting I didn't tell the police everything I knew?" There was suddenly a definite edge to her voice.

"No, on the contrary, I'm suggesting you might have said something that was overlooked or missed, and we're just trying to get another pair of eyes on this, and maybe, just maybe, we pick up on something that would allow us finally to bring Lucia's case to a close. I know it's a long shot. The odds are definitely against us. But that doesn't mean we shouldn't try to find whoever did this to Lucia and bring them to justice."

She seemed to think about that for a moment and then said, "Okay, what's your schedule like this afternoon? If you can meet with me this afternoon, we can talk."

"You name the time, and I'll meet you anywhere."

"You'll be meeting me at home. I've got two children who'll be going down for naps in about an hour. Come on over, say about half-past-one, knock on the door, and I'll be happy to tell you everything I can."

She gave me her address and hung up. I looked at the clock. That gave me ninety minutes to grab lunch. I woke Morton, took him for a short walk and then brought him back to the office. I left a note for Louie, drove down to the Pizza Shack on West Seventh, and got two slices of pizza with everything and ate them in my car. I stopped at a drugstore along the way and got a roll of Mentos to cover my pizza breath.

Camila Vasquez lived across the Mississippi River on the West side of town. I made a mental note that Lucia Ruiz's body had been found in a park over on this side of town. Camila's home was on State, just a half-block off of Cesar Chavez Street. It was one of three identical single-story stucco structures that looked to have been built right around the Second World War.

I pulled in front of the house and climbed out of my car. Camila was standing at the door before I was half-way up her front sidewalk.

"You're Dev Haskell?" She almost sounded disappointed.

"Yes, Camila?"

She nodded. "Let's just talk out here on the front steps. I finally got the kids asleep, and I don't want to risk waking them."

"Fine with me. How old are they?"

"Mateo is three and half, and Lucia is eighteen months."

"Lucia is named after—"

"Yes, and she's just like her. It's almost spooky. At eighteen months, she's controlling everyone's conversations and definitely sees herself as the person in charge."

"Sounds fun."

"Maybe in small doses. She's going to grow up and run some major corporation. In the meantime, she's driving her mother crazy. You have any kids?"

"No, I don't. I always say they're God's way of letting us know he hasn't given up on us yet."

She shook her head and said, "There are days I wonder, believe me."

"How long had you known Lucia?"

"Oh, gee, we were the same age. She was twenty-nine when she was taken from us. She'd be thirty-one this year, November as a matter of fact. Growing up, our families lived next door to each other. We were born six months apart. I was the oldest, but Lucia wasn't about to let that stop her from bossing me around. We went to kindergarten together, just over at Our Lady of Guadalupe. That was our grade school. We went to Harding for high school and then the U. I dropped out after two years, but Lucia went on to earn a pre-med degree and then did midwife training. You don't have to look very far around here to see a child she delivered in the neighborhood. She delivered our Mateo, as a matter of fact. So, you said you wanted to talk about what I told the cops?"

"I just wanted to review things with you. Was Lucia seeing anyone at the time?"

"The cops asked the same thing. She never gave much information on that front. She'd had a not-so-good relationship with a local guy, a real jerk. But she hung in there with him until he put her in the hospital."

"He was abusive?"

"That word doesn't do it justice. He was a real piece of shit. I could never figure out what she saw in him. She certainly wasn't going to straighten him out. She was in the hospital for two days, and when she was discharged, she moved in with one of her brothers, Dante."

"What's the guy's name?" I said and pulled out a notebook.

"Jack Hardy, and you don't need to write his name down. He was killed in a car accident about three months after he put Lucia in the hospital. I always wondered if it might have been her brother, Dante. But they never found the car that broadsided that slime-ball, Jack. I'd want to have a party for whoever did it. God bless them."

"Did she date anyone after that?"

"I think so. In fact, I'm sure she probably did. But like I told the police two years ago, she never mentioned it."

"How would she have met guys?"

"Mmm-mmm, probably at the bars. She could hold her own on that front."

"She ever do anything online?"

"Oh, yeah, once Jack Hardy was out of the picture, she was occasionally on Match.com. I don't know this, but if I found out it was the reason Jack beat her up, it wouldn't surprise me. Not that it makes it right. The guy really had a temper. He was a real creep."

"She never mentioned anyone?"

"Not specifically. She'd just say something really general, you know, like, I'm going to try again, or some guy contacted me, I might check him out. But, never anything specific."

"What kind of guys interested her?"

"Mmm, guys that were doing something. That's what was so screwy about pain in the ass, Jack. He didn't do shit. Well, except be a pain in the ass and treat Lucia like shit. He couldn't hold a job, at least a decent one. He was working at a liquor store, and one time some guy came in who wrote a book, and he supposedly got talking to Jack. You know, asking Jack what he did when he wasn't working. Then he offered Jack a part in a movie someone was gonna make about his book. But here's a shock, nothing ever happened, surprise, surprise. Loser Jack never got the call. I don't think he ever even saw the guy again, if he even existed in the first place. Of course, all that did was make Jack an even bigger pain in the ass, if that was possible."

A guy who wrote a book, I thought. "Hmm, did you ever hear the writer's name?"

"No, and to tell you the truth, we all thought it was probably made up. Why would anyone who wants to have a movie made from his book bring a dirt-ball like asshat Jack Hardy into the picture? Talk about a bad business decision."

"What liquor store did Hardy work at?"

"The liquor store? I forget the name. I went there once with Lucia. That was special. She ended up arguing with Jack. She's shouting at him, he's shouting back. I finally dragged her out of there before he hit both of us over the head with a bottle."

"You remember where the place was?"

"A pretty high-buck area over there by St. Thomas University. It was on a busy street, and the place had like a big grapevine and some arches and stuff painted on the side of the building. Would have probably been a nice place except that piece of shit Jack Hardy was working there. Anyway, the owner came to his senses and fired Jack a month or so after that. It turns out, they caught him on their security cameras stealing a case of Bell's whiskey and a couple cases of beer. Idiot, he didn't even have the sense to steal a good whiskey. They fired his ass the very next day and took the money for the whiskey and beer out of his paycheck. Serves him right. Like I said, Jack Hardy was a major league jerk, and if he were still around today, I wouldn't slow down if he was stupid enough to cross the street in front of me. The world's a much better place without that loser."

We chatted on for another ten minutes or so, and then Camila heard someone crying inside the house. "Oops, sorry, but it looks like the party's over. That sounds like Lucia, and I better get her before she wakes her brother. You got any other questions, give me a call and good luck. I hope I was able to help you at least a little."

She headed into the house, closing the door behind her. I climbed behind the wheel and headed back across the river. I drove through downtown on Kellogg Boulevard and then headed down Summit Avenue for three and a half miles past homes I would never be able to afford. I took a left onto Prior Avenue, and there it was a half-block off to the right. Thomas Liquors, with the side of the building covered in a gorgeous mural of a grapevine and arches. I'd purchased something there from time to time but nothing since Chuck had opened Solo Vino just up the street from me.

Eighteen

It was just like any other liquor store inside, five aisles of bottles arranged according to country and type of wine. The hard liquor was arranged on shelves on the far wall. Whiskeys, gins, vodkas, you name it. Everything from a number of top brands way out of my price range, to a number of low-priced brands I'd never heard of. Much like the beer industry some years back, there were now 'craft' distilleries springing up all over the country.

I walked up and down the aisle, carefully studying for a few minutes before I decided on a bottle of Green Spot Irish whiskey, just because I didn't have a bottle in my cabinet.

The check-out area was right next to the door, and a middle-aged woman was in the process of paying for a bottle of wine and a small package of paper napkins with a wine glass printed on the front. I waited behind her, then stepped forward as she headed out the door.

"Hi, mmm, Green Spot, a very nice choice. Anything else you need?" the guy said.

"Yeah, as a matter of fact. Just curious, a friend of mine was in a while back and ended up talking to a guy who mentioned he was a mystery writer. Would you happen to know who that could have been? He told my pal someone was going to be making a movie from one of his books. And I—"

"A movie?" he asked, taking my bottle and ringing it up. "That would have to be Mr. Hayes. Virgil Hayes, except I think he writes under a different name, some strange spelling, but I can't remember what it is. He signed a book for a guy once right here at the counter. I remember the cover was black, and it had these kind of creepy red letters for the title. I guess all his stories are set right here in town. He comes in from time to time. Nice enough guy, doesn't live too far away, somewhere over on the River Boulevard. Yeah, if you're thinking about a movie, I'd say it would almost have to be him. I guess he's got a bunch of books out there. Have to say, I've never read any, but he must be doing pretty well if he's living on the boulevard. If you want one of his books, they probably got 'em up at the bookstore on Snelling. Anything else you need?"

"No, just the bottle," I said and handed him my credit card. "Did you have a guy working here a while back, named Jack Hardy?"

The smile immediately left his face as he placed my bottle in a paper bag and tossed the receipt in after it. "Yeah, maybe two years back. He's no longer with us. Enjoy your day," he said. His tone added credibility to Camila's description of Hardy.

Just because I wasn't all that far away, I drove past Virgil Hayes's place. There was a lawn service truck with a trailer attached to the rear parked in front. One guy was riding a lawnmower back and forth across the expansive front lawn. Another was walking along the side of the house with a weed whip, trimming grass. I turned at the corner and headed down the alley just in time to see a sleek looking dark-blue car pulling into the garage. I sped up a bit to get a closer look at the driver before the garage door closed. By the time I reached the garage, the door was closing, and all I caught was the silver Mercedes logo on the trunk and a personalized license plate that read '2019 BENZ.'

I took a right at the end of the alley, drove past the liquor store again, and headed down to the office. Louie was at his picnic table, banging away on his computer. Morton was busily working on what was left of his rawhide chew, and the coffee pot was empty and still on.

As I turned off the coffee pot, Louie asked, "How's the day going?" without looking up from the keyboard.

"Still the same shit, just a different day. How'd your court appearance go?"

"We got a continuance, so that was more or less positive."

I settled in at my desk, turned on my computer, and started writing a summation of my discussions with Susan O'Mara, Tom Chambers, and Camila Vasquez.

Nineteen

About an hour later Louie said, "What do you say we end the day on a positive note and head over to The Spot for one?"

"I think that sounds like a good idea. Let me take Morton for a quick walk, and we'll meet you over there." At the sound of the word 'walk,' Morton's head suddenly popped up, and he stared at me. When I made the move to grab his leash off the windowsill, he suddenly jumped up and set his tail wagging, thumping it against the file cabinet. I attached the leash to his collar, and we headed out the door. We took a roundabout walk through the neighborhood. Morton sniffed every other tree along the sidewalk. As we walked, I kept thinking about Virgil Hayes. I wondered if Jack Hardy bragging about how he was going to be in a movie maybe led to Lucia Ruiz somehow getting together with Hayes. It seemed too farfetched at this point, but I'd keep it in the back of my mind.

My phone rang when we were a block away from The Spot.

Since the call was listed as 'unknown,' "Haskell Investigations," was how I answered.

"I'm calling to speak with Mr. Haskell, please." The 'please' sounded like it came through as a bit of an afterthought.

"Speaking."

There was a pause before the woman said, "Mr. Haskell, my name is Veronica Salucci. I'm returning a call you left for me." Then she said, "Just leave it on the desk, Susan, and I'll look at it when I'm finished here. Mr. Haskell, are you still there?"

"Yeah, still here. Are you free to talk?"

"Yes, I am," she said.

I was sizing her up as a no-nonsense type of woman. "Please, call me Dev. I contacted you in relation to the murder of Trudie Mandel back in 2015." There was a long pause, and I finally said, "Ms. Salucci?"

"Yes, I'm here. I'm sorry. You caught me off-guard hearing Trudie's name. It all seems like only yesterday. You said in your message that you're a private investigator?"

"Yes, I am, and—"

"Have you found something the police missed?"

"No, nothing like that. In fact, I'm working in conjunction with the police department. They have me looking into a series of cold cases that are all related. Miss Mandel's is one of them."

"The police said they suspected a serial killer," she said.

"Yes, they do, and I'm attempting to help them on that front."

"Forgive me for asking, but is this what you specialize in, serial killers?"

"No, but I do represent a fresh pair of eyes going over the case. Maybe picking up something, anything that might have been missed. As part of that process, I'm talking to as many friends and family members of the victims as possible. I'm trying to see if something may have possibly been overlooked or, over a period of time, maybe someone has remembered something that they thought was unimportant but it might head the investigation in a different direction."

"You sound almost desperate."

"I prefer the term focused. I'm not suggesting the police weren't. But I'm one more person who might stumble on the missing link that could suddenly point to a perpetrator."

"What do you want from me?"

"I'd just like to talk with you at a place and time of your convenience. I've gone over your interview with the police back in 2015. Maybe something, somewhere, might pop up, or possibly you said something that was missed back then, and it just might be the item that brings everything together."

"Do you know anything about light fixtures, Mr., oh, umm, I mean, Dev?"

"Light fixtures?"

"Yes, it's what we sell here. You sound like you have a knack for sales."

"I'll take that as a compliment, but I'm probably the last person on earth to know anything about light fixtures."

"Very well. I'll be wrapping up my day in about an hour. Would you have time to meet then?"

"I'll make time. You just tell me where."

"My office would work best. We're downtown in the Germania Bank building. Do you know where that is?"

"I do."

"Interesting," she said. "We're on the fourth floor. VS Industries."

"I'll see you in an hour, ma'am. Thank you in advance for your time." I disconnected, and we walked up the block to The Spot. Louie was seated on his usual stool at the far end of the bar, and when we stepped in the door, he called, "Hey, Mike," to the bartender and pointed at me.

Mike nodded and grabbed a beer glass.

"Nothing for me, Mike. I've got to head out in a few minutes," I said and walked down to Louie. As we approached, Louie reached down with two or three pork rinds in his hand. Morton hurried forward, straining at his leash. He licked up the pork rinds from Louie's hand then promptly sat and stared at Louie with a mournful look.

"You having a whiskey instead of a beer?" Louie asked.

"I wish. No, I got a call from another person in this cold case deal. I'm meeting her in a little less than an hour, and I had the wild idea that showing up smelling like beer might not be the best introduction."

"I'll bet they've got some baby bibs somewhere around here to cover the beer smell. You know, for guys like you who always slobber."

"If only that would work. No, thanks for thinking of me, but I'm going to take Morton home and then head downtown to this woman's office. You in tomorrow morning?"

Louie nodded as he took a sip. "Doing paperwork all day. I know," he said, cutting me off before I could speak. "First one in puts the coffee on."

"See you in the morning," I said. I waved at Mike on the way out the door. He was involved in a conversation with a woman and gave me a quick flick of the wrist.

Once home, I tossed the mail on the kitchen counter, let Morton out the kitchen door, and hurried upstairs to find a reasonably clean shirt. I had a nice blue button-down hanging on my closet doorknob. It still had just the slightest hint of Taffy's perfume, a spicy vanilla. I shaved, combed my hair, and put the shirt on as I hurried down the stairs. I let Morton back in, filled his water dish, tossed him a biscuit, and went out the door.

Twenty

The Germania Bank building was built in 1889, and at the time, I think it was the tallest building in town, eight stories. When Veronica made the 'interesting' comment after I said I knew where the building was, it was probably because the name of the building had changed a number of times over the last hundred-and-thirty-years. Just ten years after it was built, the Germania Bank was forced to liquidate. Close to a half-dozen name changes followed until it was placed on the National Historic register in 1974, and the name reverted back to the original Germania Bank building. I parked across the street and a half-block away. I found the office number for VS industries on the framed list of businesses next to the elevator and rode up to the fourth floor. VS Industries office was halfway down the hall behind a wooden door with frosted glass and 'VS INDUSTRIES' painted in black letters.

I stepped into a small empty lobby with a half-dozen chairs upholstered in black leather and a sign on the reception counter that said, 'PLEASE RING BELL FOR SERVICE'. A round, nickel-plated bell, the kind you hit with the palm of your hand, sat next to the sign. I hit the bell twice.

A guy maybe twenty years old strolled out a moment later. He was dressed in blue jeans and a blue striped golf shirt. "Hi, can I help you?"

"Yeah, I'm here to see Veronica Salucci. She's expecting me. Dev Haskell is my name."

"Hang on just a minute while I check," he said and disappeared around the corner. He was back about thirty seconds later and said, "If you'll follow me, please."

We walked through a room with a half-dozen cubicles. They all appeared to be empty at this time of day. He led me to a corner office, stepped aside and directed me through the door with a wave of his hand.

"Thanks," I said and entered a spacious office with a large desk littered with files and a large computer screen.

"Be with you in just a moment, Dev," a voice called from behind the computer screen. "Any trouble finding us?"

"No, not at all. I'm familiar with the city," I said, taking in the surroundings. The view looked out on Fifth and Wabasha Streets and the city beyond. A large black leather couch rested against the wall with a glass-topped coffee table placed between the couch and two wingback chairs. Off to the side was a stack of a half-dozen brown cardboard boxes with different light fixtures partially hanging out.

"Okay, finally done," the voice said, and Veronica suddenly stood and stepped out from behind her desk. She couldn't have been taller than maybe five-one or two. She was lean, but not skinny, and well-apportioned. She was attractive with black hair, dark brown eyes, and exuded a strong sense of not taking a lot of crap from anyone. She flashed sparkling white teeth as she approached in black silk slacks, a matching jacket, and a cream-colored blouse. "Nice to meet you, Dev," she said extending her hand. "Please have a seat. Hopefully, I'll be able to help in some way. Is it too strong a term to suggest the police have reopened the investigation?"

I waited as she settled into one of the winged back chairs and promptly sat in the other one. "Unfortunately, at this stage, yes, it is too strong a term. That said, I'm hoping to learn something that would encourage the police to do exactly that, reopen the investigation."

"Wonderful, what can I do to help?"

"For starters, if you could tell me about your relationship with Trudie. How did you meet? What sort of person was she? What did she like and dislike? I'm interested in anything at all that you can remember. As I mentioned, I read the transcript of your interview with the police, but anything you can think of, however irrelevant it may seem, might turn out to be just the thing that shines a new light."

"Well, we're both originally from town, but we met in college, down at Mankato State. We joined the same sorority, Theta Phi Alpha," she said and stared off to a corner of the room.

"That would have been 2002. We were both girls away from home for the first time, and we just clicked. We roomed together the next year and shared an apartment the following year. We moved back up here after college. I got hired by Brass Light Gallery, and Trudie went to work for Hennepin County. I was traveling all the time. She met Greg, her former husband, and moved in with him. We still kept in touch, but, you know, at that point, we were on different paths."

"She divorced in the fall of 2014, didn't she?"

"Yes, and for the record, it was no one's fault, really. It just happened, and looking back, you could maybe see it coming. The romance flame was just plain gone. When she and Greg divorced, Trudie and I, more or less, got back together. By that time, I'd had this company up and running for four or five years, and I offered her a job."

"She didn't take it?"

Veronica smiled. "No, she said it would probably ruin our friendship, which may have been true. Besides, she was looking at qualifying for a pension with the county in another twelve or fourteen years, and she liked what she was doing. I think after her divorce, for her last five or six months, we probably saw one another almost weekly. Nothing crazy, you know, maybe the occasional dinner out but, more often, dinner in her kitchen or mine.

Well, if it was her kitchen, she'd cook. If it was mine, it was going to be takeout, but she was okay with that."

"What can you tell me about her ex?"

"Greg? Oh, he's a really nice guy. He lives down in Dallas now. Trudie never told me, but it wouldn't surprise me to find out he moved to Dallas because he couldn't stand to be divorced from her. I'm not suggesting in any way that he's the guilty party. He wanted to try to work things out, and Trudie knew that, ultimately, it just wasn't going to work. I know for a fact, when he got the news, you know, about the incident. I know he was absolutely devastated. He was in some therapy or counseling for a while, maybe still is for all I know. He was back up here for Trudie's funeral."

"Was another guy the reason for the divorce?"

"No, that wouldn't be her style. Even though she filed for the divorce, there wasn't anything extramarital going on."

"Did she ever get back into dating anyone?"

"Yeah, some guy she worked with was interested, but she shut that down because they worked together. I know she went on a couple of dates but nothing that stands out. Usually out to dinner somewhere and then either she never heard from the guy, or she did hear from him and just begged off because she knew it wasn't going to work. I know towards the end she was into some guy, but he was traveling for business, and I don't think the relationship ever went anywhere. In fact, relationship is probably too strong a word. They had maybe two or three dates over as many weeks, and like I said, he was traveling all the time."

"She do anything online?"

"Oh yeah, I know she was into Match.com, but those seemed to be the dates where she'd meet someone, and the spark just wasn't there. I know she swore off it at least twice and then would go back on and get disappointed all over again. Although the last guy, the one traveling, she met him online. But then like I said, he was gone all the time, so it wouldn't have worked even if she'd tried to keep it up."

"She ever allude to any fears of someone following or stalking her?"

Veronica shook her head. "No, I never heard anything like that. She lived in a large complex out on Highway 61 and 36. Really good security, underground parking, she knew her neighbors on either side of her, and they all got along. I think, in the end, this was just something crazy, maybe wrong place, wrong time. You know, like she went for a walk or something and some nutcase happened to be driving by. I mean, her car was in its underground parking place. Her apartment was locked. Nothing was taken. I know there was cash in a dresser drawer, two hundred dollars I think, and a diamond pendant Greg had given her for their first anniversary or something, and those items were still in her apartment."

"This guy that was traveling for business, did she ever mention a name or what he did for business?"

She shook her head. "No, she never mentioned a name, and other than saying he traveled, that was it. As far as I know, he could have been a truck driver, or he owned a bunch of oil wells. Just the little I heard, it seemed like she might have been more interested in him than he was in her."

I pulled a business card from my wallet and handed it to Veronica. "Anything else comes to mind, don't hesitate to give me a call, please. Anytime, day or night."

"I'll be sure to do that, Dev. God, I hope you get the guy that did this to Trudie. She didn't deserve it. She was a really good person. A good friend, and, and, I really miss her," she said and then quickly regained her composure. She stood and held out her hand. "Thanks for listening to me drone on. I hope you get this guy."

"Yeah, me too."

"You ever think you might want to sell light fixtures, give me a call and we'll talk."

"Thanks, I'll keep it in mind. I can find my way out. Thanks again for your time, Veronica."

"Thank you. You know, I still miss Trudie every day and I probably always will."

Twenty-one

As I pulled into the driveway, I could see Morton looking out the front window with his head resting on the back of the couch. He watched me as I climbed out of the car and pulled the paper bag with the bottle of Green Spot from the back seat. I heard him running to the front door as I unlocked it and stepped inside.

"Hi, Morton, miss me?" I asked, giving him a good scratch behind the ears. I took the wagging tail as a positive response. "Come on. Let's get you outside."

At the sound of 'outside', he took off for the kitchen door. I let him out into the backyard. I took a small Waterford glass from a kitchen cabinet and set it on the counter. I pulled the bottle of Green Spot from the paper bag and filled the glass halfway, which amounted to probably a good free-pour double shot. I placed the cork back in the bottle and set the bottle in my liquor cabinet. This was too nice a whiskey to go pounding it down over the course of a night or two.

I let Morton back in, tossed him a biscuit, and then turned on my laptop. I wrote a summation of my conversation with Veronica Salucci, then went back and began to reread my original notes from the cold case files.

My phone rang. Amazingly, it was Taffy. I could only hope she was calling to see if I'd like to come over. "Hi, Taffy, how are you doing?"

"Oh, Dev, I'm so excited. My boss called me into his office, and I got the promotion."

"Oh, that's terrific, and no surprise. I told you." I immediately thought, 'party-time.' I'd grab a quick shower, try to find some clean clothes, stop on the way and pick up a bottle or two of wine. No, wait, as much as I hated it, I'd get prosecco. This would be great. It had been over a week since the last time we—.

"Anyway, I just wanted to let you know. I meet with my boss and the three people I interviewed with tomorrow. Oh, finally, things are starting to move. Yippie!" she shouted.

"Oh, this is so great. I'm really happy for you, but, like I said before, no surprise. I knew they'd pick you. They had to. You're the best one. How about I bring over some prosecco to celebrate. Hey, it's not too late. What do you say to me picking up some sushi, too? I can call in the order and be at your place in the next half-hour, and who knows we just might—"

"Oh, umm, thanks, Dev, but Allison is picking me up in a couple of minutes, and we're going out. I just wanted to let you know."

"You want me to meet you somewhere? We could all—"

"Mmm, that may not be the best idea. You were kind of rude to Allison the other night at the Thai Garden and…"

I was rude? I thought. The guy who paid for the hundred-dollar bottle of wine. I was rude to Allison, who gave me the finger once I paid and left. "Actually, Taffy, I don't think I was rude. As a matter of fact—"

"There you go, Dev. I call to give you some good news, and you're right back to complaining about Allison."

"Taffy, I haven't even mentioned her. You did."

"Well, you were going to, and don't even try to deny it. We're going out for a little celebration, just the two of us, and we don't need any negativity. I've got my good news, and Allison met a guy she is really into, and we do not need someone being negative and spoiling the evening. We've both worked hard to get where we are."

I could only imagine the kind of 'hard work' pain in the ass Allison did to get some guy interested in her. "Taffy, I'm not going to spoil the evening."

"I'll maybe talk to you tomorrow. Try to find a positive note between now and then," Taffy said and hung up.

I wanted to throw my phone against the wall, but then what? I'd just have to go out and buy a new one. I walked out to my liquor cabinet and grabbed the bottle of Green Spot. I brought it back to the kitchen, pulled the cork, and then carefully poured what remained in my Waterford glass back into the bottle— no use in wasting it after Taffy's phone call.

I worked for maybe another hour, then flaked out on the couch and began watching a movie of no redeeming social value. Jason Statham shooting a few hundred bad guys, it fit my mood. I woke a little after one. Morton was already upstairs in bed. I turned off the lights on the first floor and went upstairs to bed. I woke the next morning before my alarm went off. For just a moment, I caught a glimpse of blue sky between the window shade and the window trim. I thought, it looks like it's going to be a really nice day. Then, I remembered Taffy's phone call, and it was like the sky turned cloudy, and it started to rain. A hot shower didn't help much.

I went downstairs, put the coffee on, and fired up my laptop. I poured a cup of coffee and clicked on my emails. There was an email from Aaron that came through at eleven last night. *'Ben Jackson has been placed in hospice care. Give me a call in the morning.'* Damn it! Things just got worse.

Twenty-two

We were in the office early. I'd phoned Aaron twice and left a message both times. I had the coffee on and was just finishing my second cup when Aaron returned my call.

"Hi Aaron, I got your text message on Ben Jackson this morning. What's the word?"

"Not good is the bottom line, unfortunately. They've given him six weeks. Based on all the cancer, he'll be lucky if he lasts a week."

"But the chemo? I mean, didn't that do anything? He was going through all those treatments and—"

"Sometimes it just doesn't work, Dev."

"Yeah, damn it. Your text said he was in hospice. Are they back down in Florida?"

"No, they're in a hospice facility up here. One of their daughters has some connection that got him in on short notice. She knows someone. Anyway, he went in there yesterday afternoon."

"How's he doing?"

"I think about as well as can be expected. I've got a call in to his wife, Gretchen, but haven't heard back. I'd say she's got her hands full right about now. I wanted to offer her the spare room at my place, although I'm sure she'll be staying with one of their girls."

"I've got a spare room, too, if she doesn't want to be bored at your place, she can just let me know."

"Your joint? I wouldn't do that to her, Dev. God, she's got enough going on. Have you been talking to anyone on the cold cases?"

"Yeah, I've been talking to folks who knew the last three victims. Pretty much the same deal. None of the women were crazy party animals out on the town every night. One of them, Maddie Long, she's the most recent. She was the sober driver for friends when they were out. All of the victims appear to have been responsible, employed women. Probably the common denominator is they were dating guys, but what does that mean? Most women in that ten-year age group, you know twenty-five to thirty-five, are dating guys if they're not already in some kind of a relationship. Nothing appears to have been missing from their places of residence, so robbery doesn't seem to play into the motive angle. None of them had a wedding planned or were even in a relationship that may have been headed that way from what I can determine. It looks like the white slip and the wedding veil is, I don't know, something the perp has going on. I'm not giving up. It's just that's where I am at this point."

"Shit," Aaron said. "What's your day look like?"

"I'll be on the phone trying to line up more meetings with these folks. The people I've talked to have been very cooperative. I'm just not getting anything new, sorry to say."

"Dev, let's get together at the end of the day. I don't want to meet here. You pick the place, and I'll meet you for dinner. By the way, you're buying. You still owe me for the last time we were out and both your credit cards were denied."

"Gee Aaron, thanks for being so understanding."

"Later," Aaron said and disconnected.

I heard Louie groaning his way up the stairs about twenty minutes later. I filled his mug with coffee and set it on the picnic table then watched as he stepped into the office red-faced. He set his briefcase on the table, raised his hand in a semblance of a wave without uttering a word, and then collapsed in his desk chair. It was almost five minutes and a half-dozen noisy slurps of coffee before he spoke. "What time did you get in?"

"Early. I got a text message from Aaron that Ben Jackson has been moved into hospice care."

"Jackson? I thought he finished up his chemo and was set to go back to Florida. What happened?"

"I don't know, other than it didn't work. Cancer on his kidneys, lungs, liver, and pancreas. Not good."

"Where is he?"

"Hmm, Aaron never really said other than in a hospice facility. I'm having dinner with him tonight, and I'll find out. On a more positive note, Taffy apparently got the promotion. She'll be meeting with her boss and some other folks today. I'm thinking they might put her in charge of a section, and she'll have five or six people reporting to her."

"Oh, that's great news. Did you guys go out to celebrate last night?"

"No, she had some other stuff lined up."

Louie gave me a look but didn't say anything. "That's really good news. Congratulations to her."

My phone rang, saving me from any probing questions. The number had a 507 area code, southern Minnesota. "Haskell Investigations."

"Let me talk to Dev Haskell. I'm returning a call he left for me," a male voice said.

"This is Dev."

"My name is Hugh Goodman. You called regarding the murder of my sister, Marlis."

"Yes, thank you for returning my call, Mr. Goodman. I'm calling to see if you might have some time to talk with me about your sister. I'm working with the police, and we're going over a number of cases. Your sister's case is one of them."

"They never arrested anyone. Do they have some bastard in mind now?"

"Actually, no, they don't. But we're hoping someone might remember something new or might alert us to something they mentioned earlier that the police could have missed. Just one seemingly simple fact could get things going again."

"And you want to talk to me? Marlis was murdered back in 2006. I was twelve at the time."

"Yeah, I realize that, but maybe you've heard something like—"

"Heard something like someone climbing in a window or kicking her door in. Get your facts straight. Jesus Christ, you guys haven't arrested anyone in over a decade and a half. Almost fifteen damn years, and you're thinking I know something. Are you crazy? My damn sister was murdered. Our old man died from a heart attack a year later. A heart attack brought on by blaming himself for not being there to protect her. Like he ever could have been to begin with. Our mother died of a broken heart four years later. You guys still hadn't arrested anyone. Now, apparently, you've let this son-of-a-bitch kill another five women, and you still haven't done a damn thing. At what point do you start to catch on?"

"That's why I was hoping we could sit down and talk, and I could just listen to what you have to say. Maybe there's some fine point that was missed, and something you say might be just the thing that gets us focused in the right direction."

"Focused in the right direction? After all this time? And now you want to question someone who was twelve at the time. Unbelievable. You just don't get it."

"Well, then maybe you could set us straight. I'd be happy to drive down to Winona and—"

"Please, don't bother. You guys have already done more than enough damage to my family. I don't want to be anywhere near you. Do you hear me? So don't come down. Don't call me. Don't text me. And don't send me a message on a carrier pigeon. Just do me a favor and stay the hell away." The line suddenly went dead.

I felt it was a pretty safe bet I wouldn't be contacting Hugh Goodman again anytime soon.

I grabbed a bourbon bacon chicken sandwich for lunch at Shamrocks. Louie had something come up and couldn't join me, so I ate at the bar. The way the day was shaping up, I decided to stay away from alcohol, and instead, I ordered a root beer with my sandwich. I was back at the office forty minutes later, plowing through all my notes. I sent a text message to Aaron around four, telling him to meet me at Carmelo's at six.

I took Morton home around five, grabbed a shower, checked some things online, and hurried over to Carmelo's. I'd been sitting at the table for maybe ten minutes when I got a text from Aaron saying he was running a half-hour late. It was closer to an hour by the time he arrived.

"Hey, Dev, sorry I'm late. Something came up at the last minute," Aaron said as he sat down.

"Not a problem, Aaron. It must be because you were going to meet me. I'll tell you, the last twenty-four hours has been one pain in the ass situation after another." I took a sip of my Peroni beer just as our server stepped to the table.

"Would you care for a beverage?" she asked Aaron.

"I'll have whatever he's drinking," he said.

"And I'll have another," I added.

"So, Dev, what's been so bad in your life?"

"Well, don't get me wrong. I'm glad to be involved, but it's a real downer talking to friends and family of these women who've been killed. A woman last night told me she misses her friend every day and always will. Then I a get a phone call from Taffy that didn't go well. Today I'm talking with the brother of one of the victims, who basically read me the riot act over the phone. Said his father died of a heart attack and his mother of a broken heart all because we couldn't find the guy who murdered his sister."

"All of which is understandable, Dev, and, as you know, comes with the territory."

"Yeah, I know. You're right, I get that. It just isn't very fun."

"Are you ready to order?" our server asked as she set our beers down in front of us.

I ordered Fettuccine Alfredo, and Aaron ordered Primavera. We chatted about everything and nothing over our beers, and the food arrived about fifteen minutes later. We were quiet for the next five minutes until we'd had enough food to slow us down and chat casually. Aaron had two teams investigating a shooting, which thankfully, turned out to be a guy shooting himself in the foot. I told him about my phone conversation with Taffy last night, and he gave some pretty solid advice.

"You know, Dev. Maybe you should back off for a bit. You two have been going hot and heavy for months, and that's a record for you. Maybe it's the same thing for her, and she just feels like she needs to interact with more girlfriends and get some kind of balance back in her life."

"Aaron, that's a very good idea. There's only one problem. It won't work. She's not interacting with her girlfriends. She's stuck like glue to super-bitch Allison. Who, by the way, hates me ever since I told her I needed some time away from her, like for the rest of my life."

"Did you really tell her that?"

"No, but I should have. Get this…" I went on to tell him about the concert, the three-person dinner at Taffy's, the Thai Garden debacle, and last night's going out to celebrate with Allison and I wasn't invited.

"Sounds to me like the two of them have you backing off, whether you want to or not. Maybe just give them some space. They're making you do it anyway. Don't argue. Just smile and say 'Yes, dear.'"

"You think that would help?"

"Can it hurt? Obviously, trying to change Taffy's mind isn't working very well."

"Yeah, maybe."

"Amazing. You actually listen every once in a while. Not to change the subject, but are you picking up anything talking to folks on these cold cases?"

"In a word, no. Commonalities, all the women were single, dating from time to time but not going out on a date every night. They were all employed, lived in their own place, met some of their dates online. More often than not, it seems the dates they lined up didn't interest them, or the guys weren't interested in them. Thus far, everyone speaks fondly of the victims, and that seems to not be because of their unfortunate death but rather they were just very nice people. With one exception, no mention of Virgil Hayes, the author who was a person of interest."

"What was the one exception?"

I went on to tell him about Hayes probably offering Jack Hardy a role in the movie.

"Yeah," Aaron said. "The movie that was never made. Hayes was right. Someone, I forget who, optioned a book for a film. It never went anywhere, which is the case for about ninety-nine percent of books that are optioned. If I recall, Hayes got a payment for two years. Something like five grand a year, and then whoever it was couldn't find any interested parties and didn't renew the option for the third year."

"But that's still ten-grand," I said.

"Yeah, it comes to four-hundred and sixteen dollars a month. With the monthly income Hayes makes in book sales, I'm sure he never even noticed it."

We chatted for another twenty minutes, and then we were both ready to go home. I paid the bill, and we headed out the door. I was about to say goodbye, but Aaron's phone rang, and he ended up waving at me and heading for his car. I drove home, let Morton out the kitchen door for a few minutes, and then we settled in front of the tv. We watched another movie with no redeeming social value before we went up to bed.

Twenty-three

We were up the next morning before the alarm. Well, at least I was up. Morton eventually came down to the kitchen after the alarm had gone off. I was determined to make the day more positive than yesterday, and I gave him a good scratch behind the ears. I let him out the kitchen door and then went back to my computer. In the four minutes I had paid attention to Morton, an email from Camila Vasquez arrived. *'Call me when you have a moment.'*

I called her back and, with two little kids, it wasn't surprising that I ended up leaving a message. "Hi, Camila, Dev Haskell here. I got your email. Give me a call when you have time. I'm around all day. Thanks."

I let Morton back in the kitchen, fed and watered him, and wasted a half-hour hoping Camila might call. I decided against calling her back, and we drove down to the office. I was on my second cup of coffee when Louie stepped in. He was his usual red-faced self. It wasn't until he'd placed his briefcase on the picnic table that I noticed the white bakery bag that looked rather full.

"Good morning, Louie, how was your night?"

He nodded, gave the semblance of a wave, and collapsed in his desk chair with a groan. I got up, grabbed his coffee mug, and dumped the half-inch of contents into the sink. Then refilled it and set it in front of him.

After a couple of minutes, he was able to speak. “You want a caramel roll, Dev?”

“What, you don’t think I’m sweet enough?”

“Unfortunately, I only got you one.”

“I’ll take it,” I said.

Louie held the bag open for me. There were four large caramel rolls in the bag. I pulled out the top one. It was drenched in caramel, had walnuts on the top, and was still warm from the oven. It was delicious.

I was maybe halfway through the caramel roll when Louie pulled one out of the bag for himself. He took one large bite and proceeded to drip a long string of caramel across his silk tie. It landed right next to a coffee stain from a previous morning.

He chewed for a moment, then said, “How’d your dinner go last night with LaZelle?”

“Pretty well. I brought him up to date on the progress I’ve been making on the cold cases, which is next to none.”

“How did he take it?”

“What can he say? My results mirror the same thing they ran into. Everyone I’ve talked with has nothing new to add. It’s not that they’re hiding anything. It’s more like they were just thoroughly interviewed by the police, and there’s nothing new out there. He did have an interesting comment on—”

My phone suddenly rang, and I answered if halfway through the second ring. “Camila?”

“Hi, Dev, I hope I’m not catching you at a bad time.”

“No, not at all. I wanted to call you back but figured you probably didn’t need a half-dozen calls from me that you couldn’t get to.”

“Yeah, thanks for that. The kids have been up since half-past five, and I had to get them fed. God, what I could do with their energy. Hey, Mateo, leave your sister alone, or you’re going to get a time out. Mateo! Okay, thank you, much better. Oh God, and it’s barely after nine. I tell you.”

“You sent me that text message, everything okay?” I asked, trying to get her refocused.

“Oh, yeah. After we talked, I couldn’t stop thinking of Lucia. I have a journal of Lucia’s. Well, it’s not really a journal. It’s actually just three spiral notebooks. She put things in there, you know what she was doing that day, maybe what she had planned, sometimes what she ate. She mentions a couple of her dates, along with a bunch of stuff about her mom, which is pretty funny since I knew the woman. Man, she ran a tight ship. Of course, with six kids, you’d have to. God, I’ve got my two, and I don’t know how she did it. Five boys and a girl. Can you imagine? Anyway, after you stopped by, it got me thinking, and I hauled them out and started reading. She makes a comment about a guy, just that he was really hot. But I thought you might find it interesting.”

“Yeah, I do. Does she happen to mention a name?”

"No, unfortunately, but I just thought it was interesting."

"You've got these notebooks at your house?"

"Yeah, I'm looking at them right now. They're sitting on my kitchen counter."

"Would you mind if I swing by and take a look?"

"We're here all day. Maybe don't come at nap time. Once they're down, I'm usually running around trying to get the place picked up and straightened out, so it looks halfway decent for at least fifteen minutes."

"I'll be over shortly. Thanks for the email earlier, Camila. Much appreciated."

"Not a problem. I just hope it will help. Just ring the doorbell. I'll be around somewhere chasing these two."

I crammed the last of my caramel roll in my mouth and said, "I gotta run and take a look at something. You gonna be here for a bit?"

Louie nodded, gave me a wave, and pulled another caramel roll from the bag as I headed out the door. When I pulled in front of Camila's house, she was sitting on the front steps watching her kids. Mateo was racing up and down the front sidewalk on a blue mini micro scooter. His sister, Lucia, was trying to catch him and failing miserably, which only added to her brother's pleasure.

"Hi, Camila, how's it going?"

"Just trying to wear them out and get rid of some of this energy."

"You're right, the things we could do with that. God."

Mateo slowed down on the scooter until his sister was just about to reach him and then took off, which set Lucia on a screaming jag.

"Deal with it, honey. You might as well learn at a young age, that's life," Camila said. "Let me get those notebooks for you, Dev. They're just inside." She hurried up the front steps and into the house before I could even respond.

As the door closed behind her, Mateo suddenly wore an evil grin. Little Lucia turned around and began to run toward the street. I started to walk after her as Mateo shot past me on the scooter and ran into his sister, knocking her on the ground. Fortunately, she fell on the grass as opposed to the concrete. She let out a scream as Mateo raced down the sidewalk then turned around and eyed his target screaming on the grass. He pushed off, aiming directly at her and picking up speed. I beat him by two seconds and picked her up, lifting her over Mateo's head just as he rolled over the area on the lawn where she'd lain a moment ago.

"You little fu—"

"Everything all right?" Camila called from the front door.

"Oh yeah, just fine. Lucia fell, and I just wanted to make sure she was all right."

"Oh, you're so sweet. Here, I'll trade you," Camila said and held out three spiral notebooks, which I gladly traded for a crying eighteen-month-old.

"You mind if I take these back to the office? There may be pages I'll want to copy. I can get them back to you later today if you want."

She seemed to think about that for a moment, nodded, and then said, "Yeah, sure, just have them back to me by the end of the day. They're one of the few things I have of hers, and I don't want to lose them."

"Not a problem. I'll have them back to you tonight. Thanks in advance."

"Well, don't get your hopes up. Nothing really new, but still it was Lucia. I can just hear her saying some of the stuff in there. Give me a call first. Kids go down around seven, so if you could make it back by six, that would be great."

"I'll see you then," I said and fled the scene. I stopped at McDonald's, got a Quarter Pounder with cheese and bacon, a chocolate shake, and headed to the office. Louie was on his computer, typing away. The coffee pot was now empty and the burner was still on. The white bakery bag was lying flat on the corner of Louie's desk, which meant he had eaten three caramel rolls.

"Oh, man, you went to McDonald's. I would've had you grab me something if I knew you were going."

"Sorry, man. I didn't even think of it. I was going past and just drove in."

"No problem, I'll head down there in a minute. I can use the break. How'd things go for you?"

"Diaries, of a sort, from one of the victims. God forbid there'd be the name and phone number in there of the killer. Of course, while the woman runs into the house to get these, she sticks me in charge of watching her kids. The little boy tried to run his sister over on his scooter."

"That sounds a little farfetched. I'm sure—"

"I'm not kidding you, man. He runs her over from behind, knocks her down, and then as she's screaming on the ground, he turns around and heads right for her. I got her out of the way about a second before he would have nailed her. I'm telling you, the guy was gunning for her."

"Hmm, maybe a politician in the making," Louie said.

Twenty-four

I set the Lucia Ruiz notebooks aside and dined on my Quarter Pounder with cheese and bacon for the next ten minutes. I was maybe halfway through the thing when Louie switched off his computer and said, "That smells so good I'm going to get a couple. Back in fifteen minutes." He hurried out the door and down the stairs. Morton was busy with what was left of his rawhide chew and ignored me. I finished the quarter pounder, drained the chocolate shake, pulled the three notebooks in front of me, and started reading again.

The first two notebooks were worn, creased, and it dawned on me that, at this point in her life, Lucia would have still been living with Jack Hardy, and maybe she felt she had to hide the notebooks. The third one, written after she had left Hardy and moved in with her brother, was in much better condition. Her penmanship was neat, almost precise, with somewhat proper punctuation, considering it was more comments instead of sentences. The first page of the first notebook was dated November of 2017. Lucia was living with Jack Hardy, and although she didn't go into detail, you could tell it wasn't fun.

Very general terms like, "We went to Mercado for dinner. Camila stopped over tonight. Went to my mom's for a break." Occasionally, there was a descriptive term for Jack Hardy: jerk, asshole, dip-shit, pain in the ass, party pooper. Based on what Camila had told me and the comments in the notebook, I'm sure a number of people wondered what she was doing with the guy. The second notebook was more of the same, and then there was about a two-week period where nothing was written. The first entry after that, she mentioned that she had moved in with her brother Dante and 'things were a lot better.'

Louie had been back for at least an hour with two Quarter Pounders with cheese and bacon when I started in on the third notebook. The burgers were gone, and he was slowly working through a large order of fries as he typed away on his computer.

Lucia's notebook occasionally mentioned a client or, since she was a midwife, were they patients? Like the two previous notebooks, she mentioned the weight, and sex of the babies she delivered but never the mother or baby's name. Toward the end, there were a couple of dates she went on that all seemed to be one-timers, with no further contact. She listed two of the guys as 'very boring' in capital letters with two exclamation points.

Then, in June of 2018, maybe four weeks before she was murdered. She met someone she described as 'HOTTIE.' The word was in capital letters, and she had at least three dates with him. No real description, other than he had a beard. No mention of where they went other than 'go out.' For the three dates, they danced, had dinner, and saw a movie. It appeared they met once a week, but I couldn't be sure. The last line in the notebook read, 'Finally! I can't wait!!' That was it, nothing else, and one can only assume she was murdered shortly after that, maybe by this Hottie person.

I phoned Aaron LaZelle, and surprisingly, he answered. "Hi Dev, don't tell me they still have you washing dishes at the restaurant to pay for last night's dinner."

"No, I just gave them your name, your bank account number, and they were happy enough with that."

"Very funny. What can I do for you?"

"Two things actually. I forgot to ask you the name of the Hospice facility Ben Jackson is in."

"Lyngblomsten Care Center. Call and you can ask for him by name. Visiting hours for non-family are nine to five."

"You've been over there?"

"No, I'll go over tomorrow morning. I spoke to Gretchen maybe an hour ago, and she updated me."

"How's she doing?"

"She's one tough cookie, and she's hanging in there. But not fun, that's for sure. What else you got?"

I went on to tell him about reading the Lucia Ruiz notebooks and the "Finally! I can't wait!" comment. "I told Camila I'd get them back to her this evening before six, but I can make copies for you if you want. Really nothing of interest until the last few pages and then just very general terms. No description, except the guy had a beard. No mention of where they actually went out; other than the word Hottie, no names."

"You've got access to these if we need them later?"

"Yes. That's one of the reasons I want to get them back to Camila tonight. So she can trust me."

"Okay, tell you what, make a copy of those last few pages and bring them in tomorrow morning. Maybe add a name and address, just in case something happens and we need to access them in a hurry. Thanks, Dev, it's more than we had before. You know how this stuff goes."

"Yeah, very slow and inch by inch. I'll see you in the morning. Enjoy your evening." I hung up and made copies of the last ten pages in Lucia's final notebook then sat down and read them again just in case I'd missed something. Nothing stood out, and after reading through it yet another time, even the Hottie comment seemed less than impressive. I might have made too much of it in talking to Aaron.

"Did Aaron have any comment about the Hottie description?" Louie asked without looking up from the file on his desk.

"No, he's been through this enough times not to get all that excited about anything. I just reread the last few pages, and I might have sold him a bill of goods. The more I look at it, it doesn't seem that impressive and really doesn't give any information."

"But wouldn't you think, if she was dating a normal guy, he suddenly can't get hold of her, and then she's all over the news as a murder victim, wouldn't you think he'd contact the police, or the family, or at least go to the funeral?"

"Yeah, I mean, you'd hope so. But I've had more women than I can count tell me to never, ever call them again and so I haven't. I've had dates with women, and it's clearly their turn to call me, and they never did. I figured, for whatever reason, things weren't working out as far as they were concerned, and I never tried to contact them. Hell, I probably couldn't remember their names now, and they've certainly erased me from their memory."

Louie shook his head. "Who can blame them? Still the timing, her last entry and all, that would seem to add a little more weight to the subject."

"Yeah, except there isn't a name, a description, or an address. She doesn't even mention what kind of car he drove. A hottie, who the hell knows? Maybe he had a case of the flu, and he was running a temperature."

"Yeah, sure, Dev. She was referring to his temperature. There you go. You've solved the case, just solved all six as a matter of fact."

"You know what I mean. Hey, I better give Camila a call, let her know I'm bringing these back to her. You interested in going for one at The Spot?"

"I could be talked into it," Louie said.

"I'll meet you over there. Morton and I are going to return these notebooks, and then we'll see you there."

I called Camila and told her I was coming over to return the notebooks. I put Morton in the backseat, and we headed across the river to her house. It was rush hour, and the drive took twice as long. I could hear the kids making noise inside as I climbed the front steps and rang the doorbell. She answered the door thirty seconds later.

"Oh, Dev. Thanks for bringing these back so promptly. Were they any help?"

"I got a little information from them, unfortunately, nothing like a name, address, or phone number, but every little bit helps."

Camila shook her head. "I just wish there was more. I mean the way it ends, that word 'finally.' God, I had a lump in my throat. I wish she would have told me more, but she was very tight-lipped about the guy. No name, no description, nothing. At the time, I was thinking it might have been someone we knew. You know, like some football star from high school or something, but that doesn't seem to be the case. Then I was thinking maybe it was someone who was married, but to be honest, if the guy was married, she would have gotten as far away, as fast as possible. Getting involved in something like that wasn't her style. I just don't know."

"We may never know, Camila, but that doesn't mean don't keep trying. Sooner or later, something's bound to turn up." I handed her the three spiral notebooks. "I made a couple sets of copies of the last ten pages of the most recent notebook, the pages that mentioned Hottie. I'm going to give the police the copies for their file. You just never know, maybe something will click. You think of anything else, please call me."

She shook her head just as a little voice called, "Mom" from the kitchen.

"Oh, I better get back there. Apparently, I'm on call. Thanks, Dev. You keep me posted."

"I will. Thanks again, it's going to help, Camila."

She nodded and then closed her front door.

Twenty-five

Morton and I drove back to the office. I parked across the street behind Louie's car, looked up to the second floor, and noticed the lights were still on. I was a little surprised Louie was working this late, thinking he would have headed over to The Spot as soon as we'd left. We crossed the street and went up to the office. The door was locked, and I used my key to get in. The place was empty, the lights were on, the coffee pot was empty, but the burner was still on, and Louie's briefcase was gone.

I turned off the lights and the coffee maker, locked the door, and headed over to The Spot. Louie was seated on his stool at the far end of the bar talking to Mike. "That was pretty fast," Louie said as I pulled out the stool next to him. He leaned down and gave Morton a couple of pork rinds and said, "Better give me another bag, Mike. I'm almost out."

Mike pulled another bag from the rack and said, "You got time for a beer tonight?"

"You bet I do, my usual," I said.

"Everything go okay?" Louie asked as he opened the new bag of pork rinds.

"Oh yeah, no problem. I just wanted to get those notebooks back to Camila tonight. They're important to her. I'll take the pages I copied down to Aaron tomorrow. If we ever need the notebooks again, I'm sure there won't be a problem."

"Have you gotten over that woman's brother calling and bitching?"

"Hugh Goodman. Yeah, I can't blame the guy. He was just a kid when his sister was murdered. Sounds like the folks never recovered, both dead not all that long after the murder. He's understandably pissed off. I get it, but it's just that, in the long run, he's not helping."

Mike delivered my beer and picked up the five-dollar bill sitting in front of Louie. I took out a twenty from my wallet, which left me two bucks.

"Nothing of interest in those notebooks?" Louie asked.

I shook my head and took a sip. "No. Some very general comments about a guy she described as 'Hottie'. But that was it, no physical description, other than he had a beard, nothing like an address or a name, and that was actually the last thing she wrote. It could be the guy, could be some innocent schmuck who figured when he didn't hear from her again that she wasn't interested. I guess we'll never know."

My phone rang, an unknown number. "Haskell Investigations," I said just as the Rolling Stones started up on the jukebox. I slid off my stool and headed for the side door. Louie reached down and gave Morton some more pork rinds. Morton licked them off his hand and gave no indication he was interested in following me out the door.

"Yeah, I'm calling for Dev Haskell. This is Dante Ruiz." I could hear music playing in the background, not the Rolling Stones.

"Hi, Dante, thanks for calling me back. I was hoping we might be able to get together and talk. I'm looking into Lucia's murder, along with some other cases. I've reviewed the police files, but sometimes they maybe miss things. I'm hoping you might remember a comment or something, and it might just be the thing that turns the investigation around. I just finished reading—"

"You're not a cop?"

"No sir. I'm a private investigator. I'm working with the police in the hopes we can come across something that will lead us to the person who murdered your sister."

"So, what are you getting out of this?" His tone reminded me of someone who had gotten a call to change their internet service every day for the last two weeks.

"I get the satisfaction of putting one miserable bastard in jail for life. I'm not getting paid if that's what you're asking. I'm not getting a record expunged, nothing like that. I just want to get this guy and put him away."

"Okay, yeah. I'll talk with you. You doing anything tonight?"

"Tonight? No. I can get together with you. Where would you like to meet?"

"You ever hear of La Soga?"

"Yeah, I know it. You name a time." If memory served, La Soga, meant something like 'The Noose' in Spanish.

"I'll be there around eight," Dante said.

"Okay, I'll see you there. How will I know you?"

"Not to worry, I'll know you."

"Okay, see you at eight. Thanks for calling."

I stepped back into The Spot. Louie had a new drink, and there was a fresh beer waiting next to the one I hadn't finished. Louie didn't look at me. He was focused on the TV at the far end of the bar. It was tuned to the news. There was a report on some traffic incident that had apparently happened last night because the images were in the dark with cops waving flashlights around, and just now, it was still bright outside.

He took a sip and asked, "Everything okay?"

"Yeah, that call was the brother of one of the victims. I'm gonna meet with him tonight. What are you watching on the tube?" I asked and took a sip from my first beer.

"Accident last night. I caught a bit of it on the news earlier. One of my clients or, should I say, former clients. He had to do a year in the workhouse on his last DUI. His second in as many years. He should have gotten two years in prison. He hit a car with three little kids in the backseat. He blamed me for having to do any time. Told me I was fired. Still owes me fifteen hundred," Louie said and took another sip.

"Think he'll call you?"

"Nope. He's dead. Who is this brother you're meeting with?"

His sister was the fifth victim, murdered in July of 2018. As a matter of fact, she's the same woman who wrote those notebooks I was reading today. She'd been living with some dirtbag who physically abused her and put her in the hospital for a night or two. When she got out, she moved in with her brother. The guy who abused her was killed in a hit and run about three months after she was killed. I'd say more than a few folks wonder if it might have been the brother that did it. Anyway, I'm meeting him at a bar called La Soga. You know the place?"

"Only by reputation, which isn't all that sterling."

"Yeah, that's my sense. It should be interesting."

"To say the least," Louie said and followed up with another sip.

We chatted for another fifteen minutes. I finished my first beer but didn't touch the second.

"I better get going and take Morton home. I'll see you in the morning. Help yourself to that beer. I didn't touch it."

"You sure?"

"Yeah, this joint I'm going to, I'd better be on my best behavior when I go in there. Like you said, it doesn't exactly have the most sterling reputation."

"Stay safe, and I'll see you in the morning," Louie said and pulled the beer glass closer to him. Apparently,

I'd paid for the last round of drinks, because my twenty-dollar bill was now a ten. I picked up the ten off the bar and put it back in my wallet. Louie gave Morton some more pork rinds, and we went out the side door.

Once home, I tossed my mail on the kitchen counter, let Morton out into the backyard, and hurried upstairs to my bedroom. I have a rack attached to the wall in the back of my closet, and I pulled a Glock 44 and a Glock 19 off the rack. The 44 is a relatively small .22 caliber pistol that fit perfectly into the sticky holster I inserted in the front of my belt. The Glock 19 is a nine-millimeter pistol that carries fifteen rounds. I shoved the 19 into the back of my belt, pulled on a St. Paul Saints jersey, and left the jersey untucked. I gave Morton another fifteen minutes in the backyard before I coaxed him inside with the offer of a treat. He grabbed the dog biscuit on the first bounce and had it eaten before he took three steps to a distant corner. I decided to head down to La Soga a half-hour early just so I'd be able to get a sense of the clientele going in.

The place is over on the Westside, not quite a mile from Camila's house. There was a hardware store parking lot across the street from the bar. The store was closed, and I pulled into the lot. I backed into the parking space just in case I had to make a hasty retreat, then sat and watched for the next twenty minutes.

It was apparent that my gray 2014 Ford Taurus adorned with the flat black hood I'd gotten in a scrapyard was probably the worst car in a six-block area. Cadillac convertibles, a Lexus, two BMWs, spinner wheel rims, low riders, you'd think I was watching a souped-up car convention. Mostly guys were going into La Soga. The few women that did enter were drop-dead gorgeous and always had a guy on their arm who looked like he lifted weights for a living. At exactly eight, I climbed out of my beater, crossed the street, and entered the bar.

Three pool tables greeted my entrance. Each table had a game going, and I only got a quick glance from the players before they focused back on their game. One guy blocked my movement, lined up his shot, and took his time aiming. I patiently waited for him to shoot, hoping to God he'd scratch. He didn't. After he shot, he stood, looked me up and down, taking me in, maybe focused on the untucked jersey, then gave me the slightest of nods and walked around to the far side of the pool table.

Heads turned as I approached the bar, and the level of casual conversation definitely quieted down. A large muscular guy in a strappy t-shirt with maybe a gallon of ink on his skin slid off his bar stool. He downed his drink, shoved a guy out of his way, and headed for me. Things got even more quiet, and I slowly turned toward one of the pool tables, pretending to focus on the game while casually resting my right hand on the Glock 19 in the back of my belt and all the while wondering where the hell Dante was.

The tattooed giant was almost on me, and I was just beginning to pull the Glock out when he said, "You must be Haskell. Hey, leave that piece where it is, dumb shit.

I got a booth waiting for us in back. You have any problem finding the place?"

"No, no, none at all. I knew where it was, been past it a lot, but never inside. It's mmm, interesting."

He smiled at that. "Not to worry, you're safe with me. Come on back." I followed him into a back room with six tables and four booths. The tables were all occupied with guys you wouldn't want to cross and some delightfully slutty-looking women. Three of the four booths were occupied. A couple of guys nodded at Dante, and one called him, "Jeffe," as we walked by. I knew the term meant boss.

I had barely settled into the booth across from him when a woman arrived with a tray holding six shot glasses and two beers. She put the shot glasses down in front of Dante, placed a beer next to the shots, then held the second beer glass and looked at Dante. He nodded, so she set the beer in front of me and hurried off.

I raised my glass toward him and said, "To your sister Lucia, God bless. Pray that we get the bastard that did this."

He nodded, smiled, and said, "Pray that you turn him over to me when you get him." We clinked glasses, and he took a sip then set his glass down and pushed a shot across the table to me. "Don Julio forty-two, it's the best tequila" he said.

Twenty-Six

We'd been sitting in the booth for a good fifteen minutes, and we had yet to discuss Dante's sister Lucia. We had talked about life in general, his growing up next to Camila's family. He made a point of stressing he was not a fan of the police but didn't go into any detail as to why. Based on the tattoos I could see covering his muscular arms, neck, and the little I could see of his chest, not to mention the three teardrops just below his right eye, I had a pretty good idea. The teardrops were filled in, suggesting he had killed at least three people. I thought the wise decision would be to not comment.

"I read some of the notebooks your sister wrote, kind of like a journal."

"You got them from Camila, right?"

"I did. I brought them back to her earlier this evening."

"Yeah, she asked if it would be okay to let you read them. You learn anything?" he asked, then downed another shot of tequila, his third. I hadn't touched mine yet.

"I got a little information. She had three dates with a guy before she was murdered, called him Hottie in her notebook. Unfortunately, that's about all she said. No mention of a name, where the guy lived, or what he did. Oh, and she said he had a beard that she liked."

"So, you think you can find him?"

"Because he had a beard?" I asked as I looked around the room. Five guys, just in this small room, had beards. Pointing that out may not have been the best idea. "You know, maybe it just the thing to point us in the right direction," I said. "The fact that he had a beard is one more thing that narrows the field. Did she ever mention this guy to you?"

He shook his head and smiled. "No, she dated a couple of guys earlier, but when I checked them out, they weren't right for her. One was a teacher. The other sold insurance. They weren't gonna make the kind of money she'd need to be happy, so I nicely told them to get lost." I could only imagine. "She didn't mention this bearded guy to me at all. I didn't know he even existed until Camila told me about him. I thought it might have been the guy she was with before. He wasn't very nice to her."

Jack Hardy, I thought. Killed three months later when his car was broadsided. I figured there was a pretty good chance that, if Dante wasn't driving, he knew who was.

"You were kind enough to let her move in with you when she got out of the hospital."

He gave me a questioning look and took a long sip of his beer. He smiled as he set the glass down. "Let her move in?" He half-laughed. "I told her she didn't have a choice. I had someone escort her around town for the next few weeks. I didn't want Jack Hardy anywhere near her."

"Did he try to get together with her?"

"Let's just say that idea didn't work out in his favor. Once we discussed the situation, he eventually saw the light."

I could only imagine. "Were there places she liked to go, you know maybe hoping to meet someone or just hang out with friends?"

"If she came here, she would have been safe. No one would have bothered her."

No doubt I thought. "Do you know if she did any online dating?"

He grinned. "I had a guy I know block that on her computer, but I never told her, and she never asked."

Never asked because she was probably able to bypass whatever the guy had put in place to block her. "At her funeral, did any strangers show up?"

He thought about that for a moment, then shook his head. "No, well, I mean, yeah, but the usual, the ones you'd expect. Folks she worked with, people she'd gone to high school with. A couple of guys showed up whose sisters had been murdered by the same prick. We talked for a while, promised to stay in touch, but over the last year, we've drifted apart."

"You ever hear from a guy named Hugh Goodman?" I asked.

"Goodman, tall guy, balding, reddish hair?"

"I don't know what he looks like. I only talked to him on the phone."

"He have anything to add?"

I shook my head and said, "No, not really. Obviously, he's still upset. He was only about twelve when his sister was killed."

"Yeah, I know the guy you're talking about. I guess he was nice enough."

"Camila told me Lucia delivered a lot of babies in the area."

"She did." Dante glanced around the room. "Three kids to guys just in this room. She could never pay for a drink on this end of town. She was a big part of the neighborhood," he said and got a faraway look in his eye.

"Dante, are you aware of anything missing, something that might have been stolen from her? I know she was living with you, but do you know of anything that was taken, money, jewelry, credit cards?"

He shook his head. "No, nothing. In fact, she had two diamond stud earrings, half-carat diamonds. When I got them for her, I had them appraised, thirty-five hundred dollars for the pair. She was wearing them the night she was murdered. Whoever killed her was too stupid to take them."

Just the way he said it, 'When I got them,' made me think there was no point in asking where he bought the earrings. Still, in his own way, he was a guy who cared about his sister and tried to look out for her.

“Dante, I don’t really have any other questions, unless you can think of something.” I handed him my card.

He seemed to study it for a long moment before he looked up. “You just find this bastard. You need any help, you call me.”

“I will. Thank you for your time and for the beer.”

He nodded, quickly downed the last two shots of tequila, and slid out of the booth. “Let me walk you out of the room,” he said.

“Thanks, but that’s not necessary. I can—”

“It would be best,” he said and headed toward the barroom. He took about ten steps into the bar area. Everyone stepped aside to give him room. He turned, shook my hand, and said, “Call if you need something, anything at all.” I thought there might be the trace of a tear in his eye, but I couldn’t be sure.

“Thanks, Jeffe. You take care,” I said. As I walked out of the place, two pool players nodded and stepped aside. A big guy at the door, maybe a bouncer, held the door open for me, smiled, and said, “Buenos Noches, señor.”

Twenty-seven

Nice enough guy that Dante Ruiz was; after all, he bought me a beer and a shot of tequila. I once again felt like I was getting nowhere. I drove back across the river on the Wabasha Bridge and debated about going back to The Spot. Louie was probably still there, and maybe if I just took a night to unwind, something might pop into my head tomorrow. My next thought was maybe to call Taffy and see if she wanted to get together. I quickly deleted that idea. Even if she did want to see me, it probably meant the wicked witch from the west, Allison, would be there. In the end, I drove home.

Morton met me at the front door with his tail wagging, reminding me that, no matter how down I felt, he was always happy to see me. I let him out into the backyard and checked my refrigerator. There was half a pizza in there from a day or two ago, or maybe it was last week. I couldn't remember. I set it on the kitchen counter, grabbed a piece, and went over the pages I'd copied for Aaron.

Morton scratching at the door got my attention. It was now dark outside, I'd eaten the remainder of the pizza, and I knew nothing more than when I began reading. I let Morton in, tossed him a biscuit, dumped the pizza crusts in his food bowl, and started over reading the copies, again.

By the time I'd pushed away from the copies spread out across the counter, Morton had gone upstairs to bed. I'd eaten two fudgesicles for dessert, and I was still hungry. I got the coffee ready for the morning and went up to bed.

Amazingly, Morton had left me enough room. I slept fitfully and woke well before my alarm. The sun was up but just barely. I showered, dressed, and went downstairs. I was just about finished with the coffee when I heard Morton upstairs as he jumped off the bed and stretched. He made his appearance in the kitchen a few minutes later. I scratched him and let him out into the backyard. I let him back in for breakfast and phoned Aaron while Morton devoured his food in about three minutes.

"Yeah, Dev. What's up?" was how Aaron answered.

"Hi, Aaron. I was going to head down to see you shortly. I've got the copies of those pages for you."

"Okay, if you can bring them down in the next forty-five minutes, we can talk. Otherwise, I've got a meeting I'll need to get to, and we could maybe meet later this afternoon."

"I'll head down there right now. See you in a bit," I said and hung up. Morton was stretched out, apparently getting ready for an after-breakfast nap, so I left him in the kitchen and hopped in my car. I thought for a moment about picking up his morning deposit and smearing it across Manning's windshield but decided that would probably point an obvious finger at me, so I backed out of the driveway.

I parked in the visitors' lot and headed into the station. I had the copies of Lucia's pages in a manila file folder. For a change, Gary's desk was clean. No stacks of files, multiple coffee mugs, or a half-eaten sandwich. He even spotted me before I got to his desk. "Hi, Dev, how's your day going?"

"I'll tell you in a couple of minutes, Gary. I have to see Lieutenant LaZelle. You're looking all sparkly and positive."

He flashed a quick smile. "It's my birthday today. The wife always wakes me with a birthday surprise."

"Oh, really. That sounds nice. What did she give you?"

He grinned for a long moment and said, "Let me place a call to homicide and get someone to take you up."

Maybe my luck was changing because it was Detective Andretta who arrived to escort me up to homicide. He even called my name nicely then waited and held the security door for me, so I didn't have to dash across the lobby.

"Hey, detective, great to see you. Thanks for coming down to get me."

"Not a problem, how are things on your end?"

"You know, fine if you don't go into detail. I, umm, was expecting Manning. He usually escorts me up-stairs."

"Oh yeah? How's that working out?" he asked in a tone that suggested he already knew. I followed him off the elevator, waited while he punched the code into the keypad, and then followed him into homicide. "The L.T. is in his office. He told me you're supposed to go on in," Andretta said and walked back to his desk.

I walked through the section toward Aaron's corner office. I nodded at a number of people seated at their desk. A couple of them were on the phone. I noticed Manning's desk was unoccupied. There were two stacks of files on his desk with maybe a half-dozen more placed on his chair. His desk phone had three yellow Post-it notes stuck to it. I could only hope if he was around that he'd be too busy to spend time making my life miserable. I knocked on the door frame of Aaron's office.

He was on the phone, waved me in, and said, "I've got to ring off, Ben. I'll be over later this afternoon. You take care and give my best to Gretchen. You bet I'll tell him. Thanks. See you this afternoon."

"Was that Ben Jackson?" I asked.

"Yeah," Aaron said and pointed to one of the chairs in front of his desk. "He told me to put a flare under your ass and get you moving on these cold cases."

"God, I'd love it if it was that simple." I tossed the manila folder onto Aaron's desk. "Those are the last ten pages from Lucia Ruiz's notebooks. Most of it is just one liners about going to see her mom, a friend stopping over, occasionally a baby she delivered. On the last page, she mentions someone she describes as Hottie. Her final notation suggests they're getting together. She wrote, 'Finally, I can't wait.' I'm presuming she's referring to this guy, but there's no way to be sure. There's no information that would lead us to the guy. I met her brother last night and mentioned it to him, but he didn't know anything."

"Is that her brother, Dante?"

"Yeah. You familiar with him?"

"Somewhat. He's moved high enough up the food chain he doesn't have to get his hands dirty too often. Plus, he's become a lot less impulsive and, shall we say, pragmatic."

"I met him last night in a bar called La Soga. You familiar with the place?"

"Oh yeah. You might say it's his office. A very interesting clientele."

"You're telling me, Aaron. We sat in a booth in a back room, and when we were finished, he took me out to the barroom and shook hands with me, so everyone knew to leave me alone. I have to say, based on what he said, I think he did his best to keep his sister safe. When she was killed, I'm sure it got some of those individuals thinking Dante really screwed up."

Aaron shrugged, pulled the file folder closer, and opened it. He quickly flipped through the pages and looked up at me. “What the hell is all over these things, spaghetti sauce?”

“Oh, I was eating some leftover pizza. One with everything on it and double cheese. I guess maybe a little drop or two—”

“A little drop or two? There’s pizza sauce fingerprints all over these pages. Nice job.” He glanced over the pages for a minute or two then focused on the final page and frowned. He must have gone over the last page three or four times before he looked up. When he finished, he tossed the pages onto the file folder, shook his head, and said, “Shit.”

“Yeah, not much to go on. Dante wanted to know, since the guy had a beard two years ago, if we had any suspects.” Aaron actually smiled at that and shook his head. “Yeah, I know,” I said. “There were almost a half-dozen guys just in the room we were in with beards. Dante, for all his supposedly tight control, didn’t know anything about that Hottie character.”

“You talking to anyone else?”

“I got a bunch of calls out there, but I’ve already talked to everyone who called me back. I’ll place a second call to the folks I haven’t heard from and see if I can connect with some more people.”

“Yeah, do that. Okay,” Aaron said, glancing at his watch. “That’s all I got.”

“How did Ben sound?”

“Considering what he just had dumped on him, pretty damn good. I’m going to head over at the end of the afternoon. You know, if you maybe stopped by after lunch, that might help break up his day. Give him a general update. But, let me warn you, he still sounded sharp as a tack, so don't even think of bullshitting him. He'll nail you right away."

"Okay, I'll swing by this afternoon. I'll head down to the office and make some calls first. Anything else?"

"No, that should do it," Aaron said. "Andretta escort you up?"

"Yeah, it was nice for a change."

Aaron nodded and flashed a quick smile but didn't comment. "Stop by his desk and have him take you down. Hey, thanks for all you're doing, Dev."

"Be better if it led to something."

"Well then, keep at it and call those people back."

Twenty-eight

I'd lost count of the number of calls I'd made."Hi, I'm calling for Connie Sinclair. My name is Dev Haskell. I'm a private investigator working with the Saint Paul Police. We're looking into the murder of Crystal Higgins in two-thousand-eight, and I was hoping to talk to you. I'd like to see if maybe the police might have missed anything in your interview, or perhaps you remember something that may turn out to be relevant. If you could please call me at—" I went on to leave my number and hung up.

"How many of those calls do you have to make?" Louie asked. He pulled the set of earphones he'd been wearing for the past hour off his head and set them on his desk for a moment.

"I'm trying to crank through this list. It's my second call to most of these folks. You'd think they'd get the hint by now."

Louie shook his head and said, "I kind of get it. It has to be like resurrecting a very unpleasant memory, and you just want to hang onto the happy times."

I took another Bar-B-Que rib from the pile on my desk, stuck it in my mouth, and pulled the meat off the bone. I looked to make sure I'd gotten all the meat off before I tossed the bone into the wastebasket.

"I'm sorry if I'm bugging you, man. I'm going nuts just saying the same thing over and over again. I can't imagine what it's like to have to listen to me."

"It's not any worse than having to listen to you on any other day," Louie said and smiled.

"You want me to go over to The Spot and make these calls?"

"You know, that's not a bad idea, but I got a better one," Louie said, shutting down his computer.

"Oh, I'm sorry, Louie. Are you going up to the Law Library? Hey, I'll leave and you can still—"

"Get real, Dev. I'll be the one going over to The Spot. You can come over and join me when you're done with the calls. Thanks for the advice. See you over there."

Morton watched Louie tuck his laptop under his arm and head out the door. I watched out the window for a minute as he crossed the street and headed into The Spot. He seemed to pick up his pace ever so slightly the closer he got.

"Hi, I'm calling for Nancy Bruner. My name is Dev Haskell. I'm a private investigator working with…"

If I made one, I'd made another two dozen calls. I was always getting dumped into voicemail.

"Hi, I'm calling for Denise Wengler."

"This is—"

"My name is Dev Haskell. I'm a private investigator working with the Saint Paul—"

"Hello. Hello. Can you hear me?"

"Oh, oh, sorry. I, umm, I thought I got dumped into your voicemail."

"No. You just kept talking when I answered. I thought you might have been a recording. How can I help you?"

I had to quickly check my list to see who I was calling.

"Hello, are you there?"

"Yes, yes, Denise, thanks for answering. I'm working with the Saint Paul police, and we're looking into the murder of Jia Kahn. You were interviewed by the police back in 2012, and I wondered if we could meet."

"What's this about?" she said, suddenly sounding overly cautious.

"Believe me, you've done nothing wrong. We're just looking into Jia's case. I'd like to review the interview with you and see if we may have somehow missed something you said. Maybe after all this time, something might come to mind that you didn't think about or might not have mentioned in the interview."

"And you're with the police?"

"I'm working with them, but I'm actually not a police officer. I'm a private investigator, and I'm just trying to provide a fresh pair of eyes to Jia's case."

"And you want to talk to me?"

"Yes, along with anyone else who was interviewed or anyone you might think of who should have been interviewed and perhaps wasn't."

There was a long pause. I was just about to say something when she said, "Okay, do you want me to come down to the police station?"

"That won't be necessary. I'll gladly meet you anywhere, in a public place, your workplace, or your home if you would prefer that. Whatever would be best for you."

"Mmm, do you know where the state capitol is?"

"Yes, of course."

"Well, I don't work there. I'm next door in the transportation building."

"Oh, yeah, the big grey building."

"Yeah. We're up on the third floor. Communications. Just ask for me at the front desk. It would be best if we could talk before four this afternoon."

"I'll head over right now. I'm maybe fifteen minutes away."

"Tell me your name again."

"Haskell, Dev Haskell. Please, call me Dev."

"All right, Dev. I'll see you shortly."

Finally, I thought. I filled Morton's water dish and hurried out the door. I sent Louie a text message, then climbed in my car and headed up the street to the 35E entrance. Thankfully, I pulled onto the interstate at probably the slowest time of the afternoon. Not that it wasn't busy, but at least the traffic was moving. I took the Grand

Avenue exit, drove up Ramsey Hill and down Summit Avenue to the capitol area. There's an abandoned Sears store across the street from the State Transportation Building. I parked in the parking lot and ran across Rice street to the Minnesota Department of Transportation building, MN DOT, for short. An unmemorable, five-story building on the capitol plaza. I walked in the Rice Street entrance and headed for the front desk.

"Good afternoon. How can I help you?" the guy behind the desk asked and smiled.

"I'm here to see Denise Wengler. She's in communications."

"Your name, sir."

"Dev Haskell. She's expecting me."

"May I see some ID, please?"

I pulled out my wallet and showed him my driver's license.

"Please remove the license, sir."

I pulled the license out from behind the plastic window and handed it to him. He gazed at my photo, looked up at me, then placed the license in a plastic tray. He pushed a button, and the tray lit up, apparently screening something I didn't know was there. When the light turned off, he handed the license back to me, picked up the phone, and punched in three numbers.

"Yes, I have a Mr. Devlin Haskell down here to see you. He's at the Rice Street entrance. Thank you," he said and hung up. "Miss Wengler will be down in a moment if you would like to have a seat."

Twenty-nine

I grabbed a seat in a plastic chair and pulled a magazine about Minnesota Lakes from a rack on the wall. I'd just opened the magazine when a voice said, "Dev Haskell?"

Since I was the only person in the lobby area, there was no point in pretending. Denise was average height with brown hair pulled up in a bun. She wore cobalt blue pants and a light blue button-down shirt with the sleeves rolled up to her elbows.

"Hi, Denise," I said. As I approached, I held my hand out. "Nice to meet you."

She shook my hand and said, "Come on up to my office." We took the elevator up to the third floor then took a left out of the elevator to a door halfway down the hall. We entered a room with offices along a far wall and maybe thirty or forty cubicles. The cubicles were arranged two across, then an aisle and another two cubicles. I followed her over to the windows, and then we walked halfway down. She entered a cubicle and pushed a chair on wheels toward me. "Have a seat," she said as she settled into a high-back desk chair. "I've been thinking about Jia ever since we talked on the phone. She was my best friend."

"From all I've read, she sounds like a lovely person. How did you meet?"

"We grew up across the street from one another. Jia was born in Korea and adopted by the couple across the street when she was about two. We grew up together, best friends by age three. Went to grade school together, then Saint Paul Central, different colleges, but always kept in touch. She was a bridesmaid in our wedding, and she sold us the house we have now."

I noticed the diamond ring she was wearing and the picture of Denise with a guy and two little girls on the desk area behind her. I pegged the girls at maybe three or four years old. "Is that a picture of your family?"

She glanced over her shoulder. "Yeah, horribly out of date now. Brenda, the curly-haired girl on my lap, is twelve now, and Katie, on Dennis's lap, will be eleven in two months. Dennis and Denise, we're the perfect couple," she said and smiled.

"Two little girls, you're very lucky."

"There are days, believe me. Brenda is already starting her awful teen years, and Katie is right behind her."

"You purchased your home from Jia?"

"Yes, we'd been looking for a house for at least six months, and she'd shown us a number of places, but it seemed we either didn't like the house she showed us, or if we did, it was always way out of our price range. Then this house was going to come on the market, and she called us. The couple who were selling, they were older, they just liked us and actually adjusted the price so we could afford it. We essentially bought the house before it officially went on the market. All thanks to Jia."

"The family that adopted her, did they have any other children?"

"No, her mother had a series of miscarriages, and that led to Jia's adoption. They were wonderful people, lovely parents. They were both from northern Minnesota, Hibbing, I think. That's where Jia is buried. After her funeral, her parents moved back up there. I haven't seen them in years, but we still exchange Christmas cards. Have you talked with them?"

"No, I haven't."

"It's been what, eight years now, and the incident is still heartbreaking for me. I can't imagine what it's like for them. An experience I hope I never, ever have to go through."

"If Jia was your realtor, you must have been pretty close."

"Like I said, best friends since we were three. She really took care of us when we were looking for a house. Anyone else probably would have blocked our phone calls," she said and rolled her eyes. "She was always there for us. We had a lot of laughs over a glass of wine, remembering all the crazy things we used to do."

"She never married?"

"No, she had a couple of boyfriends over the years, nice guys. For whatever reason, they didn't work out. She never seemed broken-hearted if that's where you're heading. It was more like I could tell the breakup was coming because the guy was starting to drive her nuts. One guy was always going on fishing or hunting trips with pals and fitting Jia in if he didn't have anything else to do. Another was a real party animal, which sounded fun at first, but in short order, she cut him loose after he caused a car accident driving under the influence and fled the scene. The cops caught him, and that was enough for Jia. Another guy still lived with his parents. He was really nice but clearly wasn't going anywhere."

"Where'd she meet these guys?"

"Mmm, different places. Surprise, surprise, the party animal, Henry, she met him in a bar. In fact, I was with her. We were downtown at the Wood Roast Grill, and he sent a drink over to the table. He was fun to talk to, but in short order, the bar scene wasn't her thing. The fishing guy, his name was Tom, or Tim, or something like that. Anyway, she met him online. I think he was more interested in finding a woman who could clean fish and pluck geese."

"Was she seeing someone at the end?"

"I know for a fact she was, but I have no idea who. The police asked me the same thing. She'd had a few dates with some guy. Nothing out of the ordinary, I think they went out to dinner a couple of times. I know they caught a Bruce Springsteen concert at the Xcel Center just before she was killed. She was a big Springsteen fan. The concert was maybe her third or fourth date with the guy. She never told me that much about him. She knew him for no more than a couple of months if that. I forget what he did, but he traveled a lot, and…" I thought about her phrase, traveled a lot, Veronica Salucci said the same thing about the guy Trudie Mandel had been dating. Denise went on, "She liked him, and I think she liked the fact that things weren't moving too fast."

"Not moving too fast?"

"Yeah, you know, he didn't expect her to jump into bed with him on the second date. He didn't seem to be one of those kind of guys, which, let me tell you, is rare in today's world."

I thought it best not to comment on that last remark. "Did she ever mention anything about this guy, where he lived, maybe his name, what he did for a living, or what he looked like?"

"No, not really. She did say on more than one occasion that he was very good looking."

"She ever mention a beard?"

"A beard? No, but then he could have had one and she just never said anything. She was pretty private about the guy, but I mean, they were just starting to go out, so I kind of get it. Besides, with her business, you know, selling real estate, evenings could be a busy time for her. It was often the only time her clients could meet with her, evenings, well, or on the weekend. Not exactly conducive for a wild, crazy personal life."

"No and lots of hard work in between," I said.

"Yeah, but she loved doing it. Plus, she would always get in on family gossip. Oh, she had stories, believe me. There was always someone who would be a pain when she was selling an older person's home. Usually, it was whatever adult child lived out of town. He'd have all sorts of ways his siblings could spend time doing things. Then, she'd always laugh about the women who expected their kids to paint the house, fix the fence, clean the gutters, and it turned out the kids would be in their seventies. Of course, the ninety-year-old mother still thought of them as being about sixteen. I have to say, I could never do that job, but Jia actually loved it, and she was good at it, really good."

"She sounds like a wonderful person."

"Oh, she was. She was so wonderful, such a dear friend," Denise said and seemed to choke up. She cleared her throat a couple of times. "Anything else you want to know? I'm not sure how much, if any, help I was able to give you."

"It all adds up, Denise. We just don't want to miss anything."

"Well, if we're finished, I should probably escort you out and get back to work here."

"I really appreciate your time. If you think of anything, please don't hesitate to give me a call," I said and handed her my card.

She set the card on her desktop and stood. "Come on. I'll take you down to the lobby." I followed her out of the cubicle. Neither one of us spoke on the ride down to the lobby.

We stepped out of the elevator. I extended my hand and said, “Thanks again, Denise. If you think of anything, no matter how insignificant it might seem, please give me a call.”

Her eyes began to water. “Yeah, I will,” she said as she nodded then hurried back to the elevator. She stepped onto the elevator just before the doors closed and went back up to the third floor. I headed out the door toward my car in the Sears parking lot. I used to shop at this Sears from time to time. The building had been vacant for the past couple of years, and the Sears name had been taken off the building. Holes in the wall above the entrance marked the area where the neon letters had once hung. Now it was just a vast, empty parking lot.

Thirty

I climbed into my car and turned the ignition. It sputtered for a moment but suddenly came to life, and I drove back to the office. I parked behind Louie's car and headed into The Spot. It was the middle of a sunny afternoon, and there were a half-dozen guys seated at the bar. There were at least two stools between them, no one was talking, and they all sat and stared at the drinks in front of them— nothing to do and all day to do it. Cary was tending bar, and he gave me a nod as I headed toward Louie. To his credit, Louie was seated in a booth working on his computer. Believe it or not, a cup of coffee sat on the table next to the computer.

"You finally finished making those phone calls?" he said.

"Yeah, did you get the text message I sent?"

"Oh, no, I guess I left my phone on my desk. Was it important?"

"Yeah, I went to a whiskey tasting. It was really great, and when I left, they gave me a bottle for free."

"You're kidding me?"

"Actually, yeah, I am. I had to head over by the capitol and interview someone."

"How'd it go?" he asked and started typing again.

"About like you'd expect. Nice woman, misses her friend. Maybe corroborated something someone else told me the other day. But nothing really new or specific."

"You ready for a beer?"

"Actually, I'm going to head back to the office and make some more calls. I'll be over when I finish up."

"Bring my phone with you when you come, will you?"

"Yeah, be happy to. See you in a bit." I nodded at Cary on the way out and headed up to the office. Morton was stretched out on his bed, but he opened one eye as I stepped inside. Once he saw it was me, he snuggled against the cushion and closed his eyes. I picked up Louie's phone off his desk and shoved it into my pocket. I settled in behind my desk and started with the next name on my list.

"Hi, I'm calling for Mary Lee Norris. My name is Dev Haskell. I'm a private investigator working with…" I'd made close to a half-dozen calls and still wasn't getting any response.

"Hi, I'm calling for Connie Sinclair. My name is Dev Haskell. I'm—"

"Yes, this is Connie."

"Oh, hi, Connie. I'm calling regarding a cold case with the St. Paul Police department. I'm—"

"Did you call me the other day? This is about Crystal Higgins' murder, isn't it?"

"Yes, I did call, and yes, this is regarding the Crystal Higgins case."

"Did you guys finally arrest someone?"

"As a matter of fact, no, we didn't." I heard a sigh come across the phone line.

"Well then, why are you calling?"

"I'm working with the police department. I'm a private investigator, and I'm looking at Crystal's case along with some others. I've read the transcript of your interview with the police. I'd like to talk to you, just to see if the police may have missed anything, or if maybe, after all this time, something you remember comes up that maybe wasn't covered."

"I don't know what new information would come up. Crystal was murdered twelve years ago."

"Yes, I'm aware of that, but maybe the police missed something you said back then and—"

"What'd you say your name is?"

"Haskell, Dev Haskell."

"And you're not a cop?"

"No ma'am, I'm a private investigator. Here in Saint Paul."

"Are you the private investigator that has an office in that building kitty-corner to The Spot bar."

"Umm, yes, that's where my office is located."

"You're the guy that wore the kilt a couple of years ago on St. Patrick's Day, right?"

"Yes, I am." It had been St. Patrick's Day, and my memory was more than a little foggy.

“I’m the woman who asked you what you had on underneath your kilt, and you told me, ‘With a little luck maybe some lipstick later tonight.’” Fortunately, she laughed as she told me.

Oh, God. “I apologize for that comment, ma’am. There might have been some beverages involved, and I didn’t mean to—”

“Oh, relax. I thought it was pretty funny. Told all the girls about it. You calling me from your office?”

“Yes, I am.”

“I’ve gotta run some errands. How about I drive over and meet you in your office?”

“If it wouldn’t be too much trouble, that would be great.”

“Wonderful. I’ve always been kind of curious what the place looks like. I’ll see you in about twenty minutes,” she said and hung up.

I made a fresh pot of coffee. I rinsed out Louie’s coffee mug and set it next to the pot. I pulled a number of files from the file cabinet and stacked them on my desk, put the binoculars in a desk drawer, and then ran Louie’s phone over to him.

He watched me as I hurried over to the booth he was sitting in. It looked like his coffee cup had been refilled. “Where’s Morton?” he asked.

“Still sacked out.”

“You done making your phone calls?”

“For the moment. I got some woman coming over to the office on one of the cold cases. Shouldn’t take more than maybe a half-hour. Here's your phone. Morton and I will be over as soon as I finish up."

"She wanted to come to our office?"

"Yeah, in fact, she said she knows where it is and had always been curious what the place looks like."

Louie shook his head and said, "She sounds demented."

"Probably. Hey, I'll see you as soon as she leaves. Shouldn't be too long."

"Good luck," he said and went back to typing.

I hurried back across the street. I picked up a couple of beer cans around Louie's picnic table and tossed them in the wastebasket. I put the Styrofoam container with the Bar-B-Que ribs in a desk drawer since it still had three more ribs. I ran a paper towel across my desk to pick up the drops of rib sauce and the dust along the far edge. I turned on my computer, googled the police department website, and then settled into the chair behind my desk.

Thirty-one

I heard the staircase begin to creak and a moment later, the door opened, and Connie Sinclair stepped into the office. She was approximately my height and a little heavier, with reddish-brown hair and maybe two inches of white roots. She wore baggy blue jeans, a long-sleeve denim work shirt, and white slip-on shoes. She carried a worn, brown leather purse that hung over her shoulder. She took about three steps into the office, stopped, and looked around. She focused on Louie's picnic table, shook her head, smiled, and said, "I just knew it."

Morton was up and off his bed. He walked over and shoved his nose between her legs. "Oh, no doubt, your dog."

"Yeah, that's Morton," I said, coming around my desk. "I'm Dev Haskell, nice to meet you, Connie. Won't you have a seat?" I said, pointing to my client chairs. She placed her purse on the desk, pulled back the chair without the duct tape across the seat, and sat down. "Can I get you a coffee?"

"You have it made?"

"Yeah, a fresh pot. I just put it on."

“Yeah, okay,” she said and continued to look around.

I filled Louie’s mug and set it on the desk in front of her then filled my mug and sat down behind my desk.

She took a sip of coffee and looked around the office some more. “I have to say, this is just what I expected. I mean that in a nice way. The few things I’ve heard about you have always been complimentary.”

“Never enough of that, Connie. So, you and Crystal Higgins were friends?”

“Workmates actually. We were both paralegals over in Minneapolis. We met in the office, working together on a case, a bankruptcy on a big construction project. A real pain-in-the-ass senior partner had the case, and we all had to deal with his ongoing bullshit. His client was a state legislator, and the two of them were awful. Crystal and I just clicked. Nothing brings you closer together than an awful boss, and we essentially had two of them. We’d get together after work for a cocktail or two and bitch to one another just to relieve the stress. It worked, and we quickly became fast friends.”

“Did Crystal entertain much?”

“You mean, was she a party animal? Hardly. She was a smart, studious paralegal who worked very hard. God, she easily did the work of two. After her murd—umm, the incident, the firm had to put three people on to cover the work she had been doing.”

“Are you still working at the firm?”

"No, after the incident, I just couldn't deal with it anymore. The bastard we'd been working for just blew the whole thing off and gave me a lecture about getting back to work. I left a couple of weeks after that. I just couldn't take it. I work part-time in an insurance office. I'm on disability. Still see a shrink once a month. The whole thing really knocked me off the rails, and I never really got back on."

"You have any idea as to what happened? I mean, you know, why? Or maybe a suspicion of who?"

She shook her head. "No. For the longest time, I hoped it was just some nutcase who maybe saw her walking out the door somewhere and grabbed her. But to be honest, I've come to the conclusion there's about zero chance that was the case. I feel pretty certain whoever did this was someone she probably knew. Maybe didn't know her all that well, but someone who knew her well enough to plan this shit out, pull it off, and not get caught. I mean, that's kinda what the cops have been dealing with. How many are there now four or five women killed?"

"Actually, six. The most recent occurred a year ago last May. Same scenario, body found in a park. Como Park in this instance. The wedding veil, the white slip, along with some other things the police haven't made public, but it seems to make it clear it's always been the same perpetrator."

"Jesus," she said and let out a long sigh. "I wish I could tell you more, but I can't. We'd been together the

Tuesday night before. I know she had a couple of dates with some really good-looking guy, but she hadn't heard from him in like two weeks, so for whatever reason, that didn't work."

"We had our normal cocktail and bitch session. Then, forty-eight hours later, it happened. I was really worried some creep was checking both of us out that night, and for whatever reason, he grabbed Crystal. I still carry a can of mace in my purse. I took some self-defense courses. I've got cameras on the outside of my house, three locks on my front and back door, and I keep a gun in the nightstand next to my bed. I haven't been to bed with anyone in years," she said, just making a statement, not a suggestion.

"Was Crystal dating anyone?"

"The cops asked me the same thing, about a half-dozen different ways. I'll tell you the same thing I told them. No one I'm really aware of. There was the good-looking guy, but she hadn't heard from him in a couple of weeks."

"She ever mention a name, or where he lived, maybe what he did?"

She shook her head. "No, I think it was just another date that didn't work. She went out a couple of times with a guy she went to school with, but it wasn't a romance kind of thing, more like just friends. I think he took her to a Twins game, and she took him to some cooking class, pasta making, or something. They went to high school together, North High, up in North Saint Paul.

She grew up there, and that's where her apartment was. Last time I saw him was at the funeral. I think he was more screwed up than me. I haven't heard from him, umm, well since the funeral. Not even sure if he's still in town."

"You remember his name?"

"Gerry, his last name was one of those Irish names, O'Toole, O'Mara, O'Kelly, I can't remember what, exactly. He worked for some big company up here. He was a computer guy or something. There was another guy, I think, but I never met him. She had a couple of dates with him, and when I asked her how they went, the dates, she said fine and didn't say anything else. I figured she maybe ended the thing before they really got started."

"You know how she met this guy?"

"Yeah, Match.com. She was on there a bit, we both were. More when I first met her, but I'd have to say, like all of us, she had mixed results at best. You know, the guy seems great until you meet him in person, and then you just want to get out of there."

"Scary guys?"

"No, more like, I don't know, boring, I guess. I was on Match.com back in the day, and Crystal and I would trade stories. It wasn't that the guys were mean, or ugly, or you know, needed a shower. It's just that you're basically emailing back and forth, and they seem fine, maybe even interesting, and then you meet them, and before they even open their mouth, you just want to go home and watch Netflix or something. I tried getting back into it after the incident, but I couldn't do it. Now, well, it's different for a woman. A guy can seem to latch on to a woman twenty years younger. But women my age are stuck with older men. I can't bear to think of sleeping with someone old enough to be my father. I've got a bunch of nieces and nephews, and now I live the whole relationship thing through their experiences."

"Anything else you can think of that might have been a way she met someone? Maybe girlfriends introducing a brother or a neighbor?"

"Oh, there's always some of that going on, but I'm not aware of any setup Crystal had. I remember I met this really nice guy at a friend's house once. It was for a Sunday brunch, and there were four couples and then me and this guy. After a bit, the couples are all in the kitchen, and the two of us are out in the living room watching the fire. The guy smiles at me and says, "Hey, you seem really nice, and I'm sure Jackie set this up to get us together. But I met this really great woman, and I don't want to screw anything up. Let's just keep it our secret, keep everyone here happy, and you don't have to worry about contacting me, and I won't be contacting you."

"He really said that?"

"Oh, yeah. You know, it turned out to be a great afternoon. He was really funny, and I think about a year later he married the woman he mentioned. I never did tell Jackie about it. She'd be embarrassed knowing we were aware she set us up."

"That's pretty good."

"Yeah, different time, I guess. I wish I could be of more help to you. But I'm afraid I don't really have anything to add after twelve years. I've worked really hard to block the whole incident out of my mind. It was really nice to meet you again. And I've always wanted to see your office, ever since we met and you were in that kilt."

"Connie, I apologize again for my comment that night."

"You kidding, that's the most action I've had in years."

"Please stay in touch and feel free to stop in any time, Connie. It was nice to meet you officially."

"Nice to meet you, Dev. I hope you get this guy. I just wish I could have been more help."

"Well, say a prayer for us."

"I will, thanks again," she said and left. I heard the stairs creak as she went down to the ground floor and out the door. I watched as she crossed the street, climbed into a nondescript black car, and headed up the street. In a way, she was another victim of the crime. As she said, 'The whole thing really knocked me off the rails, and I never really got back on."

Thirty-two

I turned the coffee off, dumped Louie's nearly untouched mug back into the pot, and set the mug on his desk. Morton and I headed over to The Spot. Louie had changed seats. He was now out of the booth and seated on his favorite bar stool with a half-finished drink in front of him. An open bag of pork rinds rested next to his drink, and he poured some into his hand the moment we entered. Morton saw what he was doing and strained at his leash to get to Louie as fast as possible.

"Oh, Morton, good to see you, boy. Long day for you, I guess, after being stuck next to the dullest guy in town all day. Yeah, that's right. Help yourself. Go ahead. You made it. You definitely earned it, and you're back with the normal folks now."

"Yeah, right," I said. "Whatever passes for normal in here."

Mike signaled me from the other end of the bar. He was standing in front of the beer taps and raised a glass, suggesting he pour one for me. I nodded, and he pulled the tap.

"So, how'd it go?" Louie asked.

"With Connie? Oh, God love her, but more of the same. No description, no name, nothing except that Crystal may have dated some good-looking guy who she might have met on Match.com. How in the hell can one guy be the sort of person no one comments on? Wouldn't you think, if some guy was putting the moves on a woman, that she'd be telling all her friends?"

Louie shook his head. "Maybe he wasn't putting the moves on them. Maybe he was being nice, taking them out, picking up the tab, but other than a little kiss or maybe just a handshake, he was playing it low key. He's set this up enough times that now he knows what he's doing and, not all the time, but every once in a while, he can tell he's got another one on the line. She's liking the attention, liking him, and then he maybe has her over to his place for the big night, or takes her to a lake place, or he gets a hotel room. Now, she's all excited that this is the big night. Maybe he has flowers for her, or he gives her a gift, and then he drugs her, and that's it."

"But why go through all that when he could just drug her, tie her up, and put her in the trunk of his car?"

"Dev, you're thinking like a normal person, but this creep isn't normal. I don't think you'll ever make a good serial killer. Maybe a big part of it for him is to lead these women along, and now they're all excited. This is it. It's going to be the night that will always be remembered, and unfortunately, that's not far from the truth. Think about it. In a weird way, the veil and the white slip, it's their wedding night. The only problem is the woman won't be alive to remember it."

Mike set my beer on the bar and walked back to the beer taps. I picked up the glass and gulped down about a third of the glass. "Man, I never thought of it in those terms. So, let's just say he's meeting all these women online. If he works to get them into the frame of mind you described, wouldn't that also mean there were some women who didn't go the way he wanted and maybe he dropped them?"

"Yeah, certainly. Or maybe they exhibited some trait that suddenly excluded them. Maybe they had a child. Maybe they were a caregiver for a parent or some-one. Hell, maybe they liked red wine instead of white. Who knows? I'm just suggesting this guy had, or maybe has, a particular format he needs to follow. When that doesn't happen, the deal is off, and he has to start over."

"Then it seems that could also mean there were, or are, women, that he met with the intention of ultimately murdering them, and for whatever reason, they didn't fit his routine. Maybe after the first or second date, they thought this guy is a real drag, and they dumped him," I said.

"Oh, yeah. In fact, there may be a lot of women who did that. But how would you ever find them? I'd say the chances of someone, male or female, having an online date with some person that ends up not going anywhere is about a hundred percent. The odds of not fitting into some whacko serial killer's desired pattern would be huge. Six victims, Dev, there could be hundreds of women out there that, because they didn't fit into some pattern he cooked up, he decided not to pursue them."

It seemed to make sense, and we chatted over the course of another beer for me and two more drinks for Louie. Based on the pictures I'd seen of the victims, they were all attractive. They had different hair colors and styles. Not all the victims were Caucasian, and their heights and weights were varied. There was no commonality on employment, other than every victim held a professional position. Place of birth and current residence varied. Religion did not seem to be a factor.

After the better part of two hours and Morton finishing the last of the bag of pork rinds, I decided to head home.

"You in tomorrow morning?" Louie asked.

"Yeah, we should be, I— oh, damn it."

"What?"

"I told Aaron I'd swing over and see Ben Jackson in the hospice care center after the noon hour. I just completely forgot. I'll have to get over there tomorrow, but it won't be until later in the morning. I'll be in first thing."

"See you tomorrow, then. I've got a court appearance at eleven, so I'll be in sometime after nine."

"Enjoy the rest of your evening, Louie, and thanks for the thoughts on this guy. You've got me looking in some other directions. Behave," I said and waved at Mike as Morton and I headed out the door. My stomach growled as I headed to my car. I was hungry, but I craved something besides pizza. I called the Kona Grill, a Japanese place over on Grand Avenue.

"Kona Grill, how may I help you?"

"Hi, I'd like to place a takeout order."

"All right, just one moment," the woman said. Her voice sounded familiar. "Yes, okay what would you like?"

"I'll start with an order of Teriyaki Chicken skewers and a dinner order of Yaki Niku."

"Very good, anything for dessert?"

"No, that should take care of me."

"All right, this will be ready for pickup in fifteen minutes. Your name, sir?"

"First name is Dev, D-E-V. Last name is—"

"Is this, by any chance, Dev Haskell?"

"Yes it is, is this Kimi?"

"It is. I thought I recognized your voice, Dev. How have you been?"

"Good, Kimi, good. How about you?"

"Busy. I've two children now, little boys, three and one. They're driving us crazy."

"Sounds wonderful. Hey, I'll see you in fifteen or twenty minutes," I said and disconnected.

Kimi Tanaka, we went out for a while five or six years back. Her folks owned the restaurant. I enjoyed dating her, but in the end, it became clear she was looking for a lot more than I could give, and apparently, she found it. She was always nice to me, but it had been at least four years since I ran into her on the street, maybe five since I'd been in the restaurant. It would be interesting to see what she said when I went in.

With fifteen minutes before my order was ready, I decided to drive past Virgil Hayes's place. He wasn't even ten minutes away. I headed up Randolph Avenue all the way to the River Boulevard and then took a right. Hayes's house was just a few doors from the corner. Even though it was just a little after six, the front porch light was on. I took my foot off the accelerator and coasted past his house then turned at the next corner and drove down the alley. The garage door was closed, and I obviously couldn't see over the eight-foot wall. I drove to the end of the alley, took two rights, and drove past the house again. The blinds were pulled in the room to the right of the front door, but I could tell the room was illuminated. I guessed it was a living room with a fireplace based on the massive brick chimney running up the exterior wall.

I continued on to Summit Avenue then drove down Summit for the better part of three miles to Saint Alban's. I took a right, and the Kona Grill was at the corner on the righthand side. I pulled into the parking lot and hurried into the restaurant. I was more than a little excited to see Kimi, and I think it was safe to say there was probably a part of me that had never really gotten over her. I did a quick glance around but couldn't see her anywhere.

There was a high school kid with a black apron wrapped around his waist standing at the hostess counter. “Good evening, just one tonight?” he asked, reaching for a menu.

“Actually, I phoned in an order. I spoke to Kimi. Is she around?” I asked, hoping he might call her to handle my takeout.

“You’re dud?” he asked and picked up a white paper bag from behind the counter with a hand-written receipt stapled to the bag. The receipt might have said ‘Dev’, or it might have said ‘Dud.’ It has hard to tell.

“Yeah, I guess that’s my order.”

“Twenty-four ninety-five,” he said.

She didn’t even give me a discount. So much for calling an old friend. I handed him my credit card and prayed it would be accepted. He ran it through, then handed me the terminal. “Would you like to add a tip?”

Yeah right, I thought. She charged me full price and didn’t bother to say hello or thanks for coming. “No, thanks. Could I get a receipt, please?”

“But of course,” he said and smiled. He printed off the receipt and handed it to me along with the bag of food.

“Thanks,” I said, promising myself I would never go back. I climbed in the car, set the bag on the passenger seat, and headed home. Morton stuck his head between the two front seats and sniffed the bag all the way home. We went in the front door, and I let him out into the backyard. I placed my chicken skewers on a small plate and the Yaki Niku, it's ribeye steak in garlic sauce, on a larger plate. I settled onto a kitchen stool and dug in. Thinking while I ate of some private moments from five or six years ago with Kimi.

After dinner, I debated placing a third call to the people who had ignored my first two calls but decided against it. Instead, I let Morton back inside, tossed him a dog biscuit, and settled onto the couch in front of the tv.

Thirty-three

I woke when my alarm clock went off. Morton shoved his head under the pillow, as I hit the shower before heading downstairs. I'd been on the computer for the better part of an hour before Morton appeared in the kitchen. I let him outside then filled his food and water dish. Thirty minutes later, we headed down to the office. Louie was at his desk, and a full pot of coffee was on.

"I thought you were going to see Ben Jackson this morning," he said.

"I'll see him later this morning. I think I'd better call over there first, just to see how he's doing and give him a chance to get situated for the day. How'd the rest of your evening go?"

"I went home not very long after you two left. I've got court in about two hours. I'm appearing before Thompson again. She's a stickler for making sure you shaved, and God help you if there's the slightest whiff of alcohol or she suspects a hangover."

"Sounds like the voice of experience talking."

"Fortunately, other people's experience, but that's enough to make me pay attention."

I poured myself a coffee and took a sip. It was cold, and I must have made a face.

"Oh, I should have told you I just turned it on. That pot is from yesterday. Want me to pour you a mug once it's warmed up?"

"Yeah, thanks," I said and poured my mug back into the pot. "You know, I've been thinking about what you said last night, about this guy establishing his routine. I—" My phone rang. I checked the number, Denise Wengler, the woman from the Transportation Department. "Hi, Denise. How are you this morning?"

"I'm fine, Dev. I hope I'm not calling too early."

"No, not at all, just plugging away at the office. What's up?"

"I was thinking about our conversation yesterday, and to be honest, I was lying awake most of the night, racking my brain, trying to think of something Jia might have said that I never mentioned."

I held my breath for a moment. "Did something come to mind?"

"It's so basic it's embarrassing. But I figured I should pass it on."

"Please, no matter how insignificant it seems, it may turn out to be just the thing that clicks."

"Okay, well, Jia was a fanatic reader, romances usually, but not always." I wondered where this was going, probably that the guy Jia dated was really muscular and liked to walk around with his shirt off. "Anyway, she said the Match.com guy, the one who took her to the Springsteen concert, had something to do with books."

"Something to do with books?" Virgil Hayes immediately sprang to mind. "Like what, was he a librarian?"

"No, she never said. She just said he had something to do with books, or at least that's how I remember it. I wish I had more information. I know that's really vague, but it just popped into my head about four this morning, and I thought I should call. Of course, now that I've said it out loud, she could have meant he liked to read comic books or collect coloring books or something. Sorry if I'm wasting your time, Dev. I just thought, well, you know, you said to call you and—"

"No, no, much appreciated, Denise. I'll alert the police and see where this takes us. Thank you. I'm glad you called."

"You sure? I'm really sorry I can't remember more, but that was it. It sounds really stupid now. I just wanted to—"

"It's really not stupid, Denise, and I'm glad you called. Thank you."

"You're sure?"

"Yes, very sure. Much appreciated."

"Well, if anything else pops into my head, I'll be sure to say it out loud a half-dozen times before I call."

"You take care, Denise, and please call me again with anything."

"Thanks, Dev. I'll talk to you later."

As soon as she disconnected, I phoned Aaron LaZelle and left a message. "Hi Aaron, call me when you get this. I just got a call from a woman I interviewed yesterday. She remembered something that may be pertinent to the investigation. Thanks," I said and disconnected.

"That sounded like it might be positive," Louie said as he placed a steaming mug of reheated coffee on my desk. "Did she have a name or a description?"

"No, not exactly. But it just might fit. Her friend was murdered eight years ago. Denise said the woman mentioned the guy she was dating had something to do with books."

Louie made a face. "Something to do with books? Like what, he owned a bookstore, or he was an accountant and he kept the books for some business?"

"Louie, stop. You're raining on the parade here."

"Dev, she might as well have told you he put gas in his car. Something to do with books? That doesn't narrow anything down."

"It does if Virgil Hayes writes about a serial killer."

"No, it doesn't. Hayes has written crime fiction for close to twenty years. The police interviewed him twice. There's a murder in this town that goes unsolved. Hayes uses it as the main theme in a book that becomes somewhat successful. So, like anyone with half a brain, he turns the book into a series, which turns out to be highly successful, and now you think he's guilty?"

"I'm just saying the guy this woman was dating when she was murdered, apparently had something to do with books. Hayes is divorced. He's in the book business. He's been a person of interest. Doesn't it seem like this might be a reason to go back and check him out a little closer?"

Louie shook his head and said, "I think, when you asked her if he was a librarian, you might have been closer to the mark."

My phone rang, Aaron LaZelle. "Hi Aaron, thanks for returning my call so quickly."

"You got something, Dev?"

"Maybe, it's a broad statement until you examine the facts related to these murders. I met with a woman yesterday, Denise Wengler." I went on to tell Aaron about my interview with Denise and the call from her less than twenty minutes earlier.

"Has something to do with books?" Aaron said. "That could be anything. The Kahn woman was murdered in November of 2012. Dev, back then, that could have meant phone books, coupon books, music books."

"Don't forget coloring books, or he could have been a librarian," I said.

"Yeah, you're right."

"Well, don't forget, Lucia Ruiz described the guy as a Hottie and mentioned he had a beard. And her brother—"

"Dante?"

"Yeah, he said the guy she was dating at the end had a beard."

"But Dante, never actually saw the guy she was dating, did he?"

"Well, no, he didn't."

"And aren't you the guy who told me Dante mentioned the beard and you looked around the room in that dive, La Soga, and there were five or six guys with beards?"

"Well, yeah, but you think any of those guys had something to do with books?"

"I'm willing to bet at least one of them was a bookie."

"Oh, yeah, I guess."

"Let me know when you come up with something else. I'm not trying to give you a hard time, but none of this is strong enough to relaunch an investigation, Dev. I'm sorry. Say, how was Ben Jackson yesterday afternoon?"

"I didn't make it over. I got involved in a couple of interviews, and the next thing you know, it was too late to stop in and see him. I'm going to head over there later this morning."

"Just give a call first. They've got him on some schedule over there. I know he'd love to see you. Tell him about this 'doing something with books' comment. Maybe he'll have an idea. Anything else?"

"No, you've pretty much poured cold water on everything I've got."

"Well, don't go having a pity party. Thanks for the earlier call, now get back to work."

"I'll talk to you later, Aaron."

"It didn't sound like he was too impressed," Louie said.

"Hard to believe, but he was even more negative than you."

"Just trying to be logical, Dev. Look at it this way. Let's say on that slim evidence, they open an investigation of Virgil Hayes. There's about a ninety-nine percent chance they won't find anything. But let's just say he's guilty. Now, he's been alerted, and since he can conduct his book business from just about anywhere, he moves out of the state. Maybe he even leaves the country. I'm just saying the woman's comment is interesting, but you're going to need a lot more facts to build a strong case. So figure out how to get them."

"Sound advice," I said, then picked up my phone and called Ben Jackson. A woman's voice answered on the third ring.

"Hello?"

"Ben Jackson, please."

"He's not available at the moment. Can I take a message?"

"Is this Gretchen?"

"Yes."

"Gretchen, my name is Dev Haskell. I spoke with Ben a while ago, and he—"

"Are you the private investigator?"

"Yes, ma'am, I am."

"Ben and Aaron LaZelle were talking about you yesterday afternoon. I know he'll want to talk to you. Can he reach you at this number?"

"Yes, he can. I was just calling to see what the best time would be to stop by."

"Oh, I know he would like that, Mr. Haskell. He's just in the shower at the moment. I'll have him call as soon as he's able."

"Thank you. I'll look forward to his call," I said, and she disconnected.

Thirty-four

Ben called back about twenty minutes later. "Hi, Ben."

"It's about time I heard from you. What ya got?" he said and then laughed.

"Stop it. You sound like Aaron LaZell. He already poured cold water on my ideas this morning. Say, when would be a good time to come over and see you? I've got a couple of small items I'd like to discuss with you."

"Anytime today would work. They've got me on some damn meds, so I'm taking a nap from about two to four in the afternoon."

"What if I came over in about an hour?"

"That would be perfect. You know where we are?"

"Lyngblomsten Care Center, right?"

"You got it. Who the hell knew I'd end up here?"

"Ben," Gretchen's voice sounded in the background.

"Oh, sorry, that's the commanding general giving me more direction. I'll see you in a bit."

"Thanks, Ben, see you shortly," I said and hung up.

I left the office forty-five minutes later. Ben's care center was located in West St. Paul. I knew where it was, but I'd never been there. I was expecting just a building. The place was more like a campus, with gorgeous grounds, flowerbeds, trimmed hedges, and walking paths. People were seated outside in the sunlight on benches or in wheelchairs. Obviously, the place was more than a cancer care center. I entered the building and was directed up to the third floor. Ben Jackson's room was halfway down the hall.

Room is the wrong term. It was really an apartment with a small entry, a living room, kitchen area, and a bedroom. I knocked on the door, and Gretchen answered a moment later. She was clearly older, but she didn't look like an old lady. She had sparkling blue eyes, nicely done blonde hair, makeup, nice fitting black slacks, and a short sleeve sweater.

"Mr. Haskell?"

"Yes, please call me Dev."

"You look just as Ben described." I was wearing jeans and a Saint Paul Central High School sweatshirt. "Won't you come in, and please, call me Gretchen. I've never been one for formalities."

"It's very nice to meet you in person," I said.

"Get in here, Haskell, while I'm still conscious," Ben called from the couch in the living room.

"Oh, Ben, I'm going out for my walk. Anything you need before I go?"

"All's well, Gretchen. Enjoy your walk."

Gretchen lowered her voice and said," I'll leave you two to go over that case." She stepped into the hallway and closed the door. I headed over to Ben and took up one of the two chairs across from the couch. "Out on a walk. The woman's just fleeing the scene to regain her sanity for a few minutes," Ben said as I sat down.

"Looks like very nice digs they've got you in. How are you two doing?"

"As well as can be expected. These damn meds they've got me on, let me tell you, I'm not feeling the best at any particular moment. I'm basically sitting around and waiting. But enough of that shit. What have you found out?"

I went on to tell Ben about the interviews I'd had. I went through them in order of the murders. I'd burned off another set of the last ten pages from Lucia Ruiz's final notebook and handed them to Ben. He nodded as he read through them twice then set them on the coffee table between us.

"That pretty much matches my memory. Although I wasn't involved with the interviews on the Ruiz case or the most recent one, the Long woman. One of my fears right now, Dev, is that we're overdue for another murder. I'm scared to death this bastard is going to kill some other woman."

"The people I've spoken with haven't really come up with any new information. Or if they have, it's been so damn general that it's nothing that would point us in a new direction or any direction for that matter." I went on to use the example of Dante Ruiz mentioning the last person his sister was dating had a beard and that, when I looked around, there were five or six guys in the room with a beard.

He shook his head. "I'm still thinking Virgil Hayes. The guy travels a lot. He's in the book business, and did you see his picture online?"

"You mean his author site on Amazon? Yeah, dark curly hair, nice looking guy with a beard."

"And his most recent book was published before Madeline Long's murder. I don't care what they say about that being a wrongo."

"You mean a typo?"

"Yeah, whatever. As far as I'm concerned, he published detailed information regarding the murder before it had occurred. Now, just how in the hell does that happen unless the son of a bitch is involved? I'm telling you, Dev, he's our man. He's the one who's been committing these murders and damn near nothing is going to convince me otherwise."

We'd been talking and comparing notes for the better part of an hour. "How's it going, boys?" Gretchen's voice suddenly sounded as the door to the apartment opened.

"Going fine, dear, perfect timing. I was just about to throw Haskell's ass out of here," Ben said and winked at me. "Thanks for coming back and saving me, Gretchen. You are a saint."

"I'd like to hear Dev's side of the story, Ben."

"Let me hang onto these, and I'll go over them a few more times," Ben said, indicating the pages from Lucia Ruiz's notebook.

"Not a problem. You take care of yourself, Ben. Call me if I can do anything. I'll stay in touch and keep you posted as things progress. Maybe some more of the folks initially interviewed will call me back."

"Don't get your hopes up, Dev. It's pretty standard. For most of them, they just want to get as far away as possible from the event and focus on happier times."

"Yeah, I'm picking up on that. A couple of them even said as much. Okay, I'll be in touch. Gretchen, nice to meet you in person. You stay sane, and please, call me if there is anything I can do for you."

"Thank you, Dev. So nice to meet you," she said and smiled as she escorted me to the door just to make sure I left. She closed the door once I stepped into the hall. Ben was one lucky guy to have Gretchen. Which reminded me, I hadn't heard from Taffy in two days.

Thirty-five

It was close to one by the time I left the Care Center and headed back toward town. I kept playing Ben's comments around in my head and then thought of Connie's comment about Crystal Higgins dating a guy she knew in high school. The North Saint Paul high school, where Crystal Higgins went, was about fifteen minutes away on Highway 36. I'd been past it a few thousand times but had obviously never stopped. I drove through downtown, hopped on 35 E heading north, took the exit to Highway 36, and five minutes later, I pulled into the high school parking lot. There had to be at least five hundred cars in the lot, most of them nicer than my Ford Taurus. I parked and walked into the main building. The school office was just to the left.

The woman behind the counter was on the phone. She gave me a nod and signaled with her hand that she would be just a minute. She hung up a moment later, studied my Saint Paul Central sweatshirt, and frowned. "Lost?" she said but then smiled.

"Actually no," I pulled out my P.I. license and handed it to her. "I'm working with the Saint Paul police.

We're looking into the murder of Crystal Higgins. I believe she graduated from here."

"Oh, yes, she graduated back in '97. We had a big service for her when the news came out. That had to be ten years ago, now."

"Actually, twelve," I said.

"Oh, so sad, so tragic."

"Yes, it is. I was wondering if you had a yearbook from '97 that I might be able to take a look at."

"You think someone from the school—"

"No, quite the opposite. The police interviewed some people Crystal knew in high school. I just wanted to check the yearbook, see if there might be a name that was missed. Someone on a team, maybe in a play, or a choral group, a history club, anything that might shed some light on the situation. No one is suspected of anything. We're just hoping someone might know something that wasn't mentioned in the initial investigation, but it might help direct us."

"We've organized the yearbooks in another room. They go way back to 1905, our first year. Let me check and I'll be right back," she said and hurried from her desk.

The office door opened, and a kid stepped in who looked like he might be fifteen. He carried a pink slip in his left hand and didn't look too thrilled about coming into the office. He could have been me twenty years ago. I knew the drill. He'd probably be sent home for some stupid thing he'd done. He'd tell his folks classes were only a half-day. He'd deny doing whatever stupid thing he'd done, unaware his folks had already received a phone call from the school and knew exactly what he'd been up to; hiding in the girls locker room, sneaking a stale beer into school, maybe looking down some girls blouse, the list went on. I'd done them all and gotten caught on just about every one of them. "So, what did they catch you—"

"Mr. Haskell, if you'll follow me, please." She looked over my shoulder, and her eyes flared. "You wait right there, Lucas, and I'll be back." It's the sign of a repeat offender when, in a school of maybe two thousand kids, the woman at the front desk knows your name. I could only hope he'd be smarter than I was.

"In here, Mr. Haskell. I've got the yearbooks from ninety-six and ninety-seven on the table. If you need anything else, please let me know. Now, if you'll excuse me, I'll go deal with our little chronic offender." She flashed a quick smile that was anything but pleasant.

I sat down and opened the yearbook from 1997. The senior class pictures were featured in the front of the book in alphabetical order. Crystal Higgins' photo featured a dark-haired girl who, instead of having at least seventy years in front of her, barely had ten and a half before some worthless creature would take her life. She was a member of the debate team, the North choir, and the theatre club.

I paged to the 'O' page, and there he was, Gerald O'Malley. Basketball, track, the theatre club, and a member of the Three Stooges Fan Club, whatever that was. He looked like a nice enough kid. I paged through both yearbooks but never found a picture of the two of them together. I made a couple of notes then left the yearbooks on the corner of the table and stepped out to the front office.

As I rounded a corner, I passed an office labeled Vice-Principal. The door was closed, and a stern male voice on the other side of the door said, "Let me just describe what you did, Lucas, and you stop me when I get to the part where this was a good idea."

I'd heard a version of the same lecture uncountable times, and I picked up my pace until I was standing before the front desk. "Finished already, Mr. Haskell?"

"Yes, it was very helpful. Thank you. If something should occur to you or the staff that you think might be of help, please don't hesitate to call me," I said and handed her my card.

"Thank you, and if there's anything we can do, don't hesitate to call us."

I walked back to my car and drove to the office. Morton was the only one there, and he was up and standing at the door when I opened it. I grabbed his leash and took him for a brisk walk. Once back in the office, I went online and Googled Gerald O'Malley. Not that uncommon a name as it turned out. Over twenty pages of doctors, lawyers, taxi drivers, you name it. Facebook was just as jammed. After forty-five minutes, I found a guy who appeared to be a version of the yearbook photo as I remembered it. He lived in Suwanee, Georgia, about thirty miles outside of Atlanta. There was an email address for his web design business, and I sent him an email. I walked up the street to Rooster's for a Bar-B-Que pork sandwich. Twenty minutes later, I was back in the office with my sandwich, and I had a short email from Gerald O'Malley.

'Please feel free to call me.' He had attached his phone number.

I pushed my sandwich to the side and dialed the number. O'Malley answered on the second ring. "Gerry O'Malley."

"Hi, Gerry. This is Dev Haskell. Thank you for the fast response to my email."

"You're welcome. Can I ask how you got my name?"

"As part of reviewing the Crystal Higgins case, I've contacted a number of people who were originally interviewed. One of them mentioned a conversation she had with Crystal, and your name came up." I went on to give him a brief description of what Connie had told me without mentioning her name. I told him about going through the school yearbook earlier.

"Sounds like an awful lot of work. How can I help you? It gave me pause when I saw Crystal's name in your email. She was a great girl and a wonderful woman. If you're looking into her case, I hope this means you've landed on something or someone."

"Not exactly. I'm a private investigator and another pair of eyes, hoping to find something the police may have missed initially or maybe something that you might remember that didn't seem too important twelve years ago."

"Twelve years. Has it really been that long? God, I have to be honest, I've tried to put this out of my mind for the longest time and—"

"I apologize if my email brought the nightmare back."

"No, I get it. I intentionally haven't kept up to date on the investigation. Last I knew, there were four murders. I'm guessing that number is now a distant shore."

"Currently, there are six. The most recent was in May of last year. The fear is the individual may be getting ready to strike again."

"Oh, God. To be honest, Crystal and I had a few dates. I guess you could call them dates. But it was more like two high school friends just getting together for some fun. There was no hint of sex or romance if that's what you're thinking, and to be honest, neither one of us wanted that. We were just having a good time."

"Did she happen to mention anything about guys she dated?"

"No, not really, other than some funny stories about guys who were boring. I remember one guy had a calculator with him, and when it came time to pay the dinner tab, instead of just paying or splitting it fifty-fifty, he got it down to the penny. She owed something like three bucks more than he had ordered, and she had to pay it. She thought that was pretty funny."

"Any guys she liked?"

"Guys she liked? No, not really. I mean, well, there was one. She said he was a good-looking guy, umm, with a beard, but he dropped her before they really even got started. She said he was real nice, but I think they only had three or four dates. The guy traveled for business, so he probably found some woman in a little more exciting place than North Saint Paul."

"Did she say what he did that he was traveling?"

"Not that I recall. In fact, I'm not even sure she knew."

"She happen to mention a name or where he lived?"

"No, nothing like that. To tell you the truth, it was more of a passing comment than telling me about some love affair that went south. In fact, I said something like 'Good looking and a beard. That leaves me out.' She said, 'Yeah, but you're way more fun.' Anyway, that was the last time we saw one another. I got busy with work. At the time, I was with Medtronic, doing IT. They moved me down here three or four months later, and maybe two years after that, I started my own business. I met my wife. She's a Georgia girl. We've got two kids and a third one on the way."

"I'm happy for you, Gerry. It sounds like you're a lucky guy."

"Yeah, I wish I could tell you more, but there's just nothing to tell. I was never at Crystal's place. She was never in the place I was living in, which was probably a good thing. Three guys in a two-bedroom apartment, we're lucky we didn't all die of some germ infestation. The three or four times I was with Crystal, we met one another in a bar. Nothing fancy, and it would be stretching it to call the night a date."

"Gerry, thanks for your time. If anything pops up, please don't hesitate to give me a call."

"Wishing you all the best, Dev. I hope you guys get whoever did this. When you do, just shoot the bastard. I wish I had more for you, but I just don't."

"Thanks, Gerry, you take care down there."

"I will. You enjoy the winter and the forty below temperatures," he said and disconnected.

Damn it. More of the same and still nothing to go on.

Thirty-Six

At this point, my pork sandwich from Roosters was cold. It didn't matter. The thing was still delicious. Just as I was finishing up, I heard the stairs begin to creak as Louie made his way up to our office. I was licking my fingertips when he stepped through the door, red-faced and wheezing.

As he collapsed in his desk chair, I got up, grabbed his coffee mug, dumped the remnants in the sink, and poured what was left in the pot into his mug. I turned the burner off and set the mug on his desk. He pulled it toward him and took a sip.

"How'd your court appearance go?"

He flashed me the OK sign with his thumb and forefinger then took another sip and grimaced. "Oh, God, that's rough."

"I don't get it. It's only been on the burner for the last five hours."

He shook his head and took another sip. "How was Ben Jackson this morning?"

"He was good to talk to, very much on the ball. I met his wife for the first time. She's really nice, and obviously a saint for putting up with Ben all these years.

Like I said, he was good, and it sounds crazy because he's only been in that facility for two-and-a-half days, but he just, I don't know, he just seemed to look a little more frail. I can't put my finger on it, other than to say this is the first time I would have described him as more fragile looking."

Louie nodded but didn't say anything.

My phone rang. Amazingly, it was Taffy. Gee, it had only been two and a half days.

"Hello," I said, hoping I didn't sound too happy.

"Hi, Dev," she said. No mention about sorry I haven't called. Sorry I've been a pain in the ass. Sorry I spent all this time with my new best friend, Allison.

"Hi, Taffy, it's really nice to hear your voice."

"Hey, if you're going to be crabby, I don't want to talk to you."

"I'm not being crabby. It's nice to hear your voice. It's been a couple of days."

"I've been busy."

I decided not to respond. "What's the latest word on your promotion? When last we talked, you'd just gotten the word. Congratulations, again, by the way. So what's the deal? Are you going to get your own office? Will they transfer you to another department? Do you get a raise?"

"Whoa, stop with all the questions and take a breath. I thought I would give you an update tonight."

Mmm, things might be getting back to normal. This was a good start. "That sounds great. You want to pick out the restaurant? I'll pick you up, and the two of us can celebrate your win. What do you say?" I put a little emphasis on the word 'two' as in no Allison.

"I was thinking we might just have a quiet, very private dinner at my place. I have a ton of things to consider, and I'm going to need your opinion. You've been kind of hard to talk to of late."

Don't respond, focus on the 'very private dinner', a voice screamed inside my head. "What time would you like me there?"

"How does seven sound?"

"It sounds perfect. I'll be there with bells on. What can I bring?"

"Mmm, I was going to have you do a couple of steaks out on the grill. You pick the wine. I'll get the steaks, and don't wear bells. Wear something nice, not that cowboy shirt."

"Okay, I will. I'm so looking forward to this and getting back to normal."

"Normal?"

Why did I say that? "Yeah, normal. You know, me cooking steaks on the grill. You've been doing all the work lately. I just want you to sit, relax, and look like your beautiful self."

"Seven o'clock," she said.

"See you tonight, and thanks for the call, Taffy."

"Bye, bye, bye," she said and disconnected.

"What was that all about? You should see the smile on your face. Apparently, she's back talking to you," Louie said.

"Steaks at her house. Just the two of us. We're about to get caught up. Thank God."

"Well, congratulations. Good things come to those who wait."

"Yeah, well, let's just say I'm Mr. Patient."

"Yeah, sure you are, Dev."

Thirty-Seven

Morton and I headed home maybe an hour later. I let Morton out into the backyard, shaved, and took a long, hot shower. I gave Morton a treat, checked my computer for messages, and headed out the door. I drove over to Excel Pawn & Jewelry out on Rice Street. I had a pal who worked there, and I thought it might be nice to bring Taffy a little gift. I pulled up and parked in front. The one-story brick building was anything but low key. It had a blue neon sign across the front flashing 'Pawn Shop'. The two front windows had the words, 'Gold' and 'Bikes' painted in six-foot-high yellow letters across them. The word 'TVs' was painted in six-foot-high yellow letters across the double doors.

I hadn't taken more than four steps into the place when someone shouted, "Well, well, well. Look what the cat dragged in. Now, we ain't taken no stolen property from you today, Haskell."

Quandell Dickenson, we'd known one another since junior-high, best friends after our fistfight, which neither one of us won.

"Quandell, they still got you abusing people from behind the counter."

"Always, it's what I do the best. How are you, bro? Long time no see. Let me guess, you've done something stupid, again, and you need just the right piece of jewelry to get some poor woman back. Poor child, you'd think she'd know better."

"Actually, this time, I'm just being a nice guy. This one likes gold, yellow, not the white stuff. I'm thinking a bracelet. Maybe something in the twenty-dollar range."

"Twenty dollars? I don't think I have brass at that price. Let me show you a couple of items while you just sit back and dream about how this nice young lady is going to say thank you when she opens your gift."

"Nothing too crazy, Quandell. You know how—"

"Maybe just follow me," he said. He wiggled his index finger, indicating I should follow him. We walked past twenty or thirty bicycles, a long table covered with a dozen table lamps, and a rack of leather jackets. Quandell stepped behind the counter and slid the back panel open. He pulled out a tray lined in white velvet with a half-dozen gold bracelets draped across it. The one I focused on had a price tag of seven hundred dollars.

"Because you're the popular man you are, I'll knock off ten percent on any one of these."

"I'm thinking of something a little more in my price range."

"Your price range? I just told you, I'm knocking ten percent off. These are all twenty-two-carat gold bracelets. You want to make her happy, or do you want to get her even more upset?"

"Don't you have some great deal for around twenty bucks?"

"Twenty? You want some cheap-ass gold plated thing. Come on, dude. Since when did you become so cheap? Here's your choice. She's gonna look at this and climb right on top of you or take the gold-plated thing and hit you over the head. Now, which one sounds better?"

"Gold plated sounds like just the thing."

He rolled his eyes and walked down to the far end of the counter. Three cardboard boxes were piled on top of the counter. He pushed them aside and pulled out a wooden cigar box. "Here, man, take a look. These are the only gold-plated items we have. You're looking at junk if you ask me. Go ahead, see if there's anything in there that's gonna get her in the mood. If it were me, I'd just leave one of these at the front door and run for my life."

I moved the bracelets around with my finger, then spotted one on the bottom of the pile, very petite looking, and I could picture Taffy wearing it. "Yeah, this one will work," I said, focusing in on the twenty-four-dollar price tag.

"Really? You think you're gonna get your woman all charged up over this? I'm warning you, Dev. You're gonna get what you pay for here."

"This will work just fine."

He shook his head and said, "All right, let me ring you up." I followed him back to the cash register. He took my credit card and put the sale in for twenty-four dollars.

"Quandell, I thought you said you'd give me ten percent off?"

"Yeah, dude, that was on one of those twenty-two-carat numbers. You know, the kind of gift that'll get you ridden all night. This one, you'll be lucky if she don't throw your worthless ass out the door."

"You said ten percent."

"Really, dude?"

"Yeah, really."

"Okay, I pity the poor lady," he said and lowered the price to twenty-one dollars and sixty cents.

"Thanks, I really appreciate it. Oh, and I'm going to need some kind of little jewelry box, you know something she can open."

"I got just the thing. Hang on." He stepped away from the register for a moment and was back thirty seconds later with a long black box. He opened the lid and carefully placed the bracelet in the box. It fit perfectly.

"You got a way to shine that bracelet up a little?"

"I do, but I have to warn you. This is gold plated, and it will probably remove what's left of the gold. You're bound to see the silver metal underneath."

"Okay, I guess I'll go with it just the way it is."

Quandell added four bucks to the price. "What's that for?"

"The box you wanted. Dev, when in the hell did you get so cheap? You out of work or something?"

"Okay, okay, ring me up. I gotta get going here."

"Yeah, and believe me, man, I want your sorry ass out of here."

I signed the credit card receipt, we shook hands, and as I headed out the door, Quandell called, "Let me know how it works out, big spender."

Thirty-eight

I picked up two bottles of wine, pinots from Sean Minor's vineyard out in Sonoma. I pulled up in front of Taffy's building twenty minutes later. I had to ring her on the security phone twice before she answered. "Yeah?"

"Hi Taffy, it's me."

No response, but the security door buzzed, and the lock clicked. I stepped inside and took the elevator up to the third floor. Her unit was down the hall from the elevator, and in the past, she was almost always standing in her open doorway watching me approach. Not so tonight. I kept expecting her to step out into the hallway, maybe just wearing a smile, but nothing happened. I waited at the door for a long moment in case it took her a minute to remove her clothes and step out, but the door never opened, so eventually, I knocked.

"Oh, hi, Dev. Come on in," she said a half-minute later when she opened the door. She sounded like she was surprised I was standing in the hallway. I stepped into her living room and handed her the bag with the two bottles of wine. "Oh, perfect, just what the doctor ordered," she said. She gave me a peck on the cheek and hurried into the kitchen.

I noticed a stack of cardboard boxes in the corner of the living room and figured she'd probably been sent all sorts of files and maybe procedural manuals for her new position. Once I got a glass of wine in her and maybe calmed her down, she could tell me all about it.

I followed her into the kitchen. There was a crystal salad bowl on the kitchen counter, two bottles of salad dressing, French and blue cheese, my favorites. A basket with dinner rolls, a butter plate, linen napkins, silverware, and two placemats were next to the salad bowl. Something that smelled delicious was cooking in the oven.

"Why don't you open one of those wines and pour us each a glass," Taffy said as she opened the refrigerator and took out a platter with two porterhouse steaks glistening with oil and soaking up the salt and pepper. "I know, I know, before you say anything, relax. We're going to let these sit on the counter for thirty minutes before you put them on the grill. In the meantime, you can set the table out on the balcony, turn on the grill, and sip some wine. I'm going to grab a quick shower and slip into something more appropriate."

That brought a smile to my face. For a moment, I thought the night was going to be a bust. But if she was going to shower and slip into something 'more appropriate', I could only imagine. I heard the shower running as

I set our places on the glass-top table out on the balcony. I turned on the grill, sipped some wine, and fantasized about which negligée she'd be wearing, the black one or the red one. Maybe she'd pull on her world's shortest leather skirt with the slits up the side.

The shower had been off for a while, and I was now on my second glass of wine. I thought I could hear her talking in the bedroom, but maybe that was part of the deal with the new job promotion, phone calls into the evening. I sipped and waited, figuring she was probably applying makeup while talking on the phone to someone at work— more multitasking.

I finished my second glass of wine and turned down the grill. I went into the kitchen, grabbed the roll of Saran wrap, and covered the salad bowl and the dinner rolls. I poured myself another glass of wine and knocked on Taffy's bedroom door.

"I'll be out in a minute," she shouted. "Yeah, I know. You're right. No patience. Well, I'm just glad this is working out and back on track. Yes, yes, of course. No, it's not a problem. Good. All right. Bye, bye."

Her conversation didn't sound like it was too business related. I could only hope it wasn't the worst woman in the western hemisphere, Allison. I took my seat out on the balcony and waited another twenty minutes before Taffy finally came out of her bedroom. She was wearing jeans and a navy-blue sweater over a white blouse that was buttoned up to her neck. So much for my thoughts about the red or black negligée or the world's shortest leather skirt. She looked like a mom chaperoning a girl scout dance.

She stopped in the kitchen and poured herself a glass of wine. She held the bottle up to the kitchen light, checking to see how much wine was left and shook her head.

"Apparently, you're enjoying the wine?" she said, stepping out onto the balcony.

"Be more fun if you were out here. I got tired of waiting for you, so I poured myself a glass."

"A glass? It looks like you've been pounding it down."

"No, just sipping for the last hour and ten minutes."

"Oh, really, Dev. It hasn't been that long."

"Okay. I just know I was here at five minutes before seven, and it's ten after eight. So you tell me." I decided to change the subject. I picked the bracelet box off the glass-topped table. "Hey, I wanted to get you a little something in honor of your promotion. Here, congratulations. I'm very proud of you."

She set her glass on the table and looked at me wide-eyed as she took the box and opened it. "Oh, Dev, it's beautiful. Oh my God, gold. You know how I get. You didn't have to do this. Really, you didn't. You shouldn't have," she said, draping the bracelet over her wrist and extending it toward me to attach the clasp.

I set my glass down, attached the clasp, then leaned in to give her a kiss. She turned her head at the last minute, and I kissed her cheek. Hmm, so much for a wild and crazy night. She set the bracelet box on the table and said, “Why don’t you turn the grill on and warm it up. Let me just do one more thing before you put the steaks on,” she said and hurried into the kitchen.

Thirty-nine

The 'one more thing' took another fifteen minutes. I sat out on the balcony feeling like I was seated on the Titanic and the iceberg was slowly but surely approaching. I was just about ready to head into the kitchen and see if she needed some help when the intercom buzzed. Taffy didn't answer to see who was down there. Instead, she just pushed the security button and let whoever it was into the building. I started grasping at straws, trying to convince myself it was just someone from her office delivering more files. Wrong again.

A minute later, she hurried out of the kitchen and opened the front door. Squeals and shouts erupted as she and Allison hugged one another, all the while jumping up and down in a circle.

Allison, the Titanic iceberg in person. I held out hope that maybe she was just dropping something off or borrowing a roll of toilet paper. Wrong again. She handed a paper bag to Taffy, who pulled out a bottle of prosecco. I'm not a big fan of prosecco.

I wondered if things could possibly get any worse, but then Taffy pulled out a second bottle of prosecco just in time to answer my question. Five minutes later, they strolled out to the balcony together, each sipping a glass of prosecco. Taffy was carrying the platter with the two prime rib steaks and, on top of the platter, another dinner plate with silverware, and a smaller plate with a raw hamburger and two slices of cheese. She set them on the wooden side tray attached to the grill.

"Oh, hi, Dev," Allison said as she stepped onto the balcony. Her tone didn't hide her disappointment at my presence.

"Hi, Allison."

"Allison said she could join us for dinner, Dev," Taffy said.

I must have given a look that suggested I wasn't too happy with that announcement because Taffy flared her eyes at me. I was past the point of really caring. The night was a bust, and frankly, the relationship was speeding in that direction as well.

"Would you like me to get started on the grill?" I asked.

"Yeah, I think that would be a good idea, while we chat," Taffy said. The two of them headed toward the wicker couch overlooking the street below and sat down. Their backs were facing me.

As they sat, Allison said, "Now where did you get that, Taffy?" referring to the gold bracelet I'd attached around Taffy's wrist not twenty minutes ago.

"Dev gave it to me tonight. A little congratulatory gift for getting my promotion."

"Hmm, interesting," Allison said but didn't comment further. No doubt she was jealous, and the last guy to give her a gift was probably her father, as a thank you for finally moving out of the house.

They started in on their conversation, Allison's recent date. I was thinking of joining in, just so I could get the guy's name and warn him off before his life was ruined. Instead, I decided to take the high road and put the steaks on the grill. I like them rare, and I turned them at four minutes and put the hamburger on. I flipped the hamburger, took the steaks off, set them on the platter and covered them with a dinner plate. I placed the cheese slices on the burger, turned off the grill, and lowered the lid. I went into the kitchen and got the salad bowl, the dressings, and a pan of potatoes from the oven and carried them out to the balcony. I dished up everyone's plate and called the women to the table.

"Mmm, delicious. Well done, Taffy. It looks wonderful," Allison said and sat down at the place set for Taffy with the steak resting on the plate.

"Oh, I'm sorry, but that was Taffy's place. I—"

"No, that's all right, Allison. You sit there. I'll just take this one," Taffy said, sitting down in front of the other prime rib hanging over the side of the plate.

That left the cheeseburger for me. I was about to say something when Allison picked up the black box the bracelet had been in.

"That's the box for the bracelet," Taffy said.

Allison gave a funny look and turned the box over. There on the back was a white sticker that read 'EXCEL PAWN & JEWELRY.' An evil smile spread across Allison's face, and she said, "I knew it. Honey, that thing is gold plated, and it's from a pawn shop. Look," she said, taking hold of Taffy's wrist. "You can see where the gold plating has worn away. Someone else, probably a number of someones, have worn this thing. Did you disinfect this before you gave it to her, Dev?" Allison laughed.

"Dev, really?" Taffy said, unhooking the clasp and letting the bracelet fall on the table. "So not funny."

"Should we say a prayer before dinner?" I said.

No one laughed. Allison cut into her prime rib and said, "Oh, I'm sorry, but this is too rare for me."

Taffy sliced into hers and said, "Mmm, same with mine, Dev. You should probably put them back on the grill."

I had a sharp knife in one hand and a fork in the other. I took a deep breath, set the murder weapons down, picked up their plates, and tossed the steaks back on the grill. I turned on the grill, sat down, and started in on the bun-less cheeseburger. Neither woman said anything for two minutes.

When I got up to turn the steaks, Taffy said to Allison, "So things are back on track…" which apparently renewed whatever conversation they'd been involved in earlier. I placed the blackened steaks back on their plates and set the plates in front of them. “Check them out and make sure they’re done to your liking,” I said.

They each cut into the steak. “Yeah, it’s okay, I guess,” Allison said.

“Yeah, much better, Dev,” Taffy said. Neither steak now had the slightest hint of pink, and in my opinion, they were ruined.

I had one bite of cheeseburger left on my plate. I didn’t bother to sit down, but stabbed it with my fork, put it into my mouth, and then walked into the kitchen. I grabbed the unopened bottle of wine I’d brought and walked out the door. I took the elevator down to the ground floor, walked outside, and headed to my car. I could hear laughter coming from the balcony.

I climbed behind the wheel, debated about screeching my tires down the street, and decided against it. I quietly drove down the street and headed home.

Forty

The next morning after a couple of sips of coffee Louie said, "You're in early. You come straight from Taffy's?"

"Please, don't mention her name in my presence ever again."

"Oh, oh, one of those kinds of nights. What? The dinner didn't go well? You said something stupid?"

I shook my head, refilled my coffee mug, and proceeded to give Louie the details.

"You gotta be kidding me? What's with those two? That doesn't sound like Taffy."

"I don't know what it is, Louie, and I'm not going to wait around to find out. I give her a gold bracelet, hoping to smooth things over and get a fresh start, and she doesn't like the thing. Then that Allison bitch shows up and ruins what's left of the evening."

"Maybe they're thinking of having a three-way or something," Louie said. I shot him a look. "Okay, okay, just a thought, probably not the best one. I wonder if—"

The door to the office suddenly flew open. Morton half-jumped off his bed. Allison stood in the doorway and focused in on me with laser eyes. If looks could kill,

I only had seconds to live. She wore dark-gray stretch pants that left nothing to the imagination and a pink running tank top. A pink purse on a gold chain hung from her shoulder.

"Yeah, it figures. Of course, you'd be in some dive like this wasting your time. And you," she said to Louie, "I'd tell you to get your fat ass out of here, but I want a witness, so if I kill this low-life, you have to testify it was in self-defense, and I just saved our city from a total sleaze-bag."

"Hi, Allison," I said.

"Don't you 'hi' me, you worthless piece of crap. You give my close friend a cheap trinket from a pawn shop in the hope she's gonna hop in bed with you? You gotta be kidding me. I get a piece of good news I want to share with Taffy, and you throw a temper tantrum and try to ruin our night. Let me clue you in, you brainless lousy screw. We had a wonderful time once you got your worthless ass out of there. I told Taffy all about my good luck with a cool guy, the likes of which you're never ever going to be. So go ahead, spend all your time across the street in that saloon with Mr. One Too Many here," she indicated Louie. "Taffy's done with the likes of you. She's just too much of a lady to tell trash like you."

"Being a lady is something you'll never have to worry about, Allison. Now, if you wouldn't mind leaving, we're going to have to fumigate the office after being exposed to the deadly Allison germ. As always, so not a pleasure to see you."

A sneer suddenly washed across her face, and she said, "We'll just see how big you feel when she tells you she's moving to Kansas City. What? The look on your face. You didn't know? Too bad. It's part of the promotion she got. You know, the one where you gave her that cheap little pawnshop trinket to celebrate. How stupid do you think she is? She told me to toss it in the trash, just like she's gonna do to you. Hope to never see you again, ya loser," she said, then turned on her heel and walked out slamming the door behind her.

I watched out the window as she stormed across the street. Unfortunately, a car had to come to a stop and simply honked instead of running her over. Allison gave the guy the finger and climbed into her car, a white Lexus NX. There was a vertical crease in the driver's door, which made me wish someone doing seventy in a semi-truck would have broadsided her. She took off up the street, swerving into the traffic lane at the last moment, just missing a parked car by inches, and cutting off a driver. When she finally disappeared, I could only hope this was the last time I ever saw her.

"What a charming person," Louie said. "Talk about issues. That's the woman Taffy has attached herself to?"

"Yeah. I'm tempted to call her, but it wouldn't make any difference. You pick up what she said about moving to Kansas City? I saw a stack of boxes in the corner of Taffy's living room but figured it was files or manuals or something from work. I never thought she'd be packing up to move out of town."

"Well, don't beat yourself up, Dev. Seeing that Allison piece of work and then hearing about the move, it maybe answers a lot of your questions."

"Yeah, it would have been nice to hear it from Taffy, but I guess that doesn't really matter now. I need to get back to work on these cold cases anyway. This just clears my calendar and gives me more time to focus on the things that count."

"You feel like heading over to The Spot?"

I pressed the button on my cellphone. It was 10:35 in the morning. "Maybe just a little too early for me. Besides, I'm not sure it would really be the right thing to do just now."

"Yeah, I get it. I'm heading down to the courthouse. Let me know if you decide to go anywhere. I'll be back toward the end of the day."

"Thanks, Louie. Hey, good luck in court."

"Never enough of that," he said and left the office. I just sat there and thought and then thought some more.

Forty-one

My phone rang toward the end of the afternoon. Taffy. Gee, this should be fun.

"Hello, Taffy, and just how is your day going?"

"Dev, I just got off the phone with Allison. You told her she had germs? Told her she wasn't a lady?"

"Yeah, and I was being nice."

"Why would you do that? She's my friend, Dev."

"Did she happen to mention what she said to me?"

"I know she went to your office to nicely see if she couldn't get you to calm down. To not take offense. To not just walk out of my—"

"Nicely? The first thing she did was call me a piece of crap and Louie a fat ass. And by the way, she gave me the Kansas City update."

"Oh, umm, well, I was going to tell you at the proper time, but I didn't think last night was it."

"Taffy, it didn't bother you that Allison, your unannounced visitor, sat down and ate my steak? Then, complained because it wasn't done to her liking."

"Dev, she's just a little— Look, I know, I know. But her world has been turned upside down and now, right side up. She's been dating a guy, and she really likes him. They've had four dates, and everything was going absolutely wonderful, and then she doesn't hear from him."

"Sounds to me like he came to his senses."

"You're right, he did. He called her last night. He's got something special planned. Told her he just needed time to think and that he wanted to take their relationship to the next step."

"Meaning what, she can disappoint him in bed, too?"

"There, you see. And is that all you think about?"

"So he's taking her to McDonald's?"

"Honest to God, Dev. No, he's arranged a special date. He's picking her up tonight, once he gets back to town."

"Once he gets back to town. Where is he?"

"I don't know. Something to do with whatever business he's in."

"You mean he travels for his business?"

"Well, yeah, what did you think I meant?"

"How did she meet this guy?"

"That's so not important, Dev. The important thing is that tonight—"

"Did she meet him on Match.com?"

"Now I know what you're thinking, but just stop. A lot of people meet their one and only online. Maybe it's time to update to the new century, Dev. We're not living in the 1950s anymore. Not everyone goes to The Spot to find a partner."

"That's not why I go to The Spot, Taffy. Just tell me, does this guy have a beard?"

"How did you know that?"

"Is he in the book business?"

"Oh, if you know him, don't you dare call him."

"Call him? It sounds like the serial killer I've been investigating. This is exactly what he does, Taffy. He has a few dates with women, and just when they're getting all excited and thinking they may have found a nice guy, he stops contacting them for a week or two. The little we know is that he's a guy with a beard, who travels for business, and he does something with books."

"Does something with books? You mean he designs book covers? Does he sell textbooks to colleges? Or does he just read books?"

"I don't know what, exactly, he does with them, but—"

"Oh, and he has a beard. Dev, I could look out the window right now and probably see a couple of guys with beards. Hang on a minute. I'm just going to run downstairs and ask if any of them are dating Allison. Really?"

"Taffy, give me Allison's phone number, and I'll call her. At least let me warn her."

"Are you crazy? Oh yeah, after calling her all those names this morning, that's what you're going to do? Warn her? Things are finally back on track for her, so you want to ruin it. I'm sorry, Dev. I shouldn't have wasted my time. Goodbye." Click.

There was no point in calling her back. She wouldn't answer. I placed a call to Aaron LaZelle, and ended up leaving a message. "Aaron, it's Dev. I think I might have just caught a break in the cold case. Call me back as soon as possible."

Aaron returned my call five minutes later. "Aaron, thanks for calling back."

"What'd you learn?"

I went on to tell him what I'd learned from Taffy. "Wait a minute. This Allison character, is this the same woman you were bitching about the other day? The one who was inserting herself between you and Taffy?"

"Yeah, and she's been dating some guy with a beard who travels and does something with books. I'm willing to bet she's been seeing Virgil Hayes. She's head over heels about this guy. It's the perfect setup, Aaron. This is how Hayes has gotten all these women in the past. He stops contacting them, and then when they're feeling down and desperate, he suddenly reappears for a night they'll never forget."

"Well, there you go, problem solved. And here we are, not going after the guy because his fingerprints have never been found at any one of the crime scenes. Have never been found on any of the victims. His DNA has never been found on anything, anywhere. Let me give you some advice, Dev. Do not, I repeat, do not attempt to confront or threaten Mr. Hayes in any way, shape, or form. Should you do so, I will be only too happy to bring the full weight of the law down on you."

"Aaron, you're not listening. This is the guy. This is—"

"No, Dev, you're not listening. Virgil Hayes is not the serial killer. We have checked him out backward and forwards. He is not involved."

"Then how did he know so much information about the last murder and then publish it all in his book before the murder was even committed? You saw the publishing date. He—"

"Dev, that was a typo by the publishing company. They confirmed that fact. We've been over all of this too many times to count. Anything else?"

"So, you're not going to check him out?"

"Were you listening? He's been checked out, Dev, too many times to count. Now, I'm warning you as a friend. Do not go near Virgil Hayes. You're dead wrong."

Forty-two

I knew I was right. I was parked on Randolph Avenue, three houses away from Virgil Hayes's place. From where my car was, I could see his garage and any traffic going up and down the alley. I just needed to wait until he drove home with Allison after their 'special date.' Special all right, talk about a night to remember. I'd been parked out here for the past three hours, since half-past six. He had to be bringing her back soon. I considered the possibility of drugging her at the restaurant, but that didn't seem to match the circumstances of the previous murders. No, his home was the most likely place.

He'd drive her back here to his house for a 'nightcap.' There was an awfully big part of me that thought more than once it would be a better idea to let him go through with the murder and nail him after he'd removed Allison from the general population, but I'd probably feel at least a little bit guilty if I did that, maybe.

A little after ten, I was beginning to wonder if this was such a good idea. Fifteen minutes later, with nothing happening, I climbed out of my car, shoved the Glock 19 into the back of my belt, and cut across three front yards and up onto the front stoop of Virgil Hayes's house. There was a light coming from the room off to the right, the room with the fireplace. I rang the doorbell twice. A moment later, the light in the entryway came on, and the front door opened.

A clean-shaven man with curly salt and pepper hair answered the door. He had a questioning look on his face. The guy was an older version of the online image of Virgil Hayes. Maybe it was his father or an older brother.

"Yes?"

"I'm sorry to bother you so late. I'm with the Saint Paul Police is Mr. Hayes in? Virgil Hayes?"

"I'm Virgil Hayes. What seems to be the problem?"

"Mr. Hayes," I said, pulling the Glock out of my belt and shoving it in his face. "The jig is up. Where is she?"

His eyes went wide, his hands went up, and he moved backward as I stepped into the house. "What? What? What are you talking about? I don't know what you mean."

"You think I'm kidding? I'm looking for Allison. I know all about it. I gotta say, you're a hell of a lot more patient than me. Now, where is she?"

"Look, mister, I don't know who, or what, you're talking about. I don't know anyone by the name of Addison."

"Not Addison, you knucklehead, Allison. Where is she?"

"I don't know her, either. I'm afraid you're making a big mistake."

"No, you're the one who's made a mistake. Think you could get away with it again? This time, we got you. Now, where in the hell is she?"

"Look, mister, honest. I don't know what you're talking about. I've been home all night reading in my living room. I can show you. I've just been—"

"Don't bullshit me. You told her you were gonna pick her up for a special date once you got back in town this afternoon. You think I don't know what you've been up to?"

"I don't mean to question you, sir, honest, especially with that gun in my face, but I really don't know what you're talking about. I've been home all week."

"Then answer me this. How come you phoned her and told her you'd pick her up when you got back in town?"

"I didn't phone anyone. It wasn't me who called this woman, honest. What? Is she your wife? A girlfriend? I don't know anything about this. Like I said, I've been home all night. Honestly, my car is in the shop. It's getting detailed, and they're going to bring it back to me tomorrow morning. Really, I've been in the living room reading a book all evening. I had a glass of wine. I went online to check my sales for the day. That's it. Please, you have to believe me."

"Your car isn't here?"

"No, sir. They picked it up around four this afternoon, and they'll be bringing it back tomorrow morning. You can even check the garage."

"But then how were you going to pick her up?"

"Pick who up? Honest, sir, I don't know what you're talking about, and maybe, if you wouldn't mind, you could get that gun out of my face. You're making me awfully nervous."

"You're Virgil Hayes, the book guy, right?"

"Yes, and this is my house."

"Well, just when did you shave that beard?"

"My beard? I haven't had a beard in six, no wait, I think eight years."

Shit. "But the picture I saw of you online, you had a beard."

"The picture? You mean my author site? I write books, by the way. Did you read one of my books and think I have something to do with the woman who broke up with you?"

"Oh, believe me, this woman didn't break up with me."

"But then why are you here, sir? And maybe if you could lower that gun, please. Umm, would you like a beer or a glass of wine?"

"What are you drinking?" I said as I lowered my Glock. Things had suddenly gone very wrong.

"Like I told you, I'm having a glass of wine. Come on into the living room. Is it okay if I lead the way?"

"Please," I said as I shoved the Glock back in my belt.

Forty-three

Hayes led the way into his living room. Classical music was playing. A half-empty wine glass rested on a small round table next to a brown leather recliner. A Kindle rested on the chair. Hayes took a crystal wine glass from a cabinet and poured wine from a decanter into the glass.

"It's a Pinot from the Sonoma Valley," he said and handed me the glass. I didn't comment. "So, you read one of my books?"

"Actually, I've read them all. I'm somewhat familiar with the series of local cases that your books seem to be based on."

"Oh, yeah, the serial murders. I based my books on those cases, changed some names, and obviously surmised a lot, but there's a common thread throughout the series. As far as I know, no one has ever been arrested. I was loosely involved some years back, gave the police a list of what I thought the killer might be like, personality-wise. Don't know that they ever put it to use. I know I was a suspect at some point. They searched my house here. I used to have a lake place up in St. Louis County. They went through that a couple of times as well. To tell you the truth, I used their interest in me as one of my marketing ploys. It's one of the reasons I made it onto the best sellers list, well, that and my interview with Oprah Winfrey. Never enough of those," he said and shook his head.

"You said you're with the police?"

"Not exactly. I'm a private investigator, and I've been looking into the cases, going over the case files. Hoping a new pair of eyes might pick up on something. I'm really sorry, Mr. Hayes."

"Please, call me, Virgil. The Mr. sounds like you're talking to my dad."

"Okay, I'm, umm, really sorry, Virgil. My name is Dev Haskell. A woman I know seemed to fit the pattern of the victims in your books and in all the cold cases. I've interviewed a number of the victims' acquaintances. I've gone over the photos of where the bodies were found. I'm just the latest guy to try and put together what few clues there are."

"Tell me about them."

"Well, you probably know them yourself. It appears the victims meet this guy on Match.com. They have three or four dates, and just when they think things are really about to take off, he doesn't call them for a week or two. Then he's suddenly back on the scene with the promise of a super night out, and that's the last thing anyone seems to know."

"The guy apparently travels for business. He's supposed to have a beard. He's very good looking, very nice, oh, and he does something with books. But it's all such general information. Even the book thing, people have suggested the guy could be an accountant, or he collects coloring books, or that maybe he works in a bookstore."

"Well, all that used to describe me. I don't travel much anymore, at least nothing like five or six years back. I haven't had a beard in years. I'm not all that good looking, if I ever was. About all I do is still write books."

"But in your last book, you seemed to have information in it that was accurate, and the book was published before the actual murder was committed."

"Mmm, well, part of that was an error. The publication date listed had a typo. Instead of being published in 2019 like the book states, it was actually published in 2020. February of 2020, to be exact."

"Yeah, but there was some very precise information. Madeline Long was the victim."

"Oh, yes, she was murdered in May of 2019. I'll let you in on a little secret. My editor was a premed student, but for whatever reason, he didn't continue that line of study. He's given me all sorts of tips, suggestions, and ideas to make my stories that much more believable. I wouldn't be where I am today without his input. So I use what I know of the murder investigation as my general outline, and he helps me fill in the blanks, makes the story believable."

"Can you give me an example?"

“Sure, one of the common traits in all the killings is the use of a leather ligature. I originally had the victims handcuffed or tied with a rope. I think, in the first book, I actually had the victim tied to the dining room table with her hosiery. He suggested the leather bondage gear. It leaves the same marks on the wrists and ankles of all the victims, which links the murders together and has been a great way to link the books in the series. Whoever the killer is, he’s toying with the police. I have my chief protagonist doing that as well. It’s why all the victims in my books are wearing a white slip and a wedding veil, and the bodies are found in the public parks. It’s a personality trait of serial killers. They believe they’re above the fray, will never be caught. And, the fact that no one has been charged in the killings here would seem to serve as a reinforcement of that thought process.”

“Think about it for a minute, Dev. Anyone can purchase leather restraints, a nylon slip, and a wedding veil. The stuff is virtually untraceable. It all adds to the tension. Same things with the book titles, One after Midnight, Two after Midnight, not only are they easy to remember, but the titles create an immediate tension. Even if you haven’t read one of my books, it’s automatic that you’re thinking of a series of murders. It’s genius, pure genius, and all due to my editor. In fact, Jeremy suggested I have the murder happen at that exact time, one minute after midnight, two minutes after. It would dovetail nicely with the titles, but I think it wasn’t until after the third book that he made the suggestion, and I thought it was too late in the series to start that. Still an excellent idea."

"Does he happen to live here in town, your editor."

"Oh yeah, we see one another a number of times in any week. He's been traveling for the last three or four days. He does a lot of that. But I believe he was flying in sometime this afternoon. He'll be over tomorrow to review my past week's work."

"What's his name?"

"Jeremy, Jeremy Corwin. Why? Are you thinking of maybe writing a book?"

"Do you know if he's dating a woman named Allison?"

A strange look washed over Virgil's face. "Why, yes, as a matter of fact, he is. Do you know her? I met her the other day, wanted to have me sign a book. I don't mean to offend, but she is not the type of woman he should be with. In the two or three minutes we spoke, she struck me as highly narcissistic. Obviously, I have an interest in Jeremy's mental health, and having a woman like that in your life would not be good. I just need to find the right time to take him aside and—"

"Virgil, does Jeremy have a beard?"

"Oh, yeah, he's quite good looking and very fashionable. He's constantly getting a second and third look from women wherever we go. If we meet somewhere for lunch or dinner, it would not be unusual for some woman to slip him their phone number. More than once they've attempted to strike up a conversation if we're out for a drink. Amazingly, he was left at the altar. The woman he was going to marry literally ran out of the church, and there he was, left standing in a tux with his best man in front of a hundred and fifty family and friends. A lesser man might never recover, but Jeremy—"

"Virgil, he's the guy."

"What?"

"The serial killer, the beard, he travels, he's involved with books, and now that story. Virgil, he's the killer."

"What? Dev, you'd better put that wine down. You've obviously had enough. That's impossible. Jeremy is—"

"You said it yourself. Jeremy knows all sorts of inside tips, like the leather restraints. You said he was pre-med, so he'd know a bit about drugging someone with Rohypnol. That's how he was able to adjust your books to list things only the police and the killer would know, and now, that wedding story. God, he's the killer, Virgil."

"That's preposterous, with all due respect, I'm afraid you've jumped from one crazy thought to—"

"Virgil, the reason I'm here is because of the woman I know named Allison. A woman I do not like. I believe she's being set up as the next victim, and if I'm right, she's going to be murdered tonight, maybe even at seven minutes after midnight. Just tell me where Jeremy lives. I'll, I'll leave the gun here with you, but please, let me just go there. The worst that will happen is that I'll become a laughingstock, and this woman will hate me even more, if that's possible. But do you really want to take the chance that I'm wrong? Suddenly, all the broad descriptions of the killer seem to be pointing right at your friend, Jeremy Corwin."

Hayes seemed to think about that for a long moment. "I tell you what. You leave the gun here, and I'll go with you. I have a key to his unit. It's my ex-wife's condo, and he rents from me."

"Thank you, thank you, thank you," I said and handed him my Glock 19. He took it and pointed it at me. "Virgil, what the hell are you doing?"

"Just letting you know how not very fun it is to have one of these pointed at you." He said, then stepped over to the fireplace and set the Glock on the mantel. "Let's go. Is your car parked out back?"

"No, it's over on Randolph," I said, and we headed for the front door. We ran across the three front yards to Randolph and then across the street.

Virgil slowed down as he approached my Taurus. "Really, this is what you're driving?"

"Yeah, hop in. I'm having the detailing done tomorrow," I said as I climbed behind the wheel.

As Virgil jumped in, he kicked a beer can out from under the seat. "Why am I even surprised? The condo is back down on Randolph, just before you get to Hamline Avenue."

“That five-story red-brick building that looks like it was built a hundred years ago?”

“Yep, that’s the one. I think it’s only twenty-five years old. After our divorce, I purchased it with the idea that my ex would live there for a few years, and once she moved out, I could move in. She moved out after a year and a half. At the same time, my books started taking off, so I rented it out. Jeremy was doing my editing, and it just seemed natural that he’d move in. None of my books would have done half as well without Jeremy’s input.”

I sped through the Cleveland Avenue intersection and up the small hill past Saint Catherine’s University.

“I honestly hope I’m wrong, and the two of you can laugh at me and call me an idiot. But it all suddenly seems to make sense. The cops never asked you about him?”

“When they were interviewing me, it never occurred to me to mention him. I, I was taking their interest as a compliment. I’ve used the story of their interviews and searching my home and lake place as a marketing tool. You’d be surprised how well it’s worked.”

We sailed through the Fairview intersection on a yellow light.

“You might want to watch your speed here, Dev. There’s usually a police presence somewhere along this section.” I backed off the accelerator and dropped down to forty miles per hour. Still fifteen over the limit.

The light at Snelling Avenue turned red when I was still a half-block away. I slowed to a stop as cars passed in front of us. The light seemed to take forever to change. I began rolling forward as the light turned yellow for opposing traffic.

"Damn it, will you just wait five seconds before you get the both of us killed?" Hayes shouted.

"Okay, okay, I'm just worried about the time. We have to get there before seven minutes after midnight," I said.

"Which gives us fifty-eight minutes, and I can see the building just two blocks ahead."

I pulled into the visitor's parking lot. There were three other cars in the lot. None of them were Allison's Lexus. We hurried into the building's lobby.

"Let me do the talking," Virgil said and hurried to the security intercom. He pushed the button, and we waited, then waited some more.

"Push it again," I said.

"I've got a better idea," Virgil said and pulled a set of keys out of his pocket.

Forty-four

Virgil unlocked the security door and hurried to the elevator. As we entered, he pushed the button for the fourth floor. It seemed to take forever to get up to the fourth floor, and all the while, Virgil kept saying, "Come on, come on, come on," as the elevator slowly rose. Once the doors opened, he hurried into the hall. "The unit is down here to the left." I had to run a few steps to catch up to him.

Jeremy Corwin's unit was number four twenty and almost at the end of a very long hall. At this hour on a weeknight, the floor was extremely quiet. Virgil's pounding on the door reverberated back down the hallway. "Jeremy, open up. Jeremy, it's me, Virgil. Jeremy." He pounded again, this time even louder.

I heard a door open down the hall, and someone leaned out. As I turned around to look, whoever it was ducked back inside, closed the door, and then snapped the lock in place.

Virgil pounded on the door again. "Jeremy, open up. It's me, Virgil. Jeremy, open—"

"Virgil?" a muffled voice said from the other side of the door.

"Yes. Open up, Jeremy. Please."

"It's umm, late, and I'm just back in town. I'll call you tomorrow, and we—"

Virgil gave me a frustrated look and shook his head. "Jeremy, I need to see you now. Please. Open. The. Door."

"I just need some privacy tonight, Virgil. Let's talk tomorrow and—"

Virgil inserted his key in the lock, turned it, and pushed the door open. The door moved about six inches before it stopped, and Jeremy yelled, "Virgil, what the hell are you doing? I'll see you tomorrow. Do not come in. I want my privacy." He began to force the door closed, even though Virgil was attempting to keep it open. I leaned in, started pushing, and between the two of us, we began to open the door wide enough to step inside.

As Virgil stepped into the condo, Jeremy backed up, letting go of the door. I suddenly stumbled forward, and the door slammed into the wall with a bang.

"Virgil, what are you doing here? And who in the hell is this?" Jeremy said, pointing at me.

"He's a friend. Dev Haskell. He's a private investigator."

Jeremy's eyes widened, and he whispered, "Shit. Virgil, I'm just trying to get some sleep. Can't whatever it is wait until tomorrow morning?"

"Get some sleep? Dressed like that?" Virgil asked.

For his part, Jeremy was indeed handsome. Very handsome, with a neatly trimmed full beard, dark curly hair, and dark-blue eyes. He was about my height and appeared to be in fairly good physical condition. At the moment, he was dressed in very tight black leather pants, a leather vest with four brass buttons, and a black tuxedo coat with a white carnation.

We were standing in the corner of a vast living room. A gas fireplace was going. There was a couch, two chairs, and a coffee table in front of the fireplace. Beyond the chairs was a sliding double door that led out to a porch. Behind Jeremy was the kitchen. The lights were on, and what looked like a champagne bottle and two crystal champagne flutes rested on the granite-topped counter.

Jeremy took a breath and said, “I’m afraid I’m going to have to ask both of you to leave, Virgil. I don’t know what this is all about, but I want both of you out of here, now.”

“Jeremy, just what in the hell are you doing? For Christ’s sake, we were a team, a business, damn it. What in the hell is going on here?” Virgil said and headed toward the kitchen. Jeremy grabbed him by his shirt, spun him around, and sent him sailing across the dining room table. Virgil took a silver candelabra and two chairs on the far side of the table with him.

Jeremy’s back faced me for a second, and I kicked him as hard as I could in the small of his back just as he began to turn. He went down on all fours. He half-turned toward me just as the toe of my shoe caught him in the mouth. He rolled on his side, and I kicked him again. I grabbed the chair at the end of the dining room table and slammed it into his head just as Virgil came around and stopped me from hitting him again.

Virgil was bleeding from his nose and the corner of his mouth. "See if you can find her. The bedrooms are down the hall," he said, pointing past the kitchen.

I hurried down the hall and opened the door to what looked like the master bedroom. There was a fourposter bed with a folded quilt on a bench at the foot of the bed. A TV rested on the chest of drawers against the near wall. Two sets of double closet doors and a door leading into a bathroom were at the far end of the room. Nothing in the room appeared to suggest Allison.

I opened the next door, a small office with a desk and a desktop computer. The third room was dark, and I fumbled on the wall for the light switch. My feet stepped on something that seemed to crackle as I turned on the light.

The floor of the room was covered in heavy plastic, as was the bed where Allison lay. Her ankles and arms were bound to the corners of the metal bed frame with black leather restraints. She was dressed just like the previous victims in a white nylon slip with a wedding veil on her head. Her eyes appeared unfocused, but her head slowly moved from side to side, so she was still alive.

"Allison. Hey, Allison," I said, approaching slowly. Her chest rose as she took in a deep breath. I placed two fingers on her neck to check her pulse. It was slow, but it felt regular. I pulled out my phone and called 911. I ran into the master bedroom, took the quilt from the bench, and quickly covered her. I removed the leather restraints from her legs and arms. Although her ankles and wrists were red, they didn't appear to be bruised. She didn't have the ligature marks yet that I'd seen in the photos of previous victims.

I hurried back out to the living room with the leather restraints. Jeremy was in the process of sitting up with his back against the wall and his head resting on his knees. Virgil was standing a few feet away, holding a checkered towel pressed up against his nose. He held a large kitchen knife in his left hand. "Well?" he said from behind the kitchen towel.

"She's in there, drugged. I called 911. Can you call them and give them the address? I only told them the intersection. Once I get him secured, I'll go down and let them in."

"Let me have your phone," he said, taking it from my hand and punching in 911.

As Virgil talked on the phone, I took Jeremy by a handful of hair and dragged him across the floor toward the couch. "Ouch, hey, ouch, ouch, stop it. You're hurting me," he half-shouted as he attempted to crawl along behind me. I slammed his head into the front of a credenza a few times along the way. I wrapped the restraints around Jeremy's wrists and tied them to the corner legs on the couch, basically setting him up in a crucifixion position on the floor. "You so much as move, and I'll break both your arms. So help me."

"She wanted me to—" I kicked him in his side. "Uff," was the only sound he made.

"They're on the way," Virgil said. "You check on the girl. I'll buzz them in."

As I went back to check on Allison, I heard a distant siren. She seemed okay, still breathing and the slow heartbeat. "You hang in there, Allison. Taffy needs a friend. You're okay, and you're safe. You hear me? You're safe, Allison. You're—"

"You want to step back, sir, and we'll take care of this. Are you okay? That's it. Just move back, sir. Thank you, we got this," the EMT said. They were checking out Allison, and before I knew what was happening, they had her on a gurney with an oxygen mask on her face and were rolling her out of the condo.

Virgil was sitting on the couch with his head tilted back while an EMT was dabbing at his nose. "It looks like your nose is broken," she said.

I looked past Virgil, but Jeremy wasn't lying on the floor with his arms attached to the couch.

"Where is he? Where the hell did he go?"

"He's being escorted down to the police station, sir," the EMT said, still focused on Virgil's nose.

Two guys in suits suddenly entered the condo. They looked familiar, but at the moment, I could barely remember my name, let alone theirs. "He had her restrained on the bed in that last room down the hall," I said to the guy in a gray suit.

"You okay, Dev? You don't look so good."

"I'm fine, I, I think."

"Come on into the kitchen, and let's get you seated," he said and led me into the kitchen. Two uniformed cops were in there, one of them reporting to someone on the phone from the sound of it. I sat down at the counter and noticed the pink purse with the gold chain lying next to a toaster. All the contents were piled on the counter in front of the purse; a set of keys, two eyeshadows, three lipsticks, two pens, a billfold, prophylactics, a perfume spray, a visa card, and coins. The coins were neatly stacked, three quarters, two nickels, two dimes, and seven pennies. The oven was on, and a pizza, still wrapped, sat next to the stove.

A glass of water was suddenly placed in front of me. I looked up and recognized detective Andretta in the gray suit. "Oh, thanks. Nothing stronger?" I half-joked.

"You just sit here and take it easy, Dev. We're going to check out the room."

More cops seemed to be coming into the unit. I had moved into the living room at some point and was looking out a window. Virgil had been taken outside to an ambulance maybe a half-hour ago, but it was still in the parking lot, and I figured they were just keeping an eye on him.

"How are you holding up?" a familiar voice said behind me. I turned and looked at Aaron LaZelle. "You doing okay, Dev?" he said and placed an arm on my shoulder.

"Yeah, I'm fine, Aaron. Thanks. You guys have this bastard locked up?"

"No, but he will be. I just checked. He's still at Regions Hospital. Broken rib, broken nose, apparently missing a couple of teeth. Thank God, you two got here in time. Jesus Christ, I can't believe it."

"Looks like we were both kind of right. It wasn't Virgil Hayes but damn close. Virgil's down in that ambulance in the parking lot. Corwin tossed him across the dining room table."

"Yeah, I talked to him. He said you saved his life."

I shook my head. "I'm just glad we got this guy. Any news on the girl, Allison?"

"Allison Dankwell? They've got her on an IV right now. He gave her Rohypnol, but they're expecting a full recovery. They'll probably keep her through tomorrow night just to be sure, but she should be okay."

"Did he assault her?"

"You mean, rape her? No, but I'd say you two interrupted his plans. Thirty minutes later, and who knows, he probably would have killed her. He'd be busy arranging her body in some park right about now. Instead, he's handcuffed to a hospital bed with two officers watching him. He'll be locked up later this morning."

"Just take him out and shoot him," I said.

"If only it would be that easy. You stay here. I'm just going to check on the crime scene crew. Thanks for this, Dev. If it weren't for you and Virgil Hayes, well…"

Forty-five

Jeremy Corwin was charged later that afternoon. Virgil Hayes was mentioned in every news reports for the next few days, me not so much. Because of Virgil's Past Midnight book series, the news reports went viral across the US. Twenty-four-hours later, he had a two-minute trailer out there on YouTube, advertising the book series and showing the headlines from major newspapers around the country. There was even talk of a movie deal and multiple film companies competing for the rights.

I was in a bit of a fog for the next few days. I never left the house, and Louie kept the reporters at bay for twenty-four hours before they completely disappeared. I eventually felt like I was getting back to normal, whatever that was. I rolled out of bed a little after nine and hit the shower. Louie had let Morton out in the backyard an hour earlier.

"Well, he has risen, finally," Louie said as I walked into the kitchen. "Oh, wow, showered and shaved. Good to have you back, Dev."

"Yeah, thanks for looking out for me."

"You'd do the same for me. How about some French toast with maple syrup? God knows you could use the sweetening."

"Sounds good." I settled onto a kitchen stool as Louie turned on the stove.

We chatted while the scent of French toast filled the kitchen. My stomach growled in response. Louie noticed me eyeing the empty fifth of Jameson sitting on the kitchen counter. "Oh, yeah, I meant to tell you. You're out of Jameson."

"I'll get more today. After breakfast, I want to give Ben Jackson a call, then head over and see him. I should have done it three days ago."

"If you'd shown up there three days ago, they would have put you in the psychiatric care unit. You were in no shape to go around visiting people, Dev. It's good to have you back with us, man."

"You already said that."

He slid a plate with three pieces of French toast across the kitchen counter and said, "Here you go. Don't talk with your mouth full."

I phoned Ben Jackson after breakfast, and Gretchen answered.

"Hi Gretchen, Dev Haskell, can I talk to Ben, please?"

"Dev, I'm afraid he can't take a call. He's been in and out of consciousness for the last two days. They're saying a week at the longest."

"Oh, Gretchen, I'm so sorry. Would it be, I mean, could I maybe stop by? I promise I won't stay long."

"I think that would be nice, Dev. But the sooner, the better."

"I'll be there shortly," I said and disconnected.

"That didn't sound so good," Louie said.

"He's really slipped. They're giving him a week. Damn it. I should have called sooner."

"Quit beating yourself up, Dev. You couldn't call him. Go on, get over there now. I'm going to clean up the kitchen. Then I'm going to head down to the office. Stop in later if you feel like it."

I headed over to the Care Center. Gretchen answered the door after I knocked. She looked nice in navy-blue slacks, a sky-blue blouse, and a string of pearls. Her hair had recently been done. "Oh, Dev, thank you so much for coming. Ben is in the bedroom. The last few days, he's just slipped. Yesterday's low point is today's high."

"How are you doing, Gretchen?"

"Me? Oh, I'll be fine. Too busy seeing to Ben's needs to worry about myself. There'll be plenty of time for that later. Oh, this is my sister, Suzanne," she said as a woman stepped out of the kitchen area, holding two mugs of coffee. "Suzanne, this is Dev Haskell. He's the one in the paper."

"Oh, it's nice to meet you. So, you write books?"

"No, that was the other guy."

"Here, Dev, let me take you to Ben. Back in a moment, Suzi."

Gretchen led me into the bedroom. Ben was asleep or maybe unconscious. He was in a hospital bed with railings up on both sides. The bed was partially raised. Although it was warm in the room, a blanket was pulled up to his shoulders. His arms were out over the blanket, clutching the copied pages of Lucia Ruiz's journal. A blurry US Navy tattoo was on his right forearm. He looked even more pale, thin, and frail than the last time I saw him. A box of latex gloves sat on a bedside table next to him.

"Is he ever conscious?" I half-whispered.

"Not in the past two days. They said maybe a week, but I think it's going to be much sooner than that. I'll give you a couple of minutes. Go ahead and say something to him. I think he hears it."

"Thanks, Gretchen," I said as she closed the door on her way out of the room.

"Well, Ben, you did it. You got us to close the case." I gave him a short version of the arrest. Virgil Hayes unlocking the door and Jeremy Corwin standing before us dressed in black leather and a tuxedo jacket with a white carnation. Allison barely conscious, strapped to the bed in a white slip and wedding veil. "He's already pled guilty to the kidnapping and attempted murder charge. The District Attorney is going to charge him with the six murders. He'll be going away for life. Couldn't have done it without your help, Ben." I placed my hand over his and squeezed slightly. “We got this guy, thanks to you, Ben. You take care now. I’ll catch up with you soon enough. God bless.”

Forty-Six

Taffy had packed her bags and was indeed moving to Kansas City. The day after I saw Ben Jackson, we had lunch at the restaurant across the street from my place. I was thinking, you know, just in case we might want one final, memorable, 'good-bye' we could sneak over to my place. That didn't happen. She was already too focused on running the Kansas City office. In fact, she responded to three work text messages over the course of our one-hour lunch.

We politely kissed good-bye. I wished her well and had the impression she couldn't wait to get to her car. Thankfully, she never mentioned Allison, although I knew Virgil Hayes had gotten a thank you note from her. He told me he promised her a part in the movie if it was ever made. I never heard anything from her, and frankly, that was just fine with me.

Ben Jackson passed away two days later. His funeral was a formal affair with uniformed officers, a bagpiper, and an overflowing crowd in the church. The Mayor, Chief of Police, and all sorts of dignitaries were in attendance. I stood a few feet away from Gretchen at the graveside service. Afterward, I recognized a number of the people I'd interviewed giving Gretchen condolences and thanking her for Ben's continued investigation. Virgil Hayes was there, and we chatted briefly. He was anxious to get back to writing the final book in the series. Following the graveside service, there was a celebration of Ben Jackson's life at the Lexington Restaurant, a place that would have been a popular hangout for Ben and Gretchen's generation. I went but only stayed for a short while.

On the way home I heard a news report that Allison had signed a movie deal with some big wig in Hollywood. The perfect ending to a lousy day.

Forty-Seven

We were sitting at the end of the bar on our usual stools in The Spot. Louie and I were trading stories. It was nice to be back to being my old boring self. Morton was at my feet, and Louie occasionally reached down and fed him a couple of pork rinds. Mike had graciously promised me one free beer every day for a month, and I was just finishing today's freebie when a red-headed woman stepped in the front door and looked around. She was attractive, and I pegged her as being in her early thirties. There were maybe only a dozen people in the place, and four of them were women sitting in a booth. I figured that's where she was headed, but instead, she focused in on Louie and me and hurried over in our direction.

"Excuse me, are you Dev Haskell?"

I immediately ran through a list of recent screw-ups and wondered what I might have done to offend her.

"You're the guy who saved that woman from the serial killer?"

"Yeah, that's me."

"I just wanted to thank you and tell you how much I really appreciate what you did. We all do. My name is

Nancy Bruner. I worked with Maddie Long. You called a while back and left a message. I purposely ignored your call. I'm sorry. I just couldn't bear to go through that whole situation one more time. I know I should have called you back. It was stupid not to. I'm really sorry."

"Oh, look, believe me, I get it. It's very nice of you to say so, but don't worry. It's no big deal. I'm just glad the whole thing is over."

She nodded and said, "Could I buy you a beer? I'd really like to get to know you better."

The End

Thank you for taking the time to read **Cold Case.** If you enjoyed the read please consider leaving a review, it really, really helps. Thanks in advance . . .

Check out this sample of **Cash Up Front**, the next book in the Dev Haskell series.

Sneak Peek

Cash Up Front

Second Edition

MIKE FARICY

Prologue

The waiter wore a black tux and latex gloves. He smiled, turned off the gas torch, and handed a white ramekin with crème brûlée to Heidi and one to me. He said something to Heidi in French. She smiled and said, "No, Merci," and he left.

With my spoon, I tapped the melted sugar top he had just torched. It sounded like I was tapping the countertop. Crème brûlée, I loved the stuff." What did the waiter ask you?"

"He wanted to know if I'd go home with him tonight."

My eyes grew wide. I held my spoon in midair, about an inch from my mouth. "What? He really asked that?"

Heidi rolled her eyes and said, "Yeah, right, Dev. Get the hook out of your mouth."

She was wearing an exquisite blue silk dress with spaghetti straps, tight, low cut, and wonderfully short. This week, her hair was dark and gorgeous, straight and curving around her jawline. She looked like she'd just stepped out of a fashion magazine." Well, you are the most beautiful woman in the place."

"Mmm-mmm, aren't you just playing all your cards right tonight."

"Hey, it's your birthday, and by the way, I meant what I said. You are the most beautiful woman in this place." Social distancing was in effect. Tables were about ten feet apart. No tables seated more than four people. The waiters in this top-notch restaurant were wearing tuxedos, latex gloves, and face masks.

She took another spoonful of crème brûlée and got an almost orgasmic look on her face. "Oh, God help me, but I could eat a dozen of these."

"If you want another one, I'll order it."

"Oh, thanks, but I'd better not. I need to behave."

"Behave?"

"Don't worry, Dev. Relax, you'll get your reward before the night is over. This has been the most wonderful night. Thank you for making it so special."

"Like I said, it's your birthday, and you threatened me within an inch of my life if I got you a gift or a card."

"Sorry, but you know how I get about growing a year older."

"Yeah, I know how you get, just like a fine wine, better with every year. Speaking of which, would you like another glass or maybe an after-dinner drink?"

"Oh, thanks, I would, but not here, maybe once we get back to my place."

I smiled and finished my crème brûlée in six quick scoops of my spoon.

"Dev, slow down. I'm going to take my time here, and then we'll go home and attend to your needs, well, and mine too," she said and smiled.

I eventually paid the tab. Keeping my fingers crossed, my credit card wouldn't be denied. We headed out the door fifteen minutes later. I handed the valet our ticket. He nodded and headed back to the parking lot. As he disappeared, a black stretch-limo suddenly pulled out of the parking lot and stopped in front of us.

"You didn't have to do this," Heidi joked.

My first thought was it must be for someone at a groom's dinner or maybe some high-priced out of town business guy, but then the rear door opened and a muscular guy about six-five, with a shaved head and an S-curved nose stepped out and held the door open. He cleared his throat and coughed.

A voice from the back seat called "Heidi Bauer?"

"Oh my God," Heidi said as she bent over to look in. "Yes?"

"If you wouldn't mind joining me, I'd like to talk to you about an investment."

"Dev? Did you do this?"

I shook my head and looked at the guy with the 'S' curved nose. "No, honest. I don't know what this is about."

"Please, Miss Bauer, this shouldn't take more than twenty minutes or so. I'm sure you'll find my offer very much to your liking. We'll drop you off at home, and you can continue your evening."

"I'm sorry, do I know you?"

"No, at least not yet. My name is Tommy Benedetti. Please, if you wouldn't mind, I'm on a bit of a tight schedule."

"Well, I'm… You see I'm with someone and I really can't meet right—"

"Melvin, if you would please," the voice said.

The middle door suddenly opened, and two guys slid out. One of them had a skull tattoo on his right forearm with the numbers 666 on the forehead of the skull. They took three steps toward Heidi as I stepped in front of her and said, "Heidi, get back in the restaurant and call the—"

The thug with the skull tattoo gave me a quick, solid elbow in the solar plexus and a chop to the back of my neck. I collapsed on my knees, attempting to catch my breath. I looked up just in time to see the stretch-limo make a right turn out of the parking lot. I reached in my pocket for my phone only to remember it was sitting exactly where I left it so I wouldn't forget it, on the corner of my dresser.

I slowly stood, cranked my head left and right, and heard my neck crack a couple of times. A pair of headlights came out of the parking lot, Heidi's red Mercedes. The valet hopped out of the car and held the driver's door for me. I pulled a bill from my pocket and shoved it at him as I hopped behind the wheel. As I accelerated, I glanced over and realized I'd handed him a twenty. Too late to correct that mistake, he grinned and gave me a thumbs-up as I shot out of the parking lot and screeched into a right-hand turn. I raced down University Avenue swerving past everyone driving close to the speed limit. After four miles, it was obvious the stretch limo had turned off somewhere along the way. I swore, slapped the steering wheel a couple of times, slowed down, and headed over to Heidi's house.

One

I pulled in behind my car parked in front of Heidi's house. I ran up to the front door and used her keys to unlock the door. "Heidi. Heidi?" I called, hoping she'd answer. Unfortunately, she didn't. The table lamp next to the front window was on and so were the kitchen lights, just the way we'd left them.

I was standing in the living room, looking out the picture window, sipping my second Jameson. I was cursing myself for not packing a gun. The stretch limo suddenly pulled to a stop, and the same thug with the S-curved nose hopped out of the back and held the door open. Heidi slid out of the limo carrying a metal briefcase just as I hurried out the front door with a carving knife.

"Heidi? Heidi? Are you okay? Heidi?"

The thug gave me an unconcerned glance, nodded at Heidi, and slid back into the limo. The door closed as it sped up the street then turned at the corner and disappeared.

"You okay, Heidi?"

"Yeah, I'm fine, I think. I could use a drink, Dev."

“Come on. Let’s get you inside. What the hell was with those guys? Did they hurt you? Did they—”

Heidi looked at the carving knife in my right hand and said, “Dev, relax, I’m okay. He just wanted to talk, and he gave me these funds for an investment,” she said and held up the metal briefcase. The thing was silver with a black handle, rounded corners, a combination lock, and looked large enough to maybe carry a change of clothes. “Let’s just go inside, please,” she said and headed across the lawn, picking up her pace the closer she got to the front door.

She made her way into the kitchen and set the briefcase on the counter. She washed her hands with the antibacterial hand wash for two or three minutes. All the while, mumbling, “Crazy. Absolutely crazy. He said he was going to invest. Not that he wanted to, but that he was going to. God, I need a drink. This was crazy. Absolutely crazy.”

“You have some wine in the fridge?” I asked, opening the refrigerator door. There were three bottles of white wine and a bottle of prosecco lying on the top shelf.

“I’ve got vodka in the cabinet,” she said and shot another squirt of hand wash into her hand. I went out to the dining room and opened the door to the liquor cabinet. There were three different vodka bottles. I grabbed the bottle of Grey Goose and went back to the kitchen. I took a martini glass out of the cupboard and placed it on the kitchen counter.

"Just a glass and some ice," she said as she did a final rinse of her now sterilized hands.

"Okay, you want some olives or vermouth in—"

"God, never mind, I'll do it myself," she said. She grabbed the bottle out of my hand and poured an inch of vodka into the water glass next to the kitchen sink. She drained the glass and shuddered. "Oh, God," she groaned and cleared her throat. She poured two inches into the glass, grabbed two ice cubes from the freezer, tossed them into the glass then took a somewhat sensible sip.

"Feeling better? Calming down?" I asked.

"I'm not sure."

"What did that guy want? What did he say his name was, Tommy something?"

"Tommy Benedetti. He wanted to invest in Lemax Partners."

"Lemax Partners, isn't that your new fund? The one you were looking for investors?"

She shot me a look. "I'm looking for qualified investors. Not some criminal gangster who throws me into a car, hands me a bunch of cash, and tells me there's more where that came from."

"Well, it sounds like you just got the investment you were looking for. You don't have to like the guy. You just have to take—"

"Don't have to like the guy? Dev, what he's looking for is a fund to launder his illegal profits from whatever criminal enterprise he's involved in. You don't think it's even a little bit strange he obviously followed us and gave me cash as an initial investment?" she raised her chin to indicate the metal briefcase then drained her glass, shuddered, and poured two more inches of vodka into the glass.

"Did you look inside?"

"He showed me. Go ahead and open it. The combination is one, two, three."

"You're kidding," I said, looking at the combination lock. Sure enough, the dials were set in the one, two, three combination mode. I pushed the button, and the lock snapped open. I undid the toggle locks on either end and lifted the lid. The case was filled with bundles of hundred-dollar bills held together with rubber bands, crisp, fresh, hundred-dollar bills. A handwritten, torn piece of paper on each bundle had '$10,000' written on it with a black Sharpie. I counted the bundles. There were twenty. I picked up one of the bundles and fanned it, all hundreds.

"Holy shit. Talk about cash up front. How much is in here, a hundred grand?"

"No, Dev. He said two hundred grand. Two hundred thousand dollars. Remind me not to have you do any accounting for me."

"The guy just gave you two hundred grand?"

"Yes, for an investment in the Lemax Partners fund. I can't think of a faster way to get Federal authorities involved, shut down the fund, and ruin my career and reputation."

"What?"

“Dev, what do you think the odds are he earned this money in some honest way?” she said and drained her vodka glass.

“I guess about zero.”

“Yeah, right. I am so screwed.”

“Can’t you report him or just give it back to him?”

“Oh yeah, sure I can. If I decide to do that, he promised me in no uncertain terms, that I’d be dead within twenty-four hours. He expects to see a ten percent return on his investment.”

“Two thousand bucks?”

She rolled her eyes, “No, Dev, ten percent is twenty thousand dollars,” she said and shook her head. She took two more ice cubes from the freezer, placed them in the glass, and refilled the glass with vodka, spilling some onto the counter. “Oh, shit,” she said, slurring her words slightly.

Two

I woke up on the couch in Heidi's living room just after three to the sound of Heidi getting sick in the bathroom. I knocked on the bathroom door and asked, "Are you okay, Heidi. Can I get you anything?"

"No. I'll, I'll be okay in a little minute. I just need to… Oh God," she groaned and got sick again. Too bad, Grey Goose is a very good vodka. I went into the kitchen, filled a glass with water, got the aspirin bottle out of the cabinet, brought them into her bedroom, and set them on a bedside table. I turned on the light and picked up her blue silk dress from the floor. The zipper in the back was still zipped up, but the fabric had been pulled away from the zipper. One of the spaghetti straps was torn in half. I placed the dress on the bench at the end of her bed then stood next to the bathroom door listening to her groan and cough for another minute or two. So much for romance.

That was enough for me. I went back to the couch, slipped on my shoes, and grabbed the spare key from the key holder next to the back door. I set the metal briefcase underneath the kitchen table, made sure the place was locked up and drove home.

I made coffee for the morning and headed up to bed. Morton was stretched out on my bed, and I had to move him over so I could climb in. I set my alarm and was sound asleep a minute later.

I woke five minutes before my alarm went off, showered, dressed, and headed downstairs. I was on my computer and sipping coffee when I heard Morton jump off the bed. A couple of minutes later, he appeared in the kitchen and headed over to me for his morning scratch behind the ears. I let him outside, filled his food and water dish, and scrambled some eggs for myself. After breakfast, we got in the car and drove down to the office. I made a fresh pot of coffee, left a message for Louie, and headed over to Heidi's.

Thankfully, the place was still locked up. I quietly opened the door, checked on Heidi sound asleep in bed with an empty saucepan next to her, and went into the kitchen. I made a pot of coffee, plugged in my computer, and went online. I heard Heidi turning on the shower maybe an hour later. I arranged some breakfast items on the kitchen counter while she was in the shower. Nothing fancy, bread for toast and grape jelly. I set some eggs out but didn't think she'd want any. It had been at least a decade since I'd seen her as drunk as she was last night. It had been a forty-eight-hour recovery ten years ago. It would be interesting to see how she would do now.

I grabbed her untouched water glass and the bottle of aspirin from the bedside table and set them on the kitchen counter. Heidi entered the kitchen a half-hour later dressed in a light blue terrycloth bathrobe that was calf-length and cinched tightly around her waist. She sat on a stool at the kitchen counter. I pushed the glass of water and aspirin bottle toward her. She put four aspirin in her hand, tossed them into her mouth, and washed them down with three or four swallows of water.

"How's the head?"

"I was afraid earlier I was going to die; now I'm afraid I won't."

"Okay, that tells me you're going to be fine. When you're ready you should have some toast and grape jelly just to get some sugar in your system and curb that hang-over. You give me the word, and I'll cook you up some scrambled eggs and bacon for breakfast.

At the mention of breakfast, she looked like she was about to get sick.

"Or, I could not cook breakfast if that would be bet-ter."

"Mmm-mmm," she groaned and casually looked around. "Did you move that briefcase?" she asked, sud-denly sounding worried.

"I just set it under the kitchen table, so it was more or less out of sight. You want me to put it somewhere?"

"I want to get it out of my house. I think I should maybe put it in a safety deposit box for the time being."

"You have some bank in mind?"

She nodded. "I've got some contacts down at First National. I can get a safety deposit box today. If Bene-detti starts to ask any questions, I can put him off for a couple of days until I figure out exactly what I'm going to do."

"Any idea why he picked you?"

"Probably history, I've given consistently good returns for a number of years."

"I'll say."

She looked at me and shook her head. "Not funny, Dev. And I'm sorry last night didn't exactly work out the way you planned."

"What could be better than dinner and then carrying you to bed while you called me some other guys name."

She grimaced, "Oh, sorry, whose name did I say?"

"Which time?"

"Oh, God."

"Listen, I want you to have some toast and grape jelly just to get some sugar content going in your bloodstream."

"Oh, I don't—"

"Hey, trust me, Heidi. It will cut the length of your hangover time in half."

She closed her eyes and nodded. After three pieces of toast slathered in grape jelly, she actually showed some signs of life.

Two hours later, I drove her down to the First National Bank in her red Mercedes. She had her sunglasses on and more or less stared at the floor for the entire ten-minute trip. I pulled into the parking ramp, and we entered the bank on the second floor.

Dennis Constantine, the guy Heidi knew, was seated behind his desk wearing latex gloves. "Hello, Heidi," he said, ignoring me. "Long time no see. Have a seat, sign on the dotted line and we'll debit your account for the annual fee, two hundred and seventy-five dollars." As he spoke, he set two pairs of latex gloves and two face masks for us on the far side of the desk.

They exchanged pleasantries for a moment, but I had the distinct impression there may have been some personal history in the background. He phoned an underling to show us to the vault. The contents of the metal briefcase fit nicely into the safety deposit box, number 744. We pulled back in front of Heidi's house about ninety minutes after we'd first left.

"Thanks, Dev," she said as I turned off the Mercedes. "I hope you don't mind, but I'm going back to bed. You've really been nice. Sorry to ruin the evening."

"Not a problem. You just lay low and maybe no vodka tonight."

"Oh please, don't even mention that." She actually seemed to grow slightly pale behind her sunglasses.

I handed her the car keys then climbed out of the car. She pushed the fob, locking the Mercedes and headed up her front sidewalk without saying another word. I watched until she closed the door behind her, then hopped in my car and headed back to the office.

Three

Morton was the only one in the office when I returned. Louie had clearly been there because there was no more than a half cup of coffee left in the pot and the burner was still on. I dumped the remnants in the sink, made a fresh pot, and took Morton out for a brief ten-minute walk. My cellphone rang just as we were about to head back into the office.

"Haskell Investigations"

"Hi, may I speak with Dev Haskell, please?" a woman asked. Her voice wasn't what I would call high-pitched, but the lilt was definitely female.

"Speaking."

"Oh, Mr. Haskell, my name is Tracy Kelly. I got your name from a friend of mine, Gladys Wilson. You did some investigating for her four years ago."

Gladys Wilson had been married to a local state representative, Arnold Wilson. Along with the usual political chicanery, he'd managed to appoint three or four women to various positions and, in return, received some very personal benefits. I'd gotten photographs and hotel receipts for Gladys, which she used to file for divorce.

Arnold entered some sexual rehab facility for a six-week vacation, held onto his senate seat, and, last I heard, was reelected.“ Yes, I remember the case. Most unfortunate. How is she doing?”

“She’s doing very well,” Tracy said. “She’s started a therapy service for those of us who feel there may be something going on in our relationship besides our partner working long hours.”

“How can I help you, Tracy?”

“Unfortunately, I’m afraid I’m dealing with a similar circumstance. I believe my husband is having an affair.”

“I’m sorry to hear that, Tracy. There are a number of steps that can be taken. I think it would be best if we met and discussed the various options.” Other than taking Morton for a walk, I didn’t have anything scheduled for the foreseeable future. “I could clear my calendar and meet with you later today or tomorrow, and we could begin to formulate a plan based on what—”

“Unfortunately, I have a conflict. Here’s the problem. I’m getting on a plane this afternoon and flying down to Chicago to attend to some family business. I’ll be gone for a week. I fully expect Brandon, that’s my husband, I fully expect him to use the opportunity to misbehave. I’d like you to get me the evidence, photos, receipts, hopefully, the name of his participant or, God forbid, participants. Whatever you think would be appropriate to file for divorce.”

“I suppose I could do that. I can foresee a couple of, not problems, but difficulties. The more personal information I have on your husband, the better the chances are of confirming your suspicions. Places he may go to socialize, names of individuals you suspect may be involved. Where your husband is employed, things he may enjoy, you know sports, movies, maybe books, woodworking. Really anything you can think of. You said his name was Brandon?”

“Yes, Brandon Lovelace, of all things.” She followed with a small laugh. “Here’s what I’ve done. I’ve enclosed photographs and some fairly detailed personal information on him. I could have this messengered to you today. I’ll enclose the funds. Shall we say a down payment of five hundred dollars? I’ll be back next Tuesday, and hopefully, you would have some documentable evidence that I would be able to use when I take my next step.”

“Your next step being divorce?”

“Unfortunately, yes,” she said.

A down payment of five hundred dollars. I hadn’t had a client in the past six weeks. Under the circumstances, not a lot of thought was required. “Okay, I can work with that. Would you be kind enough to include your phone number? Hopefully, I won’t have to contact you, but in the event I do, I’ll have the number. Tracy, please feel free to call me at any time. Let me give you my office address.”

“Is your office still on Randolph Avenue?”

“Yes, it is.”

“Then I have the address. Gladys was kind enough to give it to me. You should have the information this afternoon.”

“All right, Tracy. I’ll look for it. Wishing you a safe flight to Chicago. Any questions or concerns, please feel free to call me. My condolences that your marriage has reached this point.”

“Thank you, but I already feel better knowing you’re involved. Thank you so much,” she said and disconnected.

Not bad, a new client who wants to pay in advance. Heidi’s sitting on two hundred grand in cash, and it was just a little after the noon hour. Things were looking up.

Four

Louie was seated behind his picnic table desk with his feet up. As I opened the door and Morton headed toward his latest chew toy Louie opened one eye. "Oh, finally. Where have you two been?"

"Just out for a quick walk," I lied. "You in court this morning?"

"Yeah, my client was the woman in detox who hit her neighbor's cars parked on the street."

"She hit two or three, didn't she?"

Louie shook his head. "Four actually, and another one a block away they're still investigating. She's eventually going to get nailed with that one, too."

"Did she get sentenced?"

Louie shook his head. "Not yet. Her license has been revoked. She'll be paying for all repairs. Her car is in the impound lot. She's going to be attending daily AA meetings in the workhouse, which, at the moment, is probably the best place for her. We've got another court date in thirty days, provided she remains on the straight and narrow."

"And if she doesn't?"

"If she doesn't? She'll be looking at some serious time, and not in the workhouse. Hell of a way to meet your new neighbors, smash up their cars. She signed a year's lease on her apartment last month and moved in. I'm guessing the landlord doesn't need the hassle, so she'll most likely be evicted in the next thirty days. Just about the time she's released from the workhouse. You look all happy. You find out the government's going to send you another stimulus check?"

"Even better, I just got off a call from a woman who wants to pay me in advance. Sending the information and a check over by messenger this afternoon."

"What does she want you to do?"

"Cheating husband, wants photos and documentation before she files for divorce."

"God, what is with people? Is he involved with some woman he's working with?"

"I don't really know. She was hopping on a plane this afternoon and couldn't come in to go over the facts personally. Hopefully, the information she sends will give me a little clearer picture. Hey, you ever hear of some guy named Tommy Benedetti?"

"It rings a bell, but I can't recall specifics. Whatever it is, my cloudy memory suggests it's nothing positive."

I went on to tell Louie about last night's event, Tommy Benedetti in the stretch limo with his thugs giving Heidi the briefcase full of cash.

“That sounds beyond crazy. Benedetti, isn’t he the guy who did something with online betting? Fixed a number of games or the odds or something?”

“You know, Louie, now that you mention it, that kind of rings a bell. I’m going to have to do a little research on him.”

“What’s Heidi think about it?”

“She’s not too happy. With everything going on in the economy, it’s not like there’s a line of potential investors waiting to get into this LeMax Fund, and then if the word got out that this character was in on the project, the thing would tank in about twenty-four hours along with her reputation. She’s going to have to figure out a way to get that money back to this guy. You wouldn’t happen to have any ideas, would you?”

Louie shook his head. “Nope, that’s way out of my league. You know who might? And believe me, I know you don’t want to hear his name.”

“Who?” I asked.

“Your pal, Gustafson.”

“Tubby Gustafson? God, I don’t want that nutcase or anyone associated with him anywhere near Heidi. Talk about ruining your reputation.”

“Yeah, but he just might be the guy who would know up-to-date information on this Benedetti character.”

Hmm-mmm, the more I thought about it, the more Louie might have a point.

“What are you thinking?” Louie asked.

"Unfortunately, I'm thinking you're probably right."

"So give him a call."

"It's too easy for him to dodge me. He'll either have one of his idiots answer the phone, provided they know how to do that, or he'll let my call drop into his voicemail and then block any future calls. No, I got a better idea. I'll go see him in person. That way, I've got at least a fifty-fifty chance of actually talking to him."

"Mind if I give you a piece of advice?"

"What is it?"

"Maybe don't mention the cash. He finds out about that and he's liable to strong-arm Heidi or something. Just tell him they had a conversation, Benedetti pressured her, and she doesn't want to get him pissed off."

"Good advice," I said, picking my keys up off the desk. You gonna be here for a while?"

"I'm here for the rest of the afternoon."

"Watch the Bow-wow till I get back."

"Not a problem, safe journey."

"Thanks, oh, and I'm expecting the file from this Tracy Kelly woman to arrive this afternoon. You mind signing for it?"

"Not a problem, good luck, and be careful," Louie said as I headed out the door.

I thought it might be a good idea to check on Heidi since her place was more or less on the way to Tubby Gustafson's house. Thankfully, Tommy Benedetti's stretch limo wasn't parked in front. I pulled in behind her

Mercedes, headed up to the door and rang her doorbell. I rang it a second time and waited. I pulled her spare key from my pocket and was about to unlock the door when it opened.

Heidi stood in front of me, not looking her best. She was still attired in her blue terrycloth bathrobe. She wore fuzzy white slippers on her feet, and as I stepped into the living room, she climbed back onto the couch and pulled a knitted blanket up to her chin. The television had John Travolta disco dancing around, wearing a black, open-collar shirt, and a white three-piece suit, Saturday Night Fever from forty-five years ago.

"How's it going, Heidi?"

"My head is still throbbing."

"Gee, and you're watching this junk? Who knew? Think there might be some tie-in?"

"You're not helping," she said.

"This movie is older than we are, Heidi."

"Ruining the mood, Dev."

"Okay, okay. Anything you need? Have you eaten anything since the toast and jelly this morning?"

"I'm really not hungry."

"I tell you what. I've got to meet with a guy. I'll pick up something for you on the way back. You have to get some food in you."

"Don't bring me McDonalds."

"I'm going to stop at a deli and get you some chicken soup. It'll calm your stomach and start to get you back on the right track. Okay?"

"Thanks, Dev."

"Maybe close your eyes and try to take a little nap."

"Enough with the direction, Dev. Hey, look, now he's wearing clothes like you."

I glanced at the TV. Travolta was in a leather jacket and a black t-shirt.

"That's an improvement," I said. "I'll see you in a bit."

To be continued...

Thanks for taking the time. I think it's a pretty safe bet things tomorrow aren't going to go the way Dev plans. Better grab your copy of **Cash Up Front,** the next book in the Dev Haskell series, to see what happens.

Books by Mike Faricy

Crime Fiction Firsts

A boxset of the first four books in four crime fiction series:

Russian Roulette; Dev Haskell series
Welcome; Jack Dillon Dublin Tales series
Corridor Man; Corridor Man series
Reduced Ransom! Hot Shot series

The following titles comprise the Dev Haskell series:

Russian Roulette: Case 1
Mr. Swirlee: Case 2
Bite Me: Case 3
Bombshell: Case 4
Tutti Frutti: Case 5
Last Shot: Case 6
Ting-A-Ling: Case 7
Crickett: Case 8
Bulldog: Case 9
Double Trouble: Case 10
Yellow Ribbon: Case 11
Dog Gone: Case 12
Scam Man: Case 13
Foiled: Case 14
What Happens in Vegas… Case 15
Art Hound: Case 16
The Office: Case 17

Star Struck: Case 18
International Incident: Case 19
Guest From Hell: Case 20
Art Attack: Case 21
Mystery Man: Case 22
Bow-Wow Rescue: Case 23
Cold Case: Case 24
Cash Up Front: Case 25
Dream House: Case 26
Alley Katz: Case 27
The Big Gamble: Case 28
Bad to the Bone: Case 29
Silencio!: Case 30
Surprise, Surprise: Case 31
Hit & Run: Case 32
Suspect Santa: Case 33
P.I. Apprentice: Case 34
Rebel Without a Clue: Case 35

The following titles are Dev Haskell novellas:
Dollhouse
The Dance
Pixie
Fore!
Twinkle Toes
(*a Dev Haskell short story*)

The following are Dev Haskell Boxsets:

Dev Haskell Boxset 1-3
Dev Haskell Boxset 4-6
Dev Haskell Boxset 7-9
Dev Haskell Boxset 10-12
Dev Haskell Boxset 13-15
Dev Haskell Boxset 16-18
Dev Haskell Boxset 19-21
Dev Haskell Boxset 22-24
Dev Haskell Boxset 25-27
Dev Haskell Boxset 28-30
Dev Haskell Boxset 1-7
Dev Haskell Boxset 8-14
Dev Haskell Boxset 15-19
Dev Haskell Boxset 20-24
Dev Haskell Boxset 25-29

The following titles comprise the Jack Dillon Dublin Tales series:

Welcome
Jack Dillon Dublin Tale 1
Sweet Dreams
Jack Dillon Dublin Tale 2
Mirror Mirror
Jack Dillon Dublin Tale 3
Silver Bullet
Jack Dillon Dublin Tale 4
Fair City Blues
Jack Dillon Dublin Tale 5

Spade Work
Jack Dillon Dublin Tale 6
Madeline Missing
Jack Dillon Dublin Tale 7
Mistaken Identity
Jack Dillon Dublin Tale 8
Picture Perfect
Jack Dillon Dublin Tale 9
Dublin Moon
Jack Dillon Dublin Tale 10
Mystery Woman
Jack Dillon Dublin Tale 11
Second Chance
Jack Dillon Dublin Tale 12
Payback Brother
Jack Dillon Dublin Tale 13
The Heist
Jack Dillon Dublin Tale 14
Jewels To Kill For
Jack Dillon Dublin Tale 15
Retirement Scheme
Jack Dillon Dublin Tale 16
The Collector
Jack Dillon Dublin Tale 17

Jack Dillon Dublin Tales Boxsets:
Jack Dillon Dublin Tales 1-3
Jack Dillon Dublin Tales 4-6
Jack Dillon Dublin Tales 1-5

Jack Dillon Dublin Tales 1-7
Jack Dillon Dublin Tales 6-10

The following titles comprise the Hotshot series;

Reduced Ransom! Second Edition
Finders Keepers! Second Edition
Bankers Hours Second Edition
Chow Down Second Edition
Moonlight Dance Academy Second Edition
Irish Dukes (Fight Card Series)
written under the pseudonym Jack Tunney

The following titles comprise the Corridor Man series:

Corridor Man
Corridor Man 2: Opportunity knocks
Corridor Man 3: The Dungeon
Corridor Man 4: Dead End
Corridor Man 5: Finger
Corridor Man 6: Exit Strategy
Corridor Man 7: Trunk Music
Corridor Man 8: Birthday Boy
Corridor Man 9: Boss Man
Corridor Man 10: Bye Bye Bobby

Corridor Man novellas:

Corridor Man: Valentine
Corridor Man: Auditor
Corridor Man: Howling

Corridor Man: Spa Day

The following are Corridor Man Boxsets:

Corridor Man Boxset 1-3
Corridor Man Boxset 1-5
Corridor Man Boxset 6-9

All books are available on Amazon.com

Thank you!

Contact the author:

- Email: mikefaricyauthor@gmail.com
- Twitter: @Mikefaricybooks
- Facebook: Mike Faricy Author
- Website: http://www.mikefaricybooks.com

Published by

MJF Publishing

www.ingramcontent.com/pod-product-compliance
Lightning Source LLC
Chambersburg PA
CBHW071411200726
48294CB00002B/358
* 9 7 8 1 9 6 2 0 8 0 3 7 8 *